For David, who always knew

Chapter 1

"Everything goes."

Kaye Bennett stood on the dewy grass in the early hours of a cool May morning and addressed the work crews scattered across the lawn. She pointed to the open front door of her family's beloved shore house and spoke in a clear voice. "I want you to take it all—every dish in the kitchen, every blanket on the bed. All of it. Get rid of it."

Three years she'd waited for this day, many times doubting it would come. Now that the moment was finally here, she was anxious to get started, to put her family's life back together. She'd spared no expense to make it happen. The sandy road in front of her house was lined with moving trucks, non-profit donation vans, and workers' personal cars, and her yard was humming with activity.

"Okay, you guys. You heard the lady. Let's go." The foreman Kaye had hired to supervise the crews grabbed a padded moving quilt from his truck and made his way into the house.

"Hang on a second." They turned as Kaye called them back. "I forgot to tell you that I put a cooler of cold drinks on the back deck and there's food in the kitchen. It's going to be hot today; pace yourself."

Then she stepped aside and allowed them to work.

The shore house had belonged to her husband's family first and Kaye had loved it from the first moment she saw it. A three-story Dutch colonial built in 1918, it was one of the first homes in Dewberry Beach, New Jersey. The house was cedar-shingled with sensible black shutters flanking each window, and it sat behind a white picket fence on a quiet sandy street. Inside, there were two big bedrooms on the third floor, each with dormer windows that overlooked a quiet salt pond and eyelet curtains that fluttered in the evening breeze. The shared bathroom was bright with natural light coming from the skylight above. Downstairs were three additional bedrooms, two bathrooms, and a sunroom in the far corner. Each room had been painted in shades of sunny yellow or cool nautical blues and had been decorated with local flea-market finds. Renovations over the years had expanded the kitchen on the ground floor, adding a mudroom to hold beach towels and coolers, and a wide deck overlooking the pond. Her husband's den faced the front of the house, with a view of the garden. In the middle was the family room with shelves and cabinets stocked with board games and puzzles for rainy days.

Purposefully missing from the shore house was a proper dining room, good china, crystal glasses, and anything that required silver polish. Formality was reserved for the Bennetts' house in Princeton. Here at the shore, sandy feet were welcome, outdoor showers the norm, and kids were allowed to play outside until the streetlights came on.

Kaye and her husband Chase had spent almost every summer of their lives in Dewberry Beach. They met when they were kids, playing together every summer holiday. Years later, they spent their first summers as newlyweds in this very house, as guests of Chase's parents. After Stacy and Brad were born, Kaye packed up the car and brought them to the shore house too. Later, when Chase's parents were ready to downsize,

Chase bought the house from them and gifted it to Kaye, who vowed to keep everything the same because it was perfect.

Three years ago, everything changed.

It began as an ordinary Saturday morning. Chase had gone into his New York City office to finish a client presentation scheduled for the following week. He was the only one in the office, but as the managing partner of a financial firm he often put in long hours. Sometime during that morning, he suffered a near-fatal heart attack and lost consciousness. If it hadn't been for the secretary who had happened to come in because she'd forgotten her headset, Kaye would have lost the love of her life.

The doctors at the hospital in New York couldn't predict the extent of the damage or if Chase would ever regain consciousness. They admitted him to ICU and Kaye never left his side. It took him three days to regain consciousness, another four to recognize his wife of thirty-five years. When the doctors warned of a very long road ahead, Kaye took steps to simplify her life so she could focus on Chase's recovery. That included leasing the shore house. The rental agent had been delighted at the prospect of offering a legacy Dewberry Beach home for the summer. It rented quickly and Kaye's only stipulation was that strangers not be allowed to use her family's things. The agent arranged for storage and filled the house with impersonal, practical furniture for tenants.

For three summers, a parade of strangers lived in her family's shore house. And although she read the income reports and the spreadsheets of expenses, she left the management to the agent because she couldn't bear to visit.

But now she was back to reclaim it.

"What about the boxes in the kitchen? You want them?" one of the volunteers called to her from the side door. "Maybe there's something in there you want to keep?"

Kaye shook her head as she walked toward the house. "The boxes in the kitchen go to the rummage sale at the church. They should be coming by to get them."

There wasn't anything in that house she wanted. In fact, she never wanted to see any of it again.

By mid-morning, most of the big furniture had been taken away. The last of the bedroom furniture had been loaded into a waiting van parked in the street. It had been wonderfully cathartic, purging the house of everything the rental agent had ordered, scrubbing it clean and filling it with her own things.

"What about that thing?" One of the workmen jerked his thumb over his shoulder toward the tiny outbuilding at the end of the side driveway.

The shed had been designed to replicate the house, with the same weathered cedar shingles, Dutch-door entrance, and flower box under a paned window. The box had been filled with blooms when Kaye let the house, but now the only sign of life was a few weak shoots struggling in the sodden earth. She'd address that, too, before her family came. She added a trip to the nursery to her growing mental list.

"You want this house cleared by three, we're gonna need to get inside-a that," the worker continued, turning to view the little shed with a critical eye. "No telling what's in there or how much we gotta haul out."

Kaye shook her head. She had insisted on the padlock when turning the house over to rent, despite the agent's objections—a shed would be a great place for guests to store surfboards, umbrellas, and beach chairs. But the shed, and what was inside, held some of her best summer memories. Strangers would never be allowed access.

"The shed isn't part of the clean-out. Just the house," Kaye answered.

Chase had wanted the shore house to sit vacant until he recovered, though neither of them knew how long that would be. He suggested that their adult children, Brad and Stacy—and Stacy's family—could enjoy the house even if he and Kaye were stuck in Princeton.

But Kaye knew better.

Her children were grown and busy with their own lives. Stacy and her husband Ryan hadn't been to the shore house for anything longer than a weekend visit since Connor was a toddler, and he was six years old now. Brad was occupied with college and everything that went with it. She had told Chase that her decision to lease out the house was a practical one, that worrying about a vacant house was the last thing she needed at the moment, and he had been satisfied.

But none of what she told him had been the truth.

Kaye refused to drive to Dewberry Beach, even for a weekend, because she was afraid to leave her husband's side. She was afraid to travel outside the protective bubble of his doctors and therapists in Princeton. She was terrified, even three years later, that Chase would suffer another heart attack.

The door of the delivery van slid open with a thump, pulling Kaye from her thoughts. Since they'd been working, the dew had burned off the grass and the crispness in the air had softened into something warmer, more in keeping with Memorial Day weekend at the New Jersey shore. The workers brightened as they peeled off their gloves to break for lunch. They even offered to help carry the delivery inside, with one man taking the case of drinks and another the tray of sub sandwiches that Kaye had ordered. They'd been working hard all morning and Kaye was happy for them to rest for a bit.

*

"Kaye, dear, how lovely to see you've come back at last."

Shielding her eyes from the early summer sun, Kaye turned toward the familiar voice to see their neighbor Mrs. Ivey making her way down the short path that connected the two yards, picking her way across the uneven ground and leaning on her cane as she walked. Kaye tracked her progress, knowing better than to offer help.

To judge Mrs. Ivey's character by her appearance would be a mistake, one that was not likely to happen twice. Though she'd never revealed her age to a living soul, Kaye guessed it to be closer to ninety than eighty. She'd been a full-time resident of Dewberry Beach and an English teacher at the middle school for more than four decades and she still felt duty-bound to call out former students for bad behavior. Kaye had heard that Mrs. Ivey had presented herself to a closed-door town council one year and told the members exactly what she thought of a recent ordinance. It was said that Mrs. Ivey reduced fourteen adult men to jelly with a single look.

"Good afternoon, Mrs. Ivey. How are you?"

Mrs. Ivey hadn't changed in all the years Kaye had known her. She wore the same printed summer dress she always had, paired with a lacy white cardigan whose lumpy cuff revealed a tissue tucked inside. Though she was not one to tolerate foolishness, it was widely known that her kitchen was open to anyone who needed a home-made cookie or a sympathetic ear, and almost everyone in town had found their way to her house at some point, usually more than once. "I thought you might be coming down today, but I wasn't entirely sure."

"I don't know how you would have known," Kaye replied gently. "I didn't know I was coming myself until just a few weeks ago."

Mrs. Ivey tilted her head, reminding Kaye of an inquisitive robin. "I knew because I'm a bit psychic; I thought I'd told you that."

"You did. I'm sorry. It must have slipped my mind." Kaye hid her smile. It was good to be back.

"Well, no wonder." Mrs. Ivey touched Kaye's forearm as she took in the activity in the front yard. "You've been very busy. This is quite a project you've set for yourself, but you've never been one to do things halfway, have you?"

"I just want things to be settled. As you know, we've had a… well, a difficult few years."

"Yes, I do know. And it's very admirable that you want everything perfect now, but be careful of expectations, Kaye." Mrs. Ivey tapped Kaye's arm. "Your Christmas letter said Chase has made a complete recovery—do you really think so?"

"Yes, yes of course I do, all back to normal," Kaye murmured, not accustomed to lying to her neighbor.

Their conversation was interrupted by the sound of a battered work truck pulling up to the curb in front of the house. The muffler rattled for a second or two after the engine stopped, something that would not have been tolerated from newer companies. But Bobby DiNapoli had been repairing canvas awnings in the Dewberry Beach community for decades and he was afforded a latitude that others were not. The truck was the same battered workhorse she remembered—faded navy blue, with a dusting of rust along the wheel wells, a sun-bleached logo with an illegible telephone number stenciled along the side of the truck, and aluminum ladders strapped to the roof. The phone number wasn't important anyway. The residents knew how to reach Bobby. Everyone else was discouraged from calling.

Expecting Bobby himself, Kaye was a bit startled to see a younger man exit the van, someone closer to her son's age than her own. He approached with a wide smile and an outstretched hand, and Kaye decided he must be Bobby's eldest son, Matty. She recognized his father's sturdy build and his mother's dark eyes. His cargo shorts were hitched just under his belly and secured with a wide canvas belt, and wisps of dark hair peeked out from the side of a Rangers hockey cap.

Kaye accepted his hand and shook it. "Matty, how nice to see you again. Thank you for coming out on such short notice."

"No problem at all, Miz. Bennett. Dad said to make your job a priority." He jerked his thumb toward the truck. "We were here last week or so to measure and we got the new awning in the back of the truck. Same color yellow, right?"

"That's right."

Part of the problem with living at the shore was the damaging winter winds and salty air. Mrs. Ivey had been vigilant in her reports to Kaye and had recently told her that the awnings hadn't been taken down at the end of the previous summer, and they'd been shredded in the winter weather. Kaye wanted to believe it was a simple mistake, a miscommunication between her and the property manager, but her more cynical side wondered if it was purposeful, retribution for ending the rental agreement.

"Thank you for rushing the order, Matty, I appreciate it."

Mrs. Ivey nudged her. "He doesn't go by 'Matty' anymore, Kaye. Not since taking over the business after Bobby and Tricia retired and moved to Boca. We must call him Matthew now."

"Is that right?" Kaye smiled. "Do you own the business now?"

"Kind of." Matthew shrugged good-naturedly. "I'm technically the owner but Dad still directs operations. Even from Florida." He turned and waved his arms at the others seated in the truck. "Let's go, you guys. I'm not paying you to sit in the truck."

Two younger versions of Bobby DiNapoli tumbled out, a little reluctantly. Matthew gestured to the back of the truck. "Jimmy, unstrap the big ladder."

Then he turned his attention back to Kaye. "We'll have the new awnings up in no time." He pointed to the side of the house. "While we were taking the old ones down, we noticed a shutter off its hinges. We'll fix that for you too, while we're up there."

"Thank you, Matty—Matthew. I appreciate it. Please bring the invoice to me and I'll pay it right away. I have my checkbook. Also, there are drinks in the cooler on the back deck, sandwiches, and pastries from Mueller's on the table inside. Help yourselves to anything you like."

One of the brothers headed immediately for the house, but Matty grabbed his hoodie and pulled him back. "Work first. I'm not kidding." He lifted his chin toward the truck. "Get the awnings and start unpacking them. Jimmy, you get the hardware."

As they watched the DiNapoli brothers work, it occurred to Kaye how quickly time passed. She remembered Matty as a boy, one of a dozen kids who came together in June and played with each other all summer. Her own son Brad had been in that group as well. They'd be outside all day, biking or crabbing or swimming or sailing, coming inside only for food or drinks before going out again. It was a comfortable constant, a rhythm she had looked forward to during the hectic months of school.

"The benefits of being a full-time resident," Mrs. Ivey commented as the boys disappeared behind the house. "You get moved to the head of the line."

"I hope so." Kaye gestured to a sad, leggy rose vine in the front yard. "Because this yard needs attention and I'm about to call in a favor from Gerta."

Gerta and her partner Corrie had maintained the yards and lawns of Dewberry Beach homes for years. They cultivated, mulched, and planted annuals into gardens before residents arrived for the season, and throughout the summer they cut the grass and deadheaded the roses. When summer was over, they tucked the gardens away for the winter by removing spent annuals and wrapping delicate shrubbery and rose bushes with burlap. They were gifted, talented women and Dewberry Beach was lucky to have them.

Apparently, though, the property manager in charge had neglected to call them—Kaye's garden needed work. Most of the rose bushes had succumbed to black spot disease and the vines were in desperate need of a good pruning. The hydrangea that Chase's mother had bought them as a housewarming gift the week they moved in was overgrown, the woody stalks split nearly to the ground. The annuals could be easily replaced, of course, with a trip to the big garden center off Highway 35—red geraniums and variegated trailing ivy for the window boxes, blue sage and wispy sea grass for the pots out front, and rosemary for the back deck. The perennials were more of a challenge. Three summers of neglect had taken their toll; she could see the insect damage from where she stood. All the plants would need to be dug up and discarded, the beds turned, replanted, and mulched. It was too big a job for her alone.

"Gerta won't be able to help," Mrs. Ivey said. "They went out of business."

"You can't be serious. When did that happen?"

"Last summer, I think. Maybe the winter before? With all the development on the vacant lots, there was too much demand for them to handle on their own. They didn't hire anyone because they liked the personal touch." Mrs. Ivey sighed. "It wasn't long before the developers lost patience, and in came the rented trucks and day workers with substandard plants and estimates so low that she couldn't compete. The developers loved it—they didn't care if the plantings died in a year or the sod burned in the sun because it wasn't watered. They put her out of business."

"That's terrible." Kaye couldn't imagine Dewberry Beach without Gerta. "Where are they now?"

"I don't know and believe me, I've asked. My own yard needs attention and I'd rather not do business with those New York people... not that I have a choice." She scowled. "When I call them, they don't come, not even for an estimate. After they drove Gerta and Corrie away, they raised their prices and are very picky about what jobs they take."

"Picky? How so?"

"They only work with builders on the big jobs, mostly the new development near the inlet."

One of the volunteers from the community center emerged from the house carrying a box. She noticed Kaye in the side yard and strode toward her, a purposeful look on her face.

Mrs. Ivey noticed too. She touched Kaye's arm gently. "Well, I'll let you get back to work. Dinner's at six and I'll make up a bed for you. I know your family comes soon, but it will be nice for us to catch up until then. I hope you don't mind indulging me."

She left before Kaye could refuse.

It took three days to reassemble the shore house into something recognizable. A full day to clear the house of everything they'd bought for rental families: furniture, board games, linens, and cookware. Another for a crew of five to clean the house, erasing all memory of other tenants. And an entire day to set Kaye's house back to the way it was. The physical work, unloading the truck from the storage unit and unpacking the boxes was only a morning's work for the crew she hired. When they left, and she was alone with her things, she took her time. She poured herself a glass of wine, flicked on the radio, tuned the dial to an old serial program, and let the memories come.

Hours later, when every painted shell and potholder was in place, Kaye finally allowed herself to rest. She wandered the rooms with an open heart. The house looked exactly the same as it had before the tragedy. If she closed her eyes, she could imagine the rustle of the morning newspaper coming from Chase's chair in the den, the clatter of silverware in the kitchen as Stacy and Brad sneaked another slice from the sheet of crumb buns.

When she was finished, she retired to her own bed knowing that Chase would join her in a few days. That night she slept more soundly than she had in the previous three years.

Early the next morning, Kaye brewed herself a pot of coffee and brought it to the back deck, her favorite place to greet the day. There, she allowed her mind to drift back to Chase's heart attack and the destruction it had left in its wake. The last three years had been the worst of her life, and despite her best efforts, she hadn't been able to shake the feeling that it wasn't over—to believe that her husband of thirty-five years and the love of her life had actually recovered and would be fine. Truthfully, it was the unexpectedness of it that haunted her; the idea that she could do everything right and still be faced with tragedy. She didn't believe the doctors, no matter how much she tried. Her more generous self might allow that they'd done their best, but she didn't really believe that either. Despite annual check-ups and following their advice on diet and exercise, the unimaginable happened and Kaye had no faith in their ability to predict his future now.

So for the past three years, she'd been bracing herself for a second attack. The one he wouldn't recover from. She knew it was coming.

It occurred to her, months after his collapse, that she should ask God's forgiveness for the things she'd said to Him, especially during those first few nights. The nights her husband lay in the ICU, his future unsure and Kaye overcome with panic. But it wasn't God who had exploited business connections and strained friendships to locate the best cardiologist in the tri-state. It wasn't God who had telephoned that very doctor at home and badgered him until he agreed to consult on Chase's case, driving to Princeton General in the dead of night. And it wasn't God who had located the rehab facility, the nutritionists, the acupuncturist, or the yoga center, made appointments at each one and forced Chase to keep them.

That was all her.

So she would deal with Saint Peter when the time came for her reckoning. She had a few things to say to him anyway.

But right now, she was too busy caring for her family.

Across the lake, an egret unfurled his wings, rising from his place on a log and lifting himself into the sky, soundless but for a soft whooshing as he crossed the water. As the first rays of the morning sun ascended the horizon, the air warmed. Mosquitos would come soon. Another thing to add to her list—she'd call the bug man as soon as the office opened, to spray the yard before the kids arrived, making sure that whatever spray he used wouldn't affect the fireflies. Stacy used to love the fireflies, used to run after them, convinced they were real fairies who had come to visit. Kaye wondered if Stacy would remember that, or if Stacy's daughter Sophie would think the same thing. She hoped so.

Kaye drew the memories of the early days of the shore house close to her, wrapping them around her like a warm blanket. Before Chase's father sold him the property, she and Chase had come to visit for the summer, first as newlyweds, then when the children were born—all of them bouncing around in that big house. Chase's mother Amara had welcomed them every year with genuine warmth and hospitality that Kaye always tried to emulate, even decades later. Amara was unflappable and utterly welcoming. It hadn't mattered to her if Stacy came down to the shore house with a classmate in tow, or if visiting slipped Brad's mind entirely. When the kids were younger and went out to play, Kaye would worry where they were, until Amara reminded her that the entire town was just six blocks across, starting with the inlet bridge to the west and ending at the ocean to the east, and that it was very difficult to get lost. She often reminded Kaye that when Chase was a boy, he was gone all day. The only way she knew which house he was visiting was by the twisted pile of bicycles casually dropped in the front yard. After that, Kaye learned to keep her worries to herself. She preferred having her family close, even if Amara might think it was silly.

Kaye allowed herself a final sip of coffee before returning her attention to the present. Now, with the house ready and her things in place, the season could officially begin. It had become a tradition, over the years, for summer families to host an informal cookout within a few weeks of their arrival, to reconnect with friends and neighbors and settle into the routine of the summer. It was a lovely tradition and Kaye always looked forward to it. This year, she hoped their party would include everyone: Chase, Stacy and her family—Ryan, Connor, and

Sophie—and Brad, Kaye's son. It would be a sort of reset on their life, a new beginning. Kaye hoped it would serve as a reminder of what was important and what could fall away.

Tomorrow, Kaye would begin the chore of stocking the kitchen. There would be trips to the cheese shop for the brie Stacy liked—and sharp cheddar for Brad—maybe a few bags of Dutch pretzels for the pantry. It was still a bit too early to place an order with Mueller's Bakery for Saturday, so she added that task to her growing list. Her grandchildren would love the crumb buns—everyone did. Chase and Stacy were partial to black and whites, Ryan to almond croissants, cupcakes for the kids; Kaye would buy all of it. She would need to go to the weekend farmers' market for vegetables because those were the freshest. Kaye imagined walking hand in hand with her grandchildren to the farmers' tents later that summer and filling a basket with anything they wanted. The corn would be ready in July, the first tomatoes at the end of June.

Kaye felt her mood lift as she planned. She'd almost accepted the notion that they might never return to the shore house, and yet here she was. If things went according to plan, the entire family would be together again, with Chase getting there first, sometime tomorrow afternoon. Though the trip was a bit more than an hour by car, Kaye didn't like the idea of Chase driving himself. She'd hired his physical therapist, Derrick, to drive him from Princeton to Dewberry Beach and had tried to find a private nurse to look in on him during the summer, but he'd refused, reminding Kaye that the doctors had released him until a November follow-up appointment. It worried her, being so far from his cardiologists, but she had finally agreed, though reluctantly. The kids would arrive shortly after Chase. The bedrooms had already been prepared for their arrival, with fresh linens on the beds and sachets tucked underneath the pillows. Lavender for Stacy and Ryan, eucalyptus for Brad, lemon for Connor, and rose for Sophie. She'd spent a ridiculous amount of time at Dewberry Beach Gifts selecting the scents, but it made her happy to do so.

She planned to take her grandchildren to Applegate's Hardware where they would select a plastic bucket and an assortment of toys for the sand, along with their very own beach towel, a tradition started when Stacy and Brad were their age. After whole days spent crabbing at the pier, or swimming at the local pool, or racing plastic boats on the salt pond, Kaye imagined the family coming together for dinners outside on the deck. New memories would be made and a whole new generation of Bennetts would come to love the shore as much as Kaye did.

Feeling the cool salty air on her skin as the breeze shifted, Kaye turned her attention to the pond just beyond the fence, watching the grass stir as a dragonfly emerged.

Yes, it would be a wonderful summer.

Kaye took her empty coffee mug inside and retrieved her fancy new cell phone from the pocket of one of Chase's old cardigans. For years she'd carried an old flip-phone, usually forgotten in her purse or left on the charger, until the day she had been needed and couldn't be reached. She'd been swimming laps in the pool that Saturday morning, her phone stowed securely in her locker and her mind on something mundane. After her swim, she'd luxuriated in a long, hot shower using the fancy glycerin soap and lotion set she'd bought herself for her birthday the week before. A whole day had stretched before her with nothing to do, and she'd toyed with the idea of booking an hour-long massage. She'd reached for her phone to book the appointment and was surprised to see fifteen text messages, all marked urgent, and a dozen voice messages, pleading with her to return the call.

That was how she'd found out that her husband had collapsed at his desk, and that if the secretary hadn't left her headset in the office by mistake, he would be gone.

To this day, the thought that jerked her from sleep and left her reeling and gasping for air was the fact that when her husband had needed her the most, she had been scheduling a massage. She'd had no feeling that he needed her, no sixth sense that the man she loved with every bit of her heart hovered, alone, between life and death.

Real life was nothing like the movies.

Kaye unlocked the phone and skimmed her contacts for her daughter's cell number. She tapped the green phone icon at the bottom of her screen.

Then she listened to it ring.

Chapter 2

Seventy miles away, in the small condominium she shared with her husband and two children, Stacy Madigan stood at the counter in the small hours of the morning, slicing oranges for her son's soccer team. She heard the chirp of her cell phone and, thinking it might be a weather update for Connor's game, glanced at the screen. When she saw it was her mother calling, she let it roll to voicemail and returned to her work.

Her husband Ryan appeared in the kitchen just in time to catch the last ring. He was normally a night owl, so she was surprised to see him up and dressed, his hair still damp from a shower. He stumbled to the cabinet to retrieve his favorite MIT ALUMNI coffee mug.

"Why is your mother calling you?"

"I don't know."

He paused, holding the carafe over his mug. "Why didn't you pick up?"

"Because my mother never calls to 'chat.' She calls to direct, organize, or interrogate. You remember I told you that my brother and I used to call her The General when we were growing up? The name still fits."

The relationship Stacy had with her mother had always been a complicated one, threaded with expectations that Stacy had never quite been able to meet. Expectations her younger brother Brad didn't seem to have. While Stacy's father had disappeared, unapologetically, into his career in the city, her mother had raised two children essentially on her own. She'd found time to look after her family, volunteer at their school, entertain her husband's clients, help out in the community, and had made it all appear effortless. Stacy, on the other hand, had always felt as if she was running three hours behind. Since she could never meet her mother's expectations, eventually she stopped trying.

"'The General?'" Ryan reached for an orange section and popped it into his mouth. "You sure you're not exaggerating? I think your mother is delightful."

It was one of the things that had attracted Stacy to Ryan in the first place: his inability to believe anyone had ulterior motives. His family, a rowdy Irish Catholic bunch from south Boston, was the same way. Seven brothers and sisters, every one of them loud and straight-talking. Ryan's family, and the way they interacted, was what made Stacy want to have a big brood of her own. She imagined chaotic Christmases like the ones at his parents' house, everyone teasing and talking over each other. It took some convincing, but Ryan finally agreed when Stacy offered to quit her job to stay at home with their children.

"First of all"—she frowned at him—"no one under sixty years old says 'delightful,' so I don't know who you've been hanging out with." She returned to her task of slicing oranges.

"And second?"

"'Second' what?" Stacy glanced up.

"You said 'first of all.' That implies a second thing. What's the second thing?"

"No idea." Stacy shrugged. At almost four months pregnant with their third child, she'd grown used to forgetting just about everything. For her, the first trimester was nausea and the second was senility.

Stacy glanced at the clock, then out the window at the gathering rainclouds. The last game of the regular season before school let out for the summer. She'd hoped for better weather. Blue skies and summer sunshine were late coming this year; most of May had been dreary and spattered with rain.

She laid her knife on the cutting board, then called down the hallway to her son's room. "Connor, let's get going. Archie and his mom will be here any minute to drive you to the game."

Turning her attention back to the task at hand, she surveyed the contents of her kitchen and mentally ran through the list she'd been given. Three oversized plastic containers packed with freshly sliced oranges, zipped plastic bags stuffed with string cheese, two cases of juice pouches—all of it covered every available inch of counterspace. Near the front door was a case of bottled water for the players and a tub of oatmeal cookies for after the game. As she arranged the snacks inside the team's logoed insulated bags, she felt a bit wistful for a simpler time, when packing a snack for her son's activities meant throwing some apple slices and graham crackers into a pocket of his diaper bag. This required planning, shopping, and prep.

She crossed the living room with the first of the bags, pausing to look out the big picture windows that overlooked the arboretum. She and Ryan had chosen this apartment specifically for the view of the canopy in the arboretum as the seasons changed: branches tipped with snow in the winter, bright-green leaves emerging in the spring, and a blanket of vibrant oranges and yellows in the fall.

"You need me to pack anything?" Ryan offered as he followed her to the kitchen.

"No, it's all done." She nudged the bag with her foot. "Can you bring this to the front door with the rest of the stuff please? Melissa will be here any minute to take the boys to the game. This is the last thing to go."

Ryan walked over and surveyed the pile by the front door with a critical eye. "You have food enough here to supply a military campaign. How many days are the kids playing for?"

"Same as usual. About an hour."

"Big production for an hour." Ryan lifted the bag and carried it to the front door. "I can't believe I'm going to say this, but when I was a kid, playing soccer meant bringing a ball to a vacant lot and kicking it around with a bunch of kids until a fight broke out. Then we went home."

"When you were a kid, Lynn and Denise weren't in charge of the snack schedule for a team of six-year-olds. At the beginning of the season, they decided it would be 'fun' if the home team supplied food for *both* teams and no one had the courage to stop them," Stacy groused as she returned to the kitchen. "Two teams, twenty kids each, three snacks per game—a welcome snack before the game, some kind of protein at half-time, and something sweet at the end, to celebrate, whether they won or not." She rinsed the knife and set it on the drainboard.

"That's a lot of eating."

Ryan's phone beeped with an incoming text message. He slipped it out of his pocket and glanced at the screen, before wandering back to the cabinet for an insulated cup.

"Melissa and I drew the line at buying boxes of hot coffee and supplying trays of pastries for the parents though. So I guess that's a win for us."

His response was noncommittal and she could tell she'd lost his attention again.

She didn't know exactly what was happening with the company Ryan and his college roommates at MIT had started three years ago, but she suspected it had something to do with the rounds of funding they'd received from venture capitalists out of Seattle. What she did know was that Ryan was becoming more distracted with his work, and she didn't like it. It reminded her of her father and his devotion to his job; she wanted better for her own family.

Connor, groggy with sleep, stumbled into the kitchen. His brown hair was tousled and his shoes were on the wrong feet. Ryan and Stacy exchanged looks. Last year, when Connor started playing soccer with his best friend Archie, the atmosphere had been much more casual, the culture more in line with a fun game for kids. Things had changed at the beginning of this season, when a small group of parents decided the boys needed "to be playing to their potential." The volunteer coach was replaced with a trio of paid coaches who scheduled practice twice a week and insisted on a pre-game warm-up an hour before every match. Stacy and Melissa had protested until things turned ugly—then they gave up. Thankfully, they had all summer to decide whether to continue.

"You want to stay home today, bud?" Stacy cupped her son's chin with her palm.

Connor shook his head. "I'm goalie today. Chad says the team needs me."

Stacy had just knelt down to fix his shoes when the doorbell rang. As Ryan went to answer it, Stacy slipped a granola bar into her little boy's hand and felt a twinge of guilt. Her mother would have made a hot breakfast.

Connor brightened when he heard his friend's voice and that made Stacy feel a bit better.

She kissed his forehead as she rose. "Have fun with Archie, and you listen to his mommy, okay?"

Connor squirmed and broke free, running toward his friend. "Okay."

Stacy followed her son to the living room. Archie's mother, Melissa, dropped her car keys into Ryan's open palm. "Thanks, Ryan."

"Any time." Ryan hoisted the strap of one of the insulated bags to his shoulder and lifted the cases of water. "You parked out front in the circle?"

"Yup." Melissa stood to the side and let him pass. "Trunk is open and the hazards are on. Can you lock it when you're done?"

"Sure thing," Ryan answered.

As Ryan left, Melissa turned her attention to Stacy. "I thought about taking the boys to the mall for pizza and a movie after the game, but if the weather is still crummy, maybe we should just stay home and order in. What do you think?"

"That sounds perfect actually. Connor's tired too and could probably use the rest. Thanks for doing all this, by the way."

Melissa shrugged. "You did it last weekend; I'm just returning the favor."

Stacy turned her attention to the darkening sky. "I wish they'd call off the game."

"That'll never happen," Melissa scoffed. "Lemme see if I can remember the exact wording from Coach Chad's introduction email." She frowned a moment, then curved her fingers into air quotes. "What the boys are playing is not just a game—they are participating in an 'elite soccer experience' offered to players to make an 'extra effort to achieve excellence.'"

"I still can't believe that."

"I'm guessing you didn't see Chad's most recent email?"

"What email?"

"He's offering a summer camp for the team to practice as a unit, in preparation for next year's season."

"They're six years old," Stacy tutted. "They should be off digging holes and playing in mud puddles, not 'developing elite skills.'"

"I agree." Melissa nodded. "That's why we're not signing Archie up."

"Good," Stacy said. "If Archie's not playing, Connor won't want to. We'll figure something else out for next year."

"Well, expect a phone call from Chad. Denise and Lynn have already signed up their boys and Chad is really pushing for the whole team to practice together. Wait until you read that email thread."

"This is the last of it." Ryan grabbed the last bag. "I'll bring it down."

Melissa smiled. "Thanks Ryan."

"Melissa, you want some coffee for the road?" Stacy asked. "Ryan brewed it fresh a little while ago."

"I would love some. I don't have nearly enough caffeine in my system." Melissa groaned and followed Stacy to the kitchen. As Stacy poured, Melissa asked, "How are you feeling?"

"Good." Stacy brought her fingertips to her stomach. "Much better actually. Morning sickness has passed, thank goodness. Now I'm just tired, so that's progress I guess."

"Why don't you let us keep Connor overnight? He can wear a pair of Archie's pajamas and Jerry can bring him home in the morning."

"Oh, you don't have to do that—" Stacy began, before her friend interrupted.

"Honestly, it's no trouble." Melissa reached for Stacy's arm. "I expect the boys'll be exhausted from the game anyway. We'll order pizza and put in a movie. They'll be asleep in no time."

Stacy laughed. "You've got this all figured out, don't you?"

"Blended family. Six kids," Melissa said. "Our lives are just a matter of controlling the chaos. And honestly"—she gave Stacy's arm a gentle squeeze— "one more is not any trouble at all. So, what do you think?"

"Awesome. Great," Stacy replied, imagining a long morning nap.

Melissa left, fortified with a fresh cup of coffee and with the boys trailing in her wake, chattering about the upcoming game. Stacy wondered if managing her own family would ever be as easy as Melissa made it appear—Stacy could barely coordinate the schedules of two children. What was she going to do in the fall when the new baby arrived?

After Melissa left with the boys, it was time to get Sophie ready for ballet. Stacy returned to the kitchen to clean up, tossing orange peels into the compost bin, throwing away the packaging from the string cheese, and wiping down the counters.

Ready for round two.

Thankfully, all she had to prep was a single snack bag, then help Sophie into her leotard. Ryan had offered to drive Sophie to her lesson and to take her out for lunch afterwards, which meant at least two blissful hours all to herself. She planned to read for a bit and then take a long nap while the house was quiet. To be honest, she did feel a twinge of guilt asking for Ryan's help with the children. It had been her idea to have a big family and she had pushed for it to happen quickly, probably before he was ready. It was only fair that she be the one who took on most of the responsibilities, even if she had to quit a job she loved to make it happen.

She peeled a few carrots and cut them into the coin shapes Sophie liked, then tucked them into the bag. Before zipping it closed, she added a packet of hummus and a bottle of water, just in case. The lesson was a short one, only about an hour, and with lunch right after it seemed ridiculous to pack a snack. But the other ballet mothers packed a snack bag, so Stacy did too. At the last minute, she tossed in a square of chocolate because her daughter loved chocolate.

She glanced at the clock again and called out a reminder: "Sophie, time to get ready. I'll be there in a second to help you with your tights."

Ryan entered the kitchen, the glow of his cell phone reflecting off his glasses as he typed a message on his screen.

"How important is it that I take Sophie to her lesson?"

"Pretty important, why?" Stacy felt a tingle of dread as she turned toward her husband. She had so been looking forward to that nap…

"Something's come up and I can't get a hold of Jeff. He hasn't been answering texts or email on his work account." He squinted as he flicked through the screens on his phone. "It's really weird that Sean's location puts him in Seattle," he muttered to himself.

"Everything okay?"

"Fine. It's fine." Ryan frowned. "Just Todd doing some saber rattling—showing off in front of the money guys."

"What does Todd want?"

"A chart—and Jeff has the data."

"A chart?" Stacy repeated, feeling a rising annoyance at Ryan reneging on a promise to her for something that seemed so insignificant. "Can't you do that from the lobby of the dance studio? I'm sure they have Wi-Fi."

"If I can't find Jeff, they'll stick me with more than just building the chart, Stace," Ryan said as he turned his attention back to the screen. "He's got user data from the past quarter and we need it for the next release of funding." Ryan tapped on the screen of his cell phone, then looked up. "But if you need me to take Sophie, I will. I'll figure something out."

"No, it's fine." Stacy took a deep breath as she rinsed the cutting board. Her nap would have to wait. "I'll take her."

"I can take her next week, I promise."

"This is the last week of lessons. The recital is Thursday."

"Good to know," Ryan said absently. "By the way, did you know the pinks are different? Apparently, it matters."

"What do you mean, 'the pinks are different'?"

"I passed Sophie in her room earlier. She said the tights you laid out are the wrong color." He shrugged, returning his attention to his work. "Last year's practice color was 'baby pink' and this year's is 'princess pink.'"

"So she's unpacked the ballet bag?"

"Yeah."

"Did you stop her?"

Ryan looked up. "Was I supposed to?"

Stacy leaned against the countertop, pressing her palms on the surface. "She's four, Ryan, and she can't put on tights by herself, so yes, you should have stopped her." As she left the kitchen to see about her daughter, she turned to ask the question that had just occurred to her. "How do you know the names of the ballet colors? That seems like an odd thing for you to know. Did Sophie tell you?"

"Nope. Jessica Steinman told me a couple of weeks ago. Her kid doesn't like the colors mixed up either."

"Jessica Steinman?" Stacy repeated, giving Ryan her full attention. "You talked to Jessica Steinman?"

"Sure. She's nice." Ryan shrugged as he sipped his coffee. "We had a whole conversation one week about shades of pink."

"Jessica Steinman is *not* nice. She's never said a single word to me. An entire year and not a single word."

Ryan gestured to the tote Stacy carried to ballet every week. It had just enough room for whatever book she was currently reading, a thermos for her decaffeinated hazelnut coffee, and a pair of noise-cancelling headphones. "You think that might have something to do with it?"

Parents weren't allowed in the practice rooms during lessons, so many of the mothers waited on chairs in the lobby. The atmosphere was clique-y and tense, and in the center of it all was Jessica Steinman, holding court. Early on, Stacy had recognized she had nothing in common with any of the dance mothers, so she had decided to spend her time with a good book and a strong cup of coffee.

Still, the implication that Stacy wasn't doing her best for her daughter stung.

"I'm re-reading *A Winter to Remember* and it's a masterpiece, I'll have you know. Almost a full year on the *New York Times* bestseller list when it was first published, and it's about to hit it again because the second book in the series comes out in the fall," she said.

"And the world can thank my brilliant wife for discovering Billy Jacob's remarkable talent," Ryan declared as he smiled.

Discovering Billy Jacob's manuscript in the slush pile was one of Stacy's proudest career accomplishments. Her first real job after graduation was as an assistant editor at Revere Publishing in Boston. Mostly she made coffee and ran errands, but occasionally she was allowed to pull submissions from the slush pile, and that was where she came across *A Winter to Remember*. The writing had been somewhat stilted and tended to veer off track, but the story itself was magical. She devoured the entire book, almost six hundred pages, in a single weekend, then rushed into her supervisor's office the following Monday. It took a lot of persuading, but eventually Stacy was allowed to work on the manuscript with Billy, provided she did so on her own time. When the story was finished the editors would read it again, with the understanding that even after all that work, the story might still be rejected.

But it wasn't.

The staff at Revere loved the story. So much so that it was fast-tracked and published just after Connor was born. She'd heard the sales were great and Revere intended to offer a contract for more books in the series. Stacy liked to imagine that she might have been allowed to edit the new books if she had returned to work from maternity leave.

But she hadn't.

*

As soon as Stacy and Sophie left for ballet, Ryan reached for his cell phone and dialed Todd, who, technically, Ryan wasn't supposed to talk to. Todd was the money guy, the representative from the venture capital firm who'd promised to take their company public, and it was no secret that he and Ryan did not agree on the way to get there.

The idea that started the company had been Ryan's. It came to him one wintery afternoon in a computer science lecture hall, presenting itself as a puzzle to be solved and would not go away. It took Ryan weeks to arrive at the solution and months more to perfect it. When it was finally ready, he showed Sean and Jeff, his roommates at the time.

Jeff was a big-data guy, a doctoral student who was excited about what Ryan's program could become. Sean, Ryan realized much later, was more interested in the dollar signs than the solution itself. Without knowing if anything would come of the idea, the three of them incorporated and agreed to let the majority decide the new company's direction. As MIT graduate students, they had access to university resources, so they booked server time to compile and test additional code that had become too complex for their laptops to handle. When the program was stable, they gave it away, just to see if people liked it.

And they did.

It was Sean who approached the venture capitalists for funding, flying to Seattle and presenting their start-up as his own without telling the other two. Afterward, he'd made the excuse that he didn't expect anything to come of the trip, so why bring it up?

Only, something had come of it. And that's when things between them began to deteriorate.

Not only was the Seattle group interested, but another firm out of San Diego had heard of their success and also wanted to invest. The amount of cash offered during the first round of funding was impressive and it was nice to be able to quit school to focus on their little company. But the second round of funding changed everything. The money came with strings this time, and oversight in the form of a slick frat boy named Todd. As the venture capitalists' representative, he initially promised to offer advice only when asked, and on the surface, that's what he did. In the shadows, he added oversight and layers of management that seemed extensive and unnecessary. But whenever Ryan pushed back, Todd added incentives—more options for Sean or equipment for Jeff—and because he was only one vote of three, Ryan lost the battle.

That's where they were now: Ryan felt like the only clear head left on a ship that had gone wildly off course. He could see the iceberg coming but no one seemed to care.

As Ryan listened to the phone ring, waiting for Todd to pick up, he felt his frustration bloom. He didn't like talking to Todd and knew this conversation wouldn't go well.

"Ryan. Glad you reached out." Todd's tone was forced, overly bright and cheerful. Ryan closed his eyes and suppressed a groan. Maybe calling wasn't a great idea. "I have a few things for you to do," Todd continued. "We need the milestone schedule to present at the partners' meeting this afternoon. Sean says you have all the customer data."

"Good morning to you too, Todd." Ryan's voice was deliberately cool.

"Sorry, pal. I didn't realize you were the kind of guy who needed flowers first." Todd's indulgent chuckle made Ryan recoil.

"The reason I'm calling," Ryan continued, "is because I got your email this morning. I don't know why you want me to build the slide-deck. We all have the same raw data, including you."

"It's Sean's opinion that you're the best one to present the data." Todd changed his tone to match Ryan's, cool and professional.

"Sean's opinion? What do you mean 'Sean's opinion'? When did you talk to him?"

"We had dinner last night, in town. He flew over for the weekend to discuss a few ideas we have. I thought he would have told you that."

"Well, he didn't."

"I guess he'll bring you up to speed later."

"I don't need him to 'bring me up to speed' later. You can tell me now," Ryan pressed.

"Fine." Todd sighed into the phone. "There's a small start-up out of UMD whose application seems to have significant overlap with yours. The partners are concerned about how quickly they're gaining market share, especially since you seem to be lagging—"

"We're not 'lagging'—" Ryan corrected.

"The partners want to you adjust the schedule. They want to capture the back-to-school market—students headed off to college in August—before the UMD guys do."

Ryan said nothing and Todd mistook his silence for interest.

"The new schedule may be challenging, but the partners are willing to allow additional funding which you can use for partner bonuses. An incentive. Sean's already on board with it." Todd dropped his voice into a conspiratorial tone that made Ryan's skin crawl. "Between you and me, I think that's the part Sean was most interested in—the toys. In fact, he and I are planning to visit a couple of car dealerships in Bellevue, maybe have something custom made and delivered by Thanksgiving."

When Ryan was a boy, his mother had taught him that it was never a good idea to respond in anger, and it was all he could do to follow her advice now. They'd pledged—Ryan, Jeff, and Sean; all three of them had pledged—to never let the money change their friendship. At their core, they were three nerdy friends who wrote a computer program because it seemed like fun, and they'd vowed that moving forward, they would make decisions together. Now, it seemed that Sean had gone back on his word.

"So what d'ya say?" Todd brayed. "The partner bonus if we make this happen could fund a nice summer vacation. Paris, maybe. I bet Sharon would love to see the Eiffel Tower."

"Stacy."

"What?"

"Stacy," Ryan repeated. "My wife's name is Stacy and she spent a year studying in Paris, so she's seen the tower."

Todd continued as if it didn't matter. "Yes, well, I'll share the spreadsheet with the new dates so you can see what we're talking about. You can adjust your team's workload accordingly."

"Nope. I don't think so, Todd."

"Excuse me?"

"You already changed our schedule back in March, adding nearly impossible deadlines. But we met all of them and I promised my team some much-needed time off. Now you want me to go back and tell them they can't have it?"

"We can talk about specifics later. Right now, what I need is a basic agreement about an accelerated schedule."

"Talk to Sean. He can do it," Ryan said. "I promised my team time off. They have families, and summer plans, and they deserve a rest. What you're asking of them is too much."

"If that's your decision, fine." Todd sighed. "I'll take another look at the UMD company and see where we stand. Maybe there's a compromise somewhere. If I can find one, will you at least look at whatever new schedule we come up with?"

He wanted to refuse. It was on the tip of his tongue to remind Todd of the deal he offered back in March, that if they met the new schedule, he wouldn't change anything else. Todd should honor his word.

But then he remembered the twenty-nine people in his department who were counting on him to protect their paychecks, their jobs, their careers. Shutting this down would be personally satisfying, but it would be detrimental to his team.

"Sure. I'll look at it." The words were bitter in his mouth.

As he hung up the phone, he felt the weight of his responsibilities press against his shoulders. Before he and Stacy were married, they'd agreed to having a big family. Stacy had done her part. She'd quit a job she loved to take care of the kids. The least he could do was make sure there was money to feed them all.

He pushed himself up from the couch and headed for his office, remembering the days when he worked on projects just because they were fun.

*

The stoplight changed from red to green and the line of cars rolled forward, a snarl of red brake lights in a ribbon of traffic. The automatic windshield wipers in Stacy's car flicked on. She leaned against the headrest, watching the blades clear a path across the glass. Sophie was napping in the back seat and the soccer game had been called off because of rain, so Melissa had treated the boys to a movie after all.

As Stacy slowed to a halt again to wait through another cycle of the stoplight, her cell phone rang. Without giving it much thought, she poked the console screen with one finger and returned her hand to the wheel.

"Hello?"

"Stacy, it's your mother." Her mother's voice was clipped, purposeful. Kaye Holloway Bennett always had a reason for calling. "I'm calling to confirm our summer plans at the shore."

"We're coming to visit the first two weeks of August. I've marked it on the calendar."

"Yes, well that's why I'm calling. Your father has asked me to arrange for a longer visit."

"Longer?"

"Yes."

"Two weeks *is* a long visit, Mom."

"Your father has asked that you come for longer than two weeks."

"You mean like for a month?"

"I mean for the whole summer. Memorial Day to Labor Day."

"But Memorial Day is next weekend."

"The children's last day of school is Friday, isn't it? That's almost a full week away. You can drive down on Saturday morning if you need an extra day."

Stacy would need more than an extra day. She pictured the family calendar on the kitchen wall, meticulously kept and updated. Oversized and color-coded, it contained every activity for the entire family—business trips, sports games, parent-teacher conferences, holiday parties, birthdays, and field trips—for the whole year. Summers were as tightly scheduled as the months before. Camps for both kids began next week, with additional activities running all the way through August. She'd booked Sophie's spot in art camp back in January, because even though the camp had been months away, it filled up quickly. Connor was just as busy as his sister, and Stacy found herself resenting the implication that her summer would be carefree.

"Are you still there?" Kaye asked. Stacy could almost see her mother's impatience.

Wasn't Stacy a little old to be summoned by her mother? It certainly felt that way.

"Dad asked for this?"

"Yes."

"Seems odd, Mom. Dad doesn't usually care."

"Well, he does this year and I've called to confirm. Can we count on you for the summer?"

"I don't know, Mom. Can we talk about this later? The traffic light's about to change and I'm in the car."

Kaye hesitated and Stacy assumed they'd been disconnected. She was about to hang up when her mother spoke. "You should know that your father asked specifically for this. It's important to him that you come, especially after what he's been through."

Stacy's father never asked for anything. It was her mother who had arranged everything for the family—birthday parties, lessons, school for Stacy and her brother, social engagements for her father. He had always seemed to be happy to go along with whatever she'd decided.

If he asked for this specifically, something had changed.

"Is Dad okay?" The car behind her beeped, impatient at the gap between Stacy's car and the one in front of her. She flicked on her blinker and pulled into a crowded grocery parking lot. "What did the cardiologist say?"

"Nothing like that, Stacy. The doctors say he's fully recovered. They've encouraged him to rest this summer and he wants his family around him, that's all."

"You can't scare me like that, Mom." Stacy let out the breath she hadn't realized she'd been holding.

"It's the first thing he's asked for in months, Stacy. After what he's suffered, I think he deserves to get it, don't you?"

"Is Brad coming too?"

"Of course your brother's coming."

"You've talked to him? I think he's still traveling," Stacy pressed. There was no way she could handle her mother, undiluted, for an entire summer; she needed her brother there too. "I haven't spoken to him in weeks."

The car behind her beeped its horn and Stacy glanced in her side mirror. She waved the driver away when she realized he wanted her parking spot. He went, but he didn't look happy about it.

"Three years," Kaye reported, as if she'd been recording her family's inattention. "We haven't been together as a family at the shore house for three summers. We have that chance now and it would mean so much to your father. You know how hard this recovery process has been for him."

"I haven't forgotten about Dad's heart attack, Mom. I came to the ICU and sat with you, remember?" Stacy winced at the sharpness of her reply. If she and her mother were to spend an entire summer together, they needed to find a way to get along. She drew a breath and tried again. "It's possible, but I'll have to check with Ryan to see what his work schedule is. I don't know how much time off he can take."

"You know, your father worked all week in the city then caught the Friday afternoon train from Grand Central Terminal to spend weekends with us. I'm sure Ryan can do the same."

"I won't ask Ryan to do that." What her mother proposed meant five days without Connor and Sophie seeing their dad. Stacy's mother may have thought the arrangement worked well, but Stacy remembered a father who was absent most of the time, and summer wasn't any different. Even when he was physically present he was distracted. She wanted more than that for her own children.

"I'm sure you'll come up with something. I've made up the blue room for you and Ryan. You remember, it gets a nice shore breeze? Bunk beds for Sophie and Connor are set up in Brad's old room."

"Mom—I'll have to let you know."

"Your father will be thrilled," Kaye continued, as if the decision had been made. "Send me a list of what the kids like to eat and I'll make sure to have it. And if you're coming on Saturday morning, don't forget traffic backs up on the inlet bridge. You should leave early."

*

They arrived home just before noon. Sophie first, bleary-eyed and wired from a nap in the car. Stacy followed, dropping her car keys on the table.

Ryan rose from his place on the couch to greet them. "Hey, Soph, aren't you going to say hello?"

Sophie paused, just for a moment. "'Lo, Daddy," she said, then continued down the hallway to her room.

Ryan moved toward his wife. As she dropped her bag and kicked off her shoes, he noticed how tired she looked.

"Why don't you go lie down? I'll order takeout."

"No, it's fine," she replied, her voice flat.

Years before—before the job, before the kids—he would have been able to tell what was wrong. Now, he wasn't sure what was wrong, but something was off.

"How was ballet?" He followed her to the kitchen.

"Fine." She opened the refrigerator and stood before it, scanning the contents. "Sophie needs a brand-new costume for the recital on Thursday, which, coincidentally, the ballet studio happened to have in stock. Lucky me."

"Your mother called."

"Called here? And you picked up?" Stacy glanced at him.

"Sure." Ryan reached into the cabinet for a bag of chips. "We had a nice chat." He opened the bag, careful to keep his tone neutral. Nothing good ever came from getting between Stacy and her mother. "She mentioned something about the shore house?"

"She called me too. She said Dad wants us all to come down for the summer."

"Aren't we already planning that?"

Stacy pointed to the family calendar. "I scheduled two weeks at the end of August. That's not the whole summer." Stacy closed the refrigerator door with a sigh. "She swears Dad's been looking forward to it, but I'm not sure I believe it."

"How do you know your father didn't ask for it? He's had a rough time of it lately. Maybe he does want to spend time with his family."

"That's what my mother said." Stacy reached for a glass and filled it with water.

"And why don't you believe it?"

"Because he's not that kind of father. Never has been. I'm pretty sure he only came to the shore on summer weekends because my mother made him. He worked so much that I don't think he would have noticed a summer without us."

"So what did you tell her?" Ryan popped a chip into his mouth and crunched.

"That's garbage; don't eat that." Stacy grabbed the bag from him and rolled it closed. "I told her I had to check with you, just to get off the phone. I'll call her back later to say you can't get the time off work and we can only come for the two weeks in August. That's enough."

"Well, let's think about it first." He leaned against the counter and folded his arms across his chest. Why shouldn't he take a break if his wife wanted to spend the summer with her family? Sean clearly had no trouble clearing his calendar and they hadn't heard from Jeff in weeks. "It might be good to get away. Spend some time by the ocean."

He thought he saw a flicker of something in his wife's expression, but it was gone in an instant. The fact remained, though, that if spending the summer with Stacy's family would allow her rest, he would make it happen.

Stacy set her glass on the counter and pointed to the calendar. "May I present our family calendar."

He squinted at it, unsure of how to respond. That calendar had hung in the same space since Connor was a baby; the only thing that changed was the year or the amount of writing on the pages. He barely noticed it anymore. He glanced from the calendar to his wife. Her expression was expectant, as if she were waiting for something, but he had absolutely no idea what it was. It didn't seem to be the right time to compliment her organizational skills.

When he didn't reply, she tapped the page, her frown deepening. "The end-of-year party for Connor's class is Thursday afternoon and I've been assigned to the task of picking up two dozen cupcakes from a bakery in exactly the opposite direction. Fine. I can do that." Stacy sliced her hand through the air. "Just this morning, Sophie's ballet recital was rescheduled from Thursday to Friday, with a mandatory rehearsal beginning at 7 a.m. via email, an 'oh by the way' as if I have nothing else to do. That's not okay." Her voice rose as she jabbed at the calendar again, this time further down. "Week after next, school lets out and summer camps start. Soccer for Connor, Art for Sophie. The reading tutor I booked for Sophie comes twice a week, leaving room for Connor to enroll in camp with Archie. Only, now, Archie doesn't want to go, which presents a whole other bucket of scheduling problems because Connor will want to do whatever Archie does."

Stacy glared at the calendar, and then at him. "My whole summer is a delicate spider web of commitments—move any one of them and it affects everything else. Do you have any idea how many phone calls it will take to cancel their camps? How much deposit money we'll lose if I cancel at the last minute?"

Ryan swallowed but said nothing. He put the bag of chips carefully on the counter.

Years ago, when they were first married and Stacy was expecting Connor, Ryan made the mistake of telling her to "calm down." Stacy's reaction was different than he'd hoped and he learned never to do it again. Instead, he paused a moment to see his wife, the woman he loved more than anything, standing before him, breathless with frustration and jabbing at a page on the wall. He saw how pale her face had become, that the dark smudges under her eyes weren't a result of smeared make-up as he'd first thought. Stacy looked utterly exhausted, as if strength of will was the only thing that held her upright. And at that moment, the only thing that mattered to him was getting her the rest she needed.

"Cancel anyway."

Stacy blinked.

"I mean it. Cancel everything." He pulled out a chair for her and guided her to it. "A whole summer at your parents' shore house sounds like a great idea. Family time. Just the break we all need."

"But…" Stacy sank into the chair and rubbed her forehead with her palm. "I think my mother's orchestrating this, using my father's recovery as an excuse to get us to come."

"Maybe so, but consider this: your mother's had a difficult few years. She's managing your father's appointments and taken care of him herself, even though we've suggested she hire help. Now that it's over, should we begrudge her a summer with her family?"

Stacy sagged against the back of the chair "My mother is expecting us to just drop everything and drive down when school's over. That's next week."

Something in Stacy's expression advised Ryan to treaded carefully, so he did. He shrugged. "It's your call. We'll do whatever makes you happy. Just don't refuse right away. Think about it first."

"What about your work? Can you really spend the whole summer away from your office?"

Ryan remembered what Todd had said about Sean's big plans for that afternoon: car shopping. They hadn't heard from Jeff in a while—for all Ryan knew, Jeff could be out doing the same thing, spending the partner bonus that would come with the new round of funding. Maybe it was time for Ryan to get away too.

"Mommy!" Sophie called from her bedroom.

"In the kitchen, Sophie," Stacy answered as she rose from her chair. "She's probably hungry. I should get lunch started."

Little feet pounded down the hallway and Sophie appeared at the door, wearing an eye patch, her pirate tunic from last year's Halloween costume, Stacy's bathrobe, and a long feather boa. Their daughter leaned forward, planted her fists firmly on her waist. "Arrrrgh."

Stacy blinked. "That's quite a costume, Soph."

"I found it in the box in your closet, Mommy. There's so many nice things in your closet."

Stacy sighed and dropped back to her chair.

"Okay." Ryan stepped forward to grab his car keys from the hook. "We're going out for lunch so Mommy can nap."

"Can I be a pirate?" Sophie looked at him and waited.

Ryan glanced at Stacy, who offered no help at all, though she seemed to be holding back a smile and that made him happy—to see a blush of color returning to her cheeks.

"'Course you can." He shrugged. "Not every day I get to have pizza with a feather-boa'd pirate."

"Can I bring my new purple rainboots?"

"They're in the hall closet. I'll get them." Stacy rose from her chair.

"I can find them," Ryan offered.

"Not in that closet, you can't." Stacy smiled, her mood improved. "Seriously, it's enough that you're taking her to lunch. Make it a long lunch and bring me something back. Nothing would make me happier."

"We should go to the shore for the summer," Ryan said impulsively. If a little thing like taking Sophie to lunch made his wife happy, he would spend the whole summer doing just that. Stacy paused at the doorway, so he continued. "As long as I have my laptop and a good internet connection, I can work from anywhere."

"Don't you have partner meetings coming up? You can't miss them."

"I can drive back if I need to—fly out to Seattle if something comes up Todd's not my boss, Stace. He doesn't get to dictate the schedule,"

Ryan finished, with more vehemence than he'd intended. "As long as we're meeting the targets in our original contract, we're fine."

Ryan was the one partner who had been against accepting outside funding. He had predicted they'd lose control of their company if they let the money guys in, and he'd been right. The changes came even before the ink on the contracts was dry. Now, there didn't seem to be anything Ryan could do about it. So he'd given up, staying only to look out for the people on his team, to make sure they were taken care of.

A summer at the shore would be a good opportunity to get away and clear his head. Figure out what to do next.

"You sure about this?" Stacy asked again. "The kids have been looking forward to their camps."

"Trading soccer camp with Chad for time at the shore?" Ryan snorted, feeling as if the weight that had been pressing against his shoulders had lifted, just a bit. "I'm pretty sure the kids'll be okay with it."

"My mother wants us to drive down next Saturday. All of us."

Ryan approached his wife and kissed her forehead. "Fine with me."

Chapter 3

From his armchair in the den, Chase Bennett could hear the hiss of tires on wet pavement as cars traveled down the tree-lined street outside his Princeton home. It had been raining all weekend, beginning shortly after Kaye had left to ready the shore house for the summer, and it had only just started to let up now, on Monday morning. He'd been able to convince her that until the shore house was ready, his time was better spent here, out of her way. His reward had been the Princeton house to himself for four whole days.

As soon as she left, Chase dug out the business reports and newspapers he'd hidden away, industry news Kaye had discouraged him from reading because she said it elevated his blood pressure. He settled in, poured himself a Scotch—another forbidden delicacy—and spread the papers across his desk, just like old times. But he found that jumping back into his profession wasn't as easy as he'd imagined. The columns of numbers in the reports looked muddled. Simple valuations that he could have calculated on the train into the city just three years ago seemed to take much longer just to understand.

By Saturday afternoon, he'd lowered his expectations considerably. His research was basic—simple internet searches for general industry news that any first-year business-school kid would understand. Even that was challenging.

On Sunday, a wave of apprehension set in, sparked by the idea that he might *never* find his way back to where he was before. That *this* was to be his new normal. He scrambled for the phone to call Kaye because for the past three years, she always knew what to say. But then he realized he'd have to disclose what he was reading, explain the business journals he'd been hiding and she wouldn't understand. So he didn't call. He spent the afternoon in front of the television, watching the Phillies play the Nationals, completely uninvested in the outcome.

By early Monday morning, he'd convinced himself that what he really needed was a change of location. He'd been cooped up in this house for three years and he was ready to join his wife at the shore. She'd left him a list of tasks to close the Princeton house for the summer, along with a reminder that each task was important. The list was thorough, and if Chase had allowed himself to think about it, he might have felt insulted by the childish level of explanation she'd added.

Turn off the water to the laundry room, in the basement. The valve is beside the washing machine, on the right. It's blue.

He'd lived in this house just as long as Kaye had. He knew how to turn off the water.

Climbing back up the basement stairs, Chase skimmed the rest of the list. Not including forwarding the mail and cancelling newspaper delivery, which Kaye had already done, it had taken him less than an hour to finish. Nothing on the list was overly complicated; it all seemed a matter of common sense. Idly he wondered if Kaye would have left the same level of detail for anyone else—for Stacy, or for

Brad—or if she would have given this list to Chase three years ago, and was disappointed to realize she wouldn't have. The heart attack he had suffered was severe but it had happened almost three years ago and he was ready to move on.

His wife, it seemed, was not.

That had presented a problem which Chase didn't quite know how to solve.

Upstairs in the kitchen, Chase pulled the coffee machine from underneath the counter and retrieved a packet of the dark roast he loved. And because he knew Kaye would not have permitted it, he had hidden it, deep in the pantry. After filling the carafe with water, he measured the grounds into the basket and flicked the switch. As the fresh coffee brewed, the rich scent filled the air. He breathed it in as he realized how much he'd missed it. All coffee, even decaf, had been forbidden to him by the cardiologist just after his illness, but Chase's lab work had been normal for months now, yet Kaye still restricted him to one cup of watery herbal tea a day.

He opened the refrigerator, reached for the carton of cream Kaye had apparently forgotten about and set it on the counter. He imagined adding a generous pour to his coffee and enjoying every bit of it.

While he waited for the coffee to brew, Chase leaned against the kitchen counter and pictured the contents of the upstairs medicine cabinet, another thing that bothered him. Kaye had kept every pill ever prescribed to him, from his initial trip to the emergency room, to his time in the ICU, and from every specialist and general practitioner he'd seen since. Three years of medication he no longer needed. Every time he opened the medicine cabinet in his bathroom, they were there, reminding him of his weakness. The collection of plastic bottles filled the entire bottom shelf, bright orange tombstones that served as souvenirs of how close he'd come to the end of his life.

Of how little time he might have left.

Impulsively, he reached under the sink for a white plastic trash bag and snapped it open. He strode up the stairs to his bathroom and faced the cabinet. Flinging open the door, he reached inside until his fingers touched the back wall, then he cupped his hand and swept everything out. Bottles fell to the countertop with a clatter, skittering onto the floor and bouncing into the sink. There were dozens of them. He gathered every last one of them up and put them where they belonged: into the garbage.

This summer would mark a new beginning for him. Kaye would get the family time she wanted—she deserved at least that—but afterward, Chase would return to work.

Suddenly optimistic, he spent the rest of the morning settled on the leather chair in his office, sipping his heavily creamed coffee and considering his options. He'd given up his share in the business, accepting a payout from his partners because, though the doctors had only suggested it, Kaye had insisted on it. If Chase himself were perfectly honest, he might allow that he wasn't able to serve clients the way he once did. The hours alone were restrictive, and he seemed to tire easily these days. However, he was confident he could find something equally rewarding in the same field, and he intended to spend the summer researching his options.

The ring of the doorbell startled him.

After folding his newspaper, he rose from his chair and went to open the door.

Tall and wiry, Derrick Cole, his former physical therapist, stood outside on the stoop, smiling broadly. Dressed in a faded blue T-shirt, jeans, and battered Converse sneakers, Derrick was stronger than he looked, stubborn to the core, and one of Chase's favorite people in the world. But it hadn't always been that way. When they'd first started working together, Chase had refused to participate. He wouldn't follow Derrick's instructions in the office or continue the exercises at home. But Derrick was patient and recognized the frustration of a man used to being in command. Now, two years later, Chase credited Derrick for teaching him how to walk again.

"Derrick? Come in please." Chase shook his friend's hand and moved to the side to let him in, all the while trying to think of a reason for Derrick's visit. Had Chase forgotten an appointment? No, they'd ended months ago.

"Mr. Bennett, you're looking well."

"Thank you. Can I offer you something to drink? I'm afraid there's not much here because I'm closing up the house for the summer." He led the way to the kitchen and filled a glass with ice. "The refrigerator still works and I have a few bottles of mineral water left. Would you like one?"

Derrick shifted his gaze to the foyer, then back to Chase. "Where are your suitcases?"

"The train doesn't leave until four."

Derrick's expression cleared, then he laughed. "She didn't tell you, did she?"

"Tell me what?"

"That you're coming with me." He folded his arms across his chest and leaned his hip against the counter. "I'm on vacation this week, driving down today to visit friends in Seaside. Mrs. Bennett hired me to drive you to Dewberry Beach because it's on the way. She told me to pick you up at eleven o'clock, to stop for lunch on the way."

"Dewberry Beach is less than an hour from here on the train."

Derrick nodded. "It is."

"My wife hired you to drive me an hour down the Parkway?" Annoyance bloomed in Chase's chest, but he pushed it away. His argument was not with this man; it was with Kaye and the way she coddled him as if he were an infant or an old man. He was neither.

"She said you needed my help," Derrick answered. "Wanted me to remind you that you're not cleared to drive yet."

"Thank you, but I don't need your help." Chase drew himself to his full height. "Since I don't plan to drive, it's immaterial if I'm cleared or not." He slipped his wallet from his pocket and opened it. "I have a car service coming to take me to the station and when the four o'clock pulls out, I plan to be on it." He withdrew a stack of bills and offered it to Derrick. "But I'd like to pay you for your time anyway. I hope this is enough."

"Nah." Derrick shook his head. "I'm good, man. You keep it."

Chase considered insisting, then didn't. He'd come to respect this man and would do as he asked. He replaced the money and his wallet, then asked a question as if the answer didn't matter. "Do *you* think taking the train is a good idea?"

Derrick lifted his chin as he considered. "You keeping up with your bands?"

"I am. I'm taking them with me to the shore."

"And you're walking every day?"

Chase nodded. He was up to almost two miles a day and had come to appreciate the quiet.

"To tell the truth, I'm happy you want to take the train." Derrick set his glass on the counter. "I know how much you've missed your independence and it's time for you to find it again, even if it looks a little different than before. Got one problem though."

"What is that?"

"You gotta be the one to tell Mrs. Bennett you're taking the train. I'm not brave enough to do it." Derrick shook his head. "Think of it as part of your recovery."

"Leave Mrs. Bennett to me. It's about time I reminded her that I'm fully recovered and should be able to do what I want."

Derrick snorted as he paused at the front door. "Good luck."

Chase took Derrick's outstretched hand and shook it. "Thank you, Derrick, for everything."

"You're welcome." Derrick nodded. "Come by any time. Even for a visit."

Chase kept busy until it was time to leave for the train. He packed a few things into the same leather duffel he'd used many times before, expecting his summer wardrobe would be waiting for him at the shore house. He dug his briefcase out of the closet and packed it as if he were going to work, adding the morning newspaper, a few business journals, and a fresh legal pad and pens for notes and ideas he planned to explore.

The car service picked him up right on time and drove him to the station. He boarded the train, found a seat in business class, and spread his work on the table in front of him. There was reassurance in leaning into the routine he'd followed for decades before his illness. And, if he closed his eyes, he could imagine that the past three years had never happened.

So that's what he did.

As the train pulled out of the station, Chase leaned his head against the glass and listened to the sound of the wheels clattering against the metal rails and found comfort in it.

This would be a great summer.

Chapter 4

They left on Sunday afternoon, two days after Stacy's mother had expected them to arrive, the car stuffed with bags of summer clothes and bathing suits, toys the kids couldn't leave behind, Stacy's books, and Ryan's work. Mail had been stopped, deliveries redirected, and the doorman had been asked to keep an eye on their apartment. With a bit of persuasion, Stacy had managed to get a few deposits returned from the summer camps that had a waiting list, which she considered a minor victory. As Connor's friend Archie wasn't attending soccer camp either, plans had been made for him to visit the shore house for a few days later in the summer.

The rain had finally stopped and the ground had begun to dry. Water drained from the streets and fat robins hopped across the lawn, looking for worms. Without apology or excuse, the sun shone bright in a brilliant blue sky, and summer in New Jersey had officially begin.

Tucked into his booster seat in the back, Connor read a children's book about the lighthouse on Barnegat Bay, one in a stack they'd selected at the bookstore before they left. He'd been delighted at the lighthouse's nickname— "Old Barney"—and even asked if he could go to see it during the summer. Then, somehow, the discussion had turned to pirates, with Sophie asking about buried treasure as she turned the knobs on her yellow plastic dump truck. She had such a vivid imagination but absolutely no interest in reading. Stacy planned to work on that over the summer.

If her father hadn't specifically asked for a family summer at the shore house, Stacy wasn't sure she'd have agreed to come. She loved the house itself, but the truth was that being so close to the ocean made her anxious, for reasons she couldn't quite place. When she was younger, she had been on the swim team at the pool so she wasn't afraid of water. Just the ocean.

As Ryan turned on to the Parkway, Stacy closed her eyes and listened to the hum of conversation in the car. The afternoon sun was warm on her face and she let her mind wander to previous summers, car trips down to the shore house when she and her brother were little. She and Brad would come home on the last day of school to find their house strangely empty and still, a row of suitcases by the front door. Their mother had already packed all the clothes they'd need for a summer at the shore: cut-off denim shorts and polo shirts, seersucker dresses and sandals for church and summer parties, tennis whites and Top-Siders for games at the club. Upstairs waiting on their beds would be new canvas totes bought especially for summer. Blue handles for Brad, pink for Stacy. Now officially free from school, they'd shed their uniforms and kick them into the closet, forgotten until September. They'd spend the rest of the day sorting through toys they couldn't bear to leave behind and fitting them into their one permitted bag.

The drive to the shore house would begin early the following morning, their mother at the wheel. They always stopped twice, though the drive from their home in Princeton to the shore house was barely over an hour. The first stop was at a corner deli close to their house;

coffee for their mother and comic books to keep them occupied. The final stop was for pancakes at the Parkway Diner, where Stacy and her brother were allowed to order whatever they wanted.

Summer days at the shore house seemed to fall into a comfortable routine and Stacy looked forward to lazy days where the biggest decision was what to have for lunch or where to stake the beach umbrella.

She must have drifted off because she woke to the motion of the car gently slowing as it exited the Parkway. The children had fallen asleep in the back seat, Connor's book open wide on his lap, Sophie's truck on the floor beneath her feet.

"You have a good nap?" Ryan asked.

"Yeah, I did." Stacy shifted in her seat and stretched. "How long was I out?"

"Not long. We're coming up on Parkway Diner—you want to stop for pancakes?"

The Parkway Diner was famous among the shore crowd. On summer weekends the wait for a table could be an hour or more but nobody seemed to mind. The restaurant had wisely provided an outdoor table with a coffee service for customers needing caffeine and a fenced side yard for kids to burn off excited energy while they waited for their turn.

Inside Stacy remembered a comfortable sameness in the way the tables were set. A long row of sticky-handled syrup dispensers lined up across the far side. In the center, a frayed wicker basket filled with small tins of grape or strawberry jelly. A red plastic squeeze-bottle held ketchup that Brad used to draw designs on his serving of scrambled eggs. They'd order the same thing every time: scrambled eggs with a side of pancakes studded with fat blueberries. Looking back, she realized it didn't matter what kind of pancakes the server brought, because the best part of breakfast at the Parkway Diner for every kid was pouring a bit from each syrup dispenser—marionberry, raspberry, blueberry, huckleberry, and maple—until their plate was flooded, their pancakes completely submerged. She and Brad ate every bit of those pancakes and, predictably, the sugar buzz hit them just as their mother pulled the car into the driveway of the shore house. Thinking about it now, Stacy wondered if that had been part of her mother's plan. Hopped up on sugar, she and Brad would disappear to chase each other around the neighborhood, leaving their mother in peace to calmly organize the house.

"I'd love to, but I think it's too late in the day," Stacy said. "Brad's supposed to arrive tonight too, and Mom's probably planned a big dinner. Best to arrive hungry."

"Hmm." Ryan's response was noncommittal as he slowed to navigate the traffic circle.

They were getting closer and Stacy felt her excitement build. Both sides of the street were dotted with surf shops and tiny neighborhood delis. Tufts of beach grass grew in the median, with a dusting of sand along the curb and on the shoulder of the road.

As they approached the Manasquan River bridge, Stacy lowered her window just a bit and inhaled. It was a game she and her brother had played in the car on the way to the shore.

The winner was the one who smelled the salt air first.

She felt the breeze from the inlet below wash over her, warm and light on her face.

"Mommy, it smells like the ocean." Connor spoke from the back seat. Stacy glanced at him in the side mirror, his eyes wide with excitement, his hair ruffling in the breeze.

"You win, bud," Stacy murmured.

The summers she and her brother had spent in Dewberry Beach had been magical and she let the memories come. Sparklers and shucking corn. Sunburns and mosquito bites. Burned hot dogs and drippy popsicles. The crash of the ocean waves as they tumbled to the shore. The sound of crickets at night, the blink of the fireflies and the heat from an outdoor fire as she held a peeled-bark stick of marshmallows too close to the flames.

The best memories came from the times she and Brad were allowed to walk to Duncan's Ice Cream after dinner. It was only four blocks or so from their house, but Stacy remembered feeling so grown up that they'd been allowed to walk there unsupervised. Her job was to hold the money, a few dollars crumpled in her fist; Brad's job was to pull the paper ticket from the machine in the shop and to step forward when their number was called. After Stacy paid, they walked home, delighting in drippy cones of whatever flavor looked good. They enjoyed a kind of freedom at the shore that wasn't permitted during the school year.

She wanted all of that for Sophie and Connor.

"Have you spoken to your brother?" Ryan asked.

"Not recently, no." Stacy adjusted the seat belt around her expanding belly. "But Mom says she did. When I talked to her earlier in the week, she said he's coming for the summer too." She glanced at Ryan. "Why?"

"No reason." Ryan's reply came too quickly, and Stacy felt her eyes narrow with suspicion.

"Why do you ask?" she repeated, staring at him.

He shrugged as he slowed for a stoplight. "It's just that I happened to see a selfie of him on Instagram a couple of days ago. The geotag was someplace in Oregon."

"Oregon? What's he doing all the way out there? What day was this?"

"I don't remember the exact day."

"Try."

"I don't know, Stace." Ryan sighed as he flicked on his blinker and turned the car onto their street. "Do you really need to have your brother there every time you visit your parents?"

"Yes." Stacy's reply came automatically. "Yes, I do."

Brad had always been her mother's favorite and Stacy had spent too much of her life trying to compete for her mother's attention. Her honors' classes and perfect grades went unnoticed while his C-minuses were noticed and applauded. During the summer, birdhouses Brad made with their grandfather in the work shed had overshadowed Stacy's swim-team medals from the club. Later, in college, Kaye encouraged Brad to travel, and he did; graduating in six years instead of the standard four. Through it all, Brad seemed oblivious to the favoritism. Had he been anything other than a genuinely good person, Stacy would have been much more resentful.

The upside of Brad absorbing their mother's attention this summer was that Stacy would be left alone. There would be much less pressure to be perfect.

They came to a stop in the driveway, their tires crunching on the white gravel.

"Bibi's house!" Connor's shouting woke his sister. He'd been three years old the last time they'd visited the shore house and Stacy didn't think he'd remember it. Apparently, he did.

Ryan stepped out to release his son from his booster seat. Stacy reached across to untangle a bewildered Sophie, who rubbed her eyes and looked around.

"Time to wake up, monkey," Stacy whispered. "We're here."

"Bibi's house?" Sophie's words were slurred with sleep.

"Yes."

"*Come on*," Connor tapped on his sister's window as he eyed the front door. He'd been told to wait for his sister, though it seemed to take considerable effort. "Bibi has presents. She always has presents."

The moment Sophie emerged from the car, Connor grabbed her hand and they ran toward the house, a burst of excited energy and chatter. Stacy hadn't seen him this happy in a while, certainly not for soccer. Maybe a summer at the shore house would be good for everyone.

"It's a good thing you're doing, coming here for your dad," Ryan offered, as he opened the trunk and pulled out a suitcase. "I know how tense things can get between you and your mother."

"I hope so," Stacy replied.

The shore house was strictly her mother's domain. Kaye was the one who packed the car and drove them down, who opened the house and stocked it with food, who issued invitations for backyard parties and scheduled events. During the summer, her father felt like a visitor. He joined the family on weekends, arriving on the Friday evening train after working all week at his office in the city, like most of her friends' fathers. Stacy remembered waiting at the town's little depot as the sun set, slapping away mosquitos in the humid evening air, listening for the deep rumbling of the engine and the shrill whistle as the train pulled in. She'd carry her father's briefcase as they walked back to the house, updating him on news of the week.

"The house looks nice, doesn't it?" Ryan set a suitcase on the graveled driveway.

It looked the same and there was comfort in that.

The shore house was set in the middle of a quiet road in an area of town whose families had summered in Dewberry Beach for generations. The house itself had originally been owned by Stacy's grandfather.

He was the one who'd planted the oak tree in the yard, the same tree whose branches now shaded the house and whose leaves still rustled in the summer breeze. The house itself, cedar-shingled and well-loved, had long ago weathered to a soft dove gray. In the front, three steps led to a wide front porch, set with white wicker furniture and a trio of rocking chairs for anyone who wanted to sit and visit. On the second floor, yellow and white striped awnings shaded front bedrooms from the afternoon sun.

The porch swing was new, Stacy noticed as she moved closer. It looked a lot like a twin bed hung from the ceiling by two lengths of fat nautical rope. The yellow cushions on the furniture seemed new too. Stacy remembered blue. She also remembered spending entire afternoons buried in the cushions of those chairs reading a book from the library, completely lost in the story.

She looked forward to doing that again.

Stacy pushed opened the gate for the white picket fence that surrounded the front yard, delighted to hear the familiar creak of the wood. The front garden was planted with clusters of white impatiens and blue lavender, same as always, and on each of the steps were big clay pots overflowing with red geraniums. Stacy remembered sticking little American flags in the soil of those pots to celebrate the Fourth of July.

"You mean the garden?" Stacy asked. "It looks the same."

"That's just it, Stace." Ryan swept his hand in a wide arc across the house. "This has been a rental for the past three summers. Do you have any idea how hard renters are on stuff they don't own? The amount of work it must have taken to transform it into something that looks the same would have been enormous."

Stacy stepped forward and looked at the house with fresh eyes.

The front garden had recently been tilled and planted. The scent of turned soil was still in the air. The wicker furniture had been scrubbed clean, with sharply creased cushions on each chair. The strangest thing was the soft cotton throw that had been casually draped across the back of a wicker chair.

Then she knew. Stacy's mother, who never seemed to care about anything but utility and practicality, had *staged* the front porch. The realization stopped Stacy in her tracks.

She glanced at Ryan for confirmation. He nodded.

She wondered what else had changed.

"C'mere." She took his hand and led him around to the back of the house.

The outdoor shower was still there. And although a shingled half-door now replaced the flimsy yellow curtain from years past, the top of the shower remained uncovered, open to whatever might fall from the sky. When they were younger, she and Brad used to fill water balloons with frigid tap water and drop them from the attic window on anyone stupid enough to use the outdoor shower. After a particularly satisfying summer of sneak attacks, their father had cobbled together a makeshift roof for the shower, using scraps of wood from their grandfather's work shed. Except that Stacy's father wasn't the carpenter her grandfather had been. The roof he built, crooked and riddled with nail holes, had leaked rainwater and collapsed the following year. Their mother eventually hired someone to have the debris removed and forbid them both from continuing their balloon war. The promise was quickly ignored, and the attacks continued. What she and Brad did do was stop shrieking when they were hit. Revenge that year was stealthy.

Stacy glanced from the outdoor shower to the attic window above. The roof was still open to the sky, the window in perfect alignment.

Brad might remember to be watchful while rinsing off beach sand, but Ryan wouldn't. He would make an excellent target. With a smile, Stacy turned to her husband.

"What's so funny?" he asked.

Stacy's smile widened as she took his hand. That water would be so cold. "Nothing. Just thinking."

Ryan had insisted on carrying the heavier bags, so Stacy grabbed Sophie's tiny pink roller and followed her husband and children into the house. Even from the driveway, she could hear the kids' excited shouts as they pounded up the stairs inside the house.

"Come in, come in." Kaye held the screen door wide. "Just leave everything right here. We'll sort it out later." Her mother moved to hug Ryan. "How was the drive in? The weather said it was still raining over by you?"

"Not too bad," Ryan answered, as he set the bags in the hallway and returned the hug.

"Where did the kids go?" Stacy glanced up the stairs.

"I've sent them to the yellow room." Kaye slipped the roller from Stacy's grasp and set it on the floor beside the suitcases. "I may have hinted about pirate treasure under their pillows so they've gone up to look."

As that moment Connor leaned over the banister and shouted down the stairs. "Bunk beds! Mommy, we have bunk beds just like Archie and his brother." His eyes widened with excitement as he caught his breath. "I get the top bunk because I'm the oldest, right, Mom? Wait until I tell Archie—he's not allowed on the top bunk."

"Bunk beds?" Stacy said, moving toward the staircase. "I'm not sure Connor's old enough for a bunk bed. We brought the fold-up bed for Sophie. I thought she'd sleep in our room."

"For the entire summer?" Kaye scoffed. "Stacy, don't be ridiculous. The children need their own room. Both beds have rail-guards and the steps on the ladder to the top bunk are extra-wide. The man at the store assured me the children will be fine."

"Well, if the man at the store said it's safe, who am I to argue?" Stacy muttered under her breath, annoyed at herself for not being more assertive with her mother.

"But you're welcome to check if you want," Kaye added, in a tone that made Stacy wonder if her mother's hearing was sharper than she had remembered.

"I'm sure it's fine, and if it's not, we have options," Ryan said as he slipped his arm around Stacy. "I'm looking forward to seeing Chase. Is he on the deck?"

Kaye nodded, her expression softening. "Yes, in fact he is. Come on back."

Stacy and Ryan followed Kaye into the house, through the kitchen and onto the deck. The deck was one of the best features of the house and the last thing Stacy's paternal grandfather, Santos Bennetti, added before he stopped working altogether. He had been an exceptionally talented woodworker, with skills he accepted as a gift from God. He honored that gift by offering his services to anyone who needed them, whether they were able to pay or not. He supported his family, putting all six children through school, with work he did for the carriage trade, but he fed his soul with work he did for his friends.

Back then, the best cedar came from the Pine Barrens, a swath of land so vast that it spanned seven counties along the coast of New Jersey. The soil there was sandy and acidic, useless for anything but the most determined trees. When the craftsmen realized that determined trees produced the strongest wood, everyone wanted Pine Barren timber, especially the owners of the posh new marina a few towns over.

It just so happened that the men working at the marina were friends of the family, skilled dockworkers who had no problem "redirecting" some of the materials ordered for the marina to the alley behind Santos's house. The men and their families would join Santos on Saturdays, bringing lawn chairs, food, and beer. Santos would make them whatever they wanted out of the wood they'd "found" for him. At the end of the summer, they all chipped in to build a deck for the friend who never charged them for his work.

Years later, the deck was still the best part of the house. Men who knew how wood fit together had built it and it looked as good today as it did the day it was christened. They built it large enough to accommodate an oversized dining table and groups of wide chairs, and they angled it in such a way that it overlooked the pond beyond the yard. The salt pond was where a lanky white egret lived and families of loud mallards made their home. At the end of the day, family and friends could gather to watch the sun make its descent through the tree branches and listen as the air stilled.

It was her father's favorite place to sit.

"Look who's here," Kaye announced as she stepped onto the deck.

Stacy's father was seated in one of the slatted Adirondack chairs that faced the pond. A green market umbrella provided shade and a pale glass of iced tea sat forgotten on a side table nearby. He rose, folding his newspaper and slipped it under his chair.

"Hi, Dad." Stacy wrapped her arms around her father and hugged him.

"How ya doing, kiddo?" His deep voice vibrated against Stacy's ear.

Her father used to be a brick of a man, with a chest Stacy could barely get her arms around and an oversized personality that dominated the room. It was still unnerving to see the physical changes his illness had wrought, even after his recovery. He was much too thin, his clothes falling in soft folds from his shoulders, and his once-enviable head of hair had thinned and grayed.

"Good, Dad. I'm good," Stacy answered as she pushed back, careful not to meet his eye in case he could read her thoughts. "How are you? That's the more important question."

"Can't complain," he said benignly, as he reached for Ryan's outstretched hand. "And how are you, Ryan? How's the master of industry?"

Ryan laughed. "Not quite a master yet, but the company is doing well."

"I've heard good things about those Seattle VCs. You'll get your money's worth out of them, that's for sure."

"Glad to hear it."

As Ryan and her father chatted, Stacy allowed her thoughts to wander. Though she and her parents lived within a couple hours' drive of each other, she hadn't seen her father much since he'd been released from the hospital. She'd grown used to news of his recovery reaching her through Kaye and she passed messages back to her father the same way. But it was wrong to do so. Stacy should have made more of an effort to visit her father or help with his care. Even with two small children to look after, she could have found the time.

Growing up, Stacy had idolized her father. Even though he missed more sporting events than he attended, couldn't pick her friends out of a line-up, and barely made it to her college graduation in time to see her cross the stage, he was there when Stacy needed him the most.

And that was all that mattered to her.

Stacy had gone into labor unexpectedly with Sophie when Ryan was in Seattle on business. There were complications after the birth that were so concerning that doctors debated whether to airlift both mother and child to Princeton General. In the flurry of activity that followed, with Kaye in the hallway making phone calls and Ryan scrambling to come home, it had been her father who sat beside her bed and held her hand. He told her he knew that Sophie would eventually become a healthy, active little girl, and he distracted her with funny stories of his own childhood. When her father told her that everything would be okay, she believed him. The following afternoon, Ryan arrived at the hospital after traveling all night and her father quietly faded into the background, allowing Ryan to take charge of his young family.

But even then, her father didn't leave the hospital.

Stacy learned years later that her father had claimed a chair in the waiting room and stayed there. Every night. Every day. For a full week. Her father didn't leave the hospital until Sophie was out of the NICU and had been cleared to go home. And even then, Stacy suspected that, had Ryan allowed it, her father would have followed them home.

Behind them the screen door slapped shut and Connor bounded out of the house, his face alight with joy. Sophie followed closely behind, carrying an oversized red purse over her shoulder and wearing a looped beaded necklace underneath her pirate boa.

Connor ran up to Stacy, his fists full of treasure. She smiled at her son then redirected him to his grandfather. "Did you say hello to Grampy?"

"'Lo, Grampy," Connor said, his face flushed with excitement.

"What d'ya got there?" her father asked.

"All of this." Connor tipped his hands to show. "It was all under my pillow."

"You know"—Chase's eyes twinkled as he lowered his voice—"they say this house is filled with treasure. I've heard that pirates used it as a hide-out years ago and it's filled with secret cubbyholes, so you never know what you'll find."

Stacy remembered the story of her own grandfather "finding" boxes of galvanized marine nails along with Pine Barren timber in the alley behind the house and snorted. "I bet."

"Excuse me, ma'am." As Stacy's father addressed Sophie his smile widened. "If you happen to see my granddaughter, would you send her out to us?" He held his hand flat. "She's about this tall and looks surprisingly like you. Her name is Sophie."

Sophie lifted the eye patch. "It's me, Grampy. I'm Sophie."

"Oh, pardon me. So you are." He shook his head ruefully. "I guess I didn't recognize you all dressed up. Where ya going?"

"Out to dinner. Then to a play."

"Is that so?"

As her father concluded his conversation with Sophie, Connor brought his treasure to Stacy. "This was on *top* of my pillow, Mommy, but I don't know what it is. Sophie got one too."

"Let's see what you got." Ryan sat down on the chair opposite Connor and pulled Sophie onto his lap. She was more delicate than her brother, extracting the contents from her purse one by one instead of dumping it all.

"What's this, Mommy?" Sophie asked.

Stacy knelt on the floor and slipped it on her daughter's wrist. "It's a rope bracelet, Sophie. You put it on your wrist on the first day of summer vacation and wear it all summer long."

"Even in the water?" Connor asked.

"Even in the water," Stacy said. "Every day the sun and the water soften the rope and shrink it to fit your wrist, until you forget that you even have it on. On the last day of summer vacation, before you leave the shore, you get together with your friends and cut the bracelet off."

"And then what?" Sophie asked.

"And then you remember all the fun you had at the shore," Stacy added quickly.

If you were a kid, the first thing you did when you arrived at Dewberry Beach was run to Applegate's Hardware store and buy your bracelet. If you were lucky and you arrived early, you could find one with a colored cord woven into the design. If not, you made do with all-white and pretended that's what you wanted in the first place. Every kid had one and wore it everywhere—to the beach, in the pool, on the courts—all summer long. Cutting it off marked the end of summer and was just as significant. Some of the older kids gave the fragments to a holiday crush, but Connor and Sophie were too young to know about that part.

Stacy glanced at her mother, the only one who would have known about the bracelets and was touched by her thoughtfulness. "Thanks, Mom."

"You're welcome."

While Ryan and her father talked, Stacy followed her mother into the kitchen to help her with dinner. They took the long way around, through the mudroom instead of the dining room, which seemed a bit odd, but maybe Stacy was just tired.

Through the open windows, she heard the kids shrieking as they ran around the yard. Despite naps, they were wired from the trip down and their new surroundings. Hopefully a good dinner and a warm bath would make them sleepy enough to go to bed at a reasonable time. She was tired herself and hoped Brad would arrive soon so they could eat.

"Can I help set the table?"

"It's already set, but you can make the salad." Kaye pointed to the cutting board and knife on the countertop. "Everything you need is in the crisper in the refrigerator."

Stacy suppressed a groan. Making the salad was the worst job. If Brad were here, she would have pulled older-sister privilege and made him scrape and chop the vegetables. But he was running late, as usual, so making the salad fell to her. She made her way to the refrigerator and opened the drawer. In retaliation, she'd make Brad do the dishes—all of them. Even scrub the pots with steel wool pads. When he was finished, she'd inspect his work and make him wash them again, because big sisters could get away with things like that.

Her mother pulled a deli tray from the refrigerator and lifted the plastic lid. On the tray was an assortment that seemed different than their usual. Instead of the typical selection of cured meats, aged cheeses, and mayo-based pasta salads, there was lighter fare: sliced turkey, shredded baked chicken, and vegetables like celery, cucumbers, and carrots. It struck Stacy again how much her parents' lives had changed since her father's heart attack.

"How's Dad feeling?" Stacy asked, as she held a colander of mushrooms under the faucet.

"Brush off the mushrooms, Stacy. Don't rinse them or they'll get waterlogged."

Stacy turned off the tap.

Her mother wiped her hands on a tea towel and paused to consider the question. "Your father thinks he's healthier than he is." She folded the towel, placing it neatly on the countertop. "Selling his stake in the business was hard for him, even though it was the right decision."

"What's he going to do now?"

"He's going to retire, Stacy." Her mother's words were clipped, as if any other option was ridiculous. Stacy knew her well enough to recognize the end of a discussion.

It was strange to imagine her father retired. He'd loved his job and had told Stacy that he'd found the work rewarding, more so because he'd earned the opportunity himself. Both Stacy's parents came from working-class families and had put themselves through school. Chase worked for his father during the day to earn tuition and attended college classes at night. After graduating with a degree in finance, he found a job on Wall Street in New York City and worked his way up. He started his own business, fulfilling a need so specialized that Stacy wasn't exactly sure what it was but knew he loved it.

To quit entirely instead of pulling back must have been hard for him.

They worked in silence for a while, Stacy lost in her own thoughts.

She reached for a pepper. "Can I leave the red peppers off the salad, Mom? Connor doesn't like them."

Kaye frowned. "Of course not. Your father likes them and Connor needs to learn the world will not change for him."

Stacy stiffened. "I wasn't really looking for a life lesson here, Mom. And Connor will learn what Ryan and I decide to teach him."

She glared at her mother and her mother glared back.

Her mother was the first to yield. "You do what you want, Stacy." Her mother adopted the same grating tone that had worked Stacy's nerves for years. "I think it's never too early to learn the world doesn't care what you prefer. How will that boy navigate the world if he's coddled?"

Stacy bit back a remark, though she didn't want to. One of the resentments of Stacy's life was being forced to "go along" for the sake of everyone else. Like tolerating peppers in her salad when she didn't want them or pretending to be cheerful when she wasn't. It seemed that she was always making sure everyone around her was happy except herself, and she refused to teach that lesson to her children.

However, now wasn't the time to pick a fight with her mother. If they were to get along this summer, allowances must be made. Her grip tightened as she sliced discs of cucumber, willing Brad to arrive. When she finished, she plated a small salad for Connor—without peppers—and brought it to the table, then returned with the larger bowl for the family.

As she placed it on the table, she noticed the count seemed off. There was a high chair for Sophie, a booster seat for Connor, and four regular place settings. One missing.

Her mother had forgotten to set a place for Brad.

No big deal. Stacy pulled another placemat from the buffet drawer and made room on the table.

She had been rummaging around for a matching napkin when her mother entered the room.

"What are you doing?" Kaye asked, her tone wary.

"It looks like we're one place short," Stacy answered, her attention on the contents of the drawer. "It's okay. I've got it."

"You needn't bother. Brad won't be joining us tonight after all." Her mother's words were deliberately casual as she set a basket of rolls in the center of the table and turned to leave.

"Mom."

Kaye paused at the door, her expression unreadable.

Stacy closed the drawer slowly, then faced her mother. "You said Brad was coming. When I spoke to you last week, you said he'd be here for the summer."

"He *is* coming. He's just late."

"How late?" Stacy pressed. "Will he be here tomorrow? The day after? What did he say when you talked to him?"

"I don't know why the specifics matter so much to you, Stacy." A hint of color rose in her mother's cheeks. "But since they do, I'll tell you that I've left several messages for your brother. I'm still waiting for him to return my calls."

The air between them crackled with tension.

"So you haven't actually spoken with him?" Stacy finished, biting off each word. "You lied to me."

"Honestly, Stacy. You get worked up over the smallest thing. Your brother will come. Tomorrow, or the day after—this week or next." Kaye fluttered her hand through the air. "What difference does it make exactly when?"

Stacy felt the breath leave her body. An image of the family calendar came to Stacy, carefully balanced with summer activities. Each week carefully orchestrated to allow the perfect mix of play for the kids and rest for her. All cancelled. The weeks of summer camp, the reading tutor she'd hired for Sophie, the sleepovers and playdates and birthday parties they'd all been looking forward to. She'd cancelled them all. Ryan, too, had restructured his work just to be here, and he'd done it without complaint. What they had in place of the summer she'd planned was a summer here, weeks and weeks of sparring with her mother. An endless summer of criticism and unmet expectations, and she just didn't have the energy for it.

If she gave voice to her thoughts now, she'd regret it, so she said nothing. She felt a surge of anger so powerful that it could only be contained by pressing her teeth together until she imagined her jaw might crack. She wasn't strong enough to stand against her mother. Not without her brother.

Stacy watched Kaye turn to leave the dining room, as if the discussion were finished. Her mother always got the end result she wanted—how it came about never mattered.

A thought came to her so unexpectedly that it stopped Stacy in her tracks. *What if Dad didn't ask for this?* The shore house was her mother's domain. What if she was the one who'd decided on a family summer, and what if she had orchestrated it all, with the lie that the visit was necessary for her father's health?

That was too much to consider. She turned on her heel and left the dining room.

Outside, she crossed the back deck and strode across the length of the yard, stopping only when she could go no further. She stopped at the farthest corner of the empty lot next to the property, lowered herself to the ground, and sat with her back to the house, feeling like a petulant toddler but not caring. Instead, she stewed, furious that her mother had lured her to the shore under false pretenses. Angry with herself for allowing herself the hope that this visit would be any different from all the others. And sad that her mother seemed to be perfectly willing to shatter what was left of their relationship.

Of course, staying for the summer was now out of the question.

Stacy fished her cell phone from her pocket, tapped the icon for her brother, and listened to it ring. After four, it rolled to voicemail.

"Brad, it's me." She slapped away a cloud of gnats that had begun to swarm around her head. "I'm here at the shore house because Mom told me you were going to be here. That's how she got us here, telling me you were coming for the summer, but I don't think you know anything about it." Her nose had started to run. She sniffed loudly.

"Ryan seems to think you're traveling so I hope you get this. Call me when you do—call collect if you have to. I'm not staying down here alone. I can't take concentrated Mom, and no one else understands like you do." She cleared her throat and summoned her best Big Sister Voice. "You better call me."

No matter how badly her father may or may not have wanted the family together at the shore house, Stacy could not imagine an entire summer without her brother serving as a buffer against her mother.

"You okay?" Ryan stood before her, silhouetted in the fading evening light.

"Brad's not coming."

"What makes you say that?"

"My mother admitted that she never talked to him. She lied."

"Wow." Ryan sat on the grass next to her. "That's unfortunate."

"I think it's more than 'unfortunate,' don't you?

"I know you and your mother don't usually get along, but even I can see she's trying."

"She lied to me."

"She twisted the truth a bit," Ryan agreed. "What else would have gotten you here?"

"I don't know," Stacy huffed. "Maybe tell the truth for once? The complete truth?"

Ryan scoffed. "You're saying that if your mother said, 'Please come down to the shore house for the summer, I miss you and want to see my grandchildren,' it would have been enough for you to cancel everything and drive down?"

"That's not the point, Ryan," Stacy retorted, purposely avoiding his question. "She does this all the time. In fact, I don't think Dad even cares that we're here."

"Oh, I think he might." Ryan plucked a blade of grass. "You didn't see him talking to Sophie. I've never heard him talk like that—pirate treasure? What was that?"

Stacy snorted. "Yeah, that was… new."

"He's never really had a chance to know the kids."

Stacy wanted to point out that her parents knew where they lived and could visit any time, but Ryan raised his hand to stop her. "For whatever reason—he hasn't been around them much. But we're all together now. It took a lot to get us here, so maybe we should think about staying for just a little longer?"

They sat in silence for a while, watching the shadows deepen into twilight and hearing the birdsong give way to crickets. Ryan's phone beeped twice with messages, but he didn't check them and Stacy was grateful.

"Stace?"

"Yes?"

"These mosquitos are eating me alive. Can we go inside now?"

"Fine." Stacy felt the pull of a smile. "But we leave the shore when I want to. Even if I wake up in the middle of the night and decided that's it. We leave."

"Deal."

"And you have to help me up."

"Okay."

"But you have to pretend that I'm not getting fat."

"I would never." Ryan pulled Stacy to her feet and they walked back to the house.

Chapter 5

She handled that badly.

When Kaye heard the back door close, she knew where Stacy was headed and she knew better than to follow. Promising Stacy that Brad would be staying at the shore house with them had been a miscalculation, but in her defense, Kaye had been sure he would call before Stacy and her family arrived for the summer. What boy goes so long without calling his mother? Especially one who's traveling.

As she plated the cookies from the bakery, Kaye saw her summer slipping away, like a child's plastic bucket being pulled into the surf. Over the past three years her life had been upended, along with her husband's, and she'd had a lot of time to think. Maybe too much. There were things to make up for, memories to erase—or at least to replace. Kaye needed the time with her family to make sure it happened.

"Are those cookies for us, Bibi?" Connor asked. He stood, wide-eyed and dimple-cheeked, his head barely reaching the countertop. She was glad to see he wore the rope bracelet she gave him. At least he'd have that when Stacy made them all leave, as she undoubtedly would. The only question was when.

"They are, once you've had your dinner," Kaye replied as lightly as she could manage. "Do you like cookies?"

"Chocolate is my favorite." Connor nodded, looking so much like Brad when he was little that Kaye could almost imagine her son standing before her. Connor's face had lost the baby-ness she remembered. He was becoming a real little man, with green eyes like his mother and wavy brown hair like his father. Sophie had changed so much that Kaye almost didn't recognize her. When was the last time they were all together? Christmas? No, before that. Thanksgiving.

That had ended badly too.

"But I don't like fruit cookies." Connor grimaced as he continued. "Someone brought jammy ones to my soccer game for after and they weren't good."

"Well, there are no fruit cookies here. And in the future, I will remember not to buy them."

"Do you have black and whites?" Stacy entered the kitchen from the back deck, followed by Ryan. Her expression was unreadable, but at least she'd come back and Kaye knew she had Ryan to thank for that.

"I will always have black and whites." Kaye dropped her gaze and focused on her work. "They're your favorite."

"C'mon, bud, let's get washed up for dinner." Stacy cupped her son's head and directed him to the powder room.

After they'd left, Kaye glanced at her son-in-law, her gratitude overflowing. "Thank you."

Dinner that night was quick, the conversation stilted, and Kaye got the feeling that even though Stacy had returned to the house, all was not forgiven. While Ryan and Chase chatted about Ryan's work and Chase's retirement, Stacy busied herself with the children. Kaye hoped she would decide to stay a few more days, if only to rest. She looked pale, her face drawn. Three children in six years really was too much, but it was impossible to tell Stacy anything.

After dessert, Stacy took the children upstairs to get ready for bed. On the way down the hallway, Kaye overheard Connor say that he planned to sleep with his rope bracelet on and Sophie ask if she could sleep with her new red purse.

Kaye had hoped she would be the one to read them a bedtime story on their first night at the shore house. She'd bought picture books especially. But when the moment came, she wasn't brave enough to ask.

It was not quite dawn the following morning when Kaye began making plans to salvage the rest of the summer. Dinner the previous night had not gone as she'd imagined, and she knew that Stacy would pack up her family and leave if things didn't change drastically. Kaye telephoned her son twice before bed and then again early this morning, past caring if she woke him up.

But he didn't answer. And he hadn't responded to her texts.

She'd spent a restless night, shocked at the turn of events, examining them from every angle. What caught her most off-guard was her daughter's extreme reaction to Brad's absence, but with the morning came perspective. After all, Kaye may have played a part in setting her daughter's expectations. While Stacy may have had reason to be frustrated with her, Kaye could honestly say that she'd done her best to get in touch with Brad. She'd left messages—many of them—but he hadn't returned any of her calls. And really, what else was there to do but leave messages?

Kaye reached for a loose thread on the chenille bedspread. As she worked it loose, her annoyance touched on her husband. He never understood the tension between Kaye and Stacy and he was no help now when Kaye tried to explain her side of it. All he said was "why did you tell her Brad was coming if he wasn't?" When she refused to reply, he rose and dressed for his morning walk, leaving Kaye alone and no closer to a solution.

Outside, the sky lightened from a soft pink and the birds began to waken. For all Kaye knew, her daughter could be packing her suitcases at this very moment and Kaye's chance would be lost.

Without a clear plan, or the hope of one, she slipped on her robe and made her way downstairs. In the kitchen, she spooned coffee into the filter, added water, and switched on the machine. By the time the coffee had finished brewing, she had a breakfast buffet arranged. A bowl of fresh strawberries from the organic market, fat and ripe and shockingly overpriced. A platter of sliced honeydew and clusters of purple grapes. And, best of all, an entire sheet of crumb buns from Mueller's Bakery.

She'd just set a cold pitcher of cream out when she heard stirrings from the rooms upstairs; a door opening and a pair of little feet running down the hallway, Ryan's deep voice calling after. Then giggling and another door slamming. When the kids were young, Kaye forbade them to slam doors—now she felt as though she'd miss the sound of it.

Stacy was the first one down, still in her robe, her hair swept into a loose ponytail. She stumbled into the kitchen to pour herself a cup of coffee. By way of reconciliation, Kaye restrained herself from reminding Stacy that caffeine wasn't good for the baby.

"There's milk in the refrigerator, for the kids. I bought almond milk for Connor," Kaye offered. Maybe Stacy wanted a fresh start as much as she did? "If he still has the allergy."

After sliding the carafe back into the machine, Stacy closed her eyes. Kaye watched her daughter's chest rise as she inhaled, a deep breath that seemed to go on forever. Finally, Stacy opened her eyes as she exhaled. "Why do you do this, Mom?"

"Do what?"

"All this." Stacy's arm swept the kitchen. "The almond milk, the organic strawberries. Do you think all of this will somehow make up for lying to me about Brad coming?"

"Lying is such a strong word, Stacy. I don't appreciate you using it. As for the rest, well, I thought you and the kids might like some breakfast. That's all."

"You know what, Mom?" Stacy paused, and this time it was Kaye who held her breath. "Never mind." Stacy turned her attention back to her coffee. Kaye felt her daughter slipping away and didn't know the words to bring her back.

"Morning, all." Ryan entered, carrying a giggling Sophie over his shoulder like a sack of potatoes, with Connor following closely behind. Kaye had always admired how effortlessly he interacted with his children. Chase was never like that. He didn't know how to play with his children.

The boys were dressed casually in white T-shirts and loose-fitting cargo shorts with sunglasses on a string around their necks. Sophie was a bit more elegant, in a sundress, a floppy hat, her red purse, and a pair of Kaye's satin evening gloves. So they weren't leaving any time soon. That was a good start. A gift.

"What are your plans today?" Kaye asked Ryan. She'd get a straight answer from her son-in-law; sparring with her daughter was not always fruitful.

"The kids want to see the beach, so I thought I'd take them," Ryan replied, cutting a slab from the sheet of pastry and setting it on a plate.

He cut a smaller square for Connor. "This is awesome, bud. Wait till you taste it."

"Not too much," Stacy warned as she added fruit to the plate. "Pour them some milk too. Unless you want them wired all morning."

"Aren't you going with them?" Kaye asked Stacy.

"Stacy doesn't like the ocean—never has. We happen to be one of the very few couples who didn't spend their honeymoon lounging at a beach resort," Ryan answered for her, as Stacy's attention was on helping Sophie fill her plate. "You're welcome to come with us if you want, Kaye?"

Kaye's breath caught. Her daughter was still afraid of the ocean, even years later. Kaye had thought Stacy had forgotten…

"No, thank you." Kaye's breezy reply was forced. "I have things to take care of here."

"Where's Dad?" Stacy asked.

"He went for his walk already."

"Maybe I'll see if I can catch up with him. Do you know where he went?"

"He left early—by now he'll be on his way to Johnson's Marina to see the new boats. You can probably catch him there."

Chapter 6

It had been Stacy's intention to pack up the car and leave first thing this morning. Furious with her mother for lying, she was not at all interested in spending even one more day in her company. It was Ryan who'd changed her mind. He suggested that her mother was doing her best, that maybe she didn't know any other way to get the family together. And because the end result made her father happy, maybe Kaye could be forgiven.

It was something to think about.

But Stacy couldn't quite bring herself to forgive her mother's manipulation, so she did what she always did when her mother drove her crazy. Stacy sought out her father.

She dressed quickly, pulling on a pair of maternity shorts and an oversized T-shirt. Before venturing downstairs, she grabbed one of Ryan's flannel shirts because the fabric was soft and the smell was comforting. She made her way downstairs and was outside and across the back deck by the time the screen door slapped shut behind her, breathing in the crisp salty air as she walked down their street toward town. She took the shortcut through the empty lot beside their house, the same one she and Brad used when they were kids. She could still see a faintly worn path across the patchy grass. As she walked through the dewy grass, she could feel the moisture collect on the toes of her white canvas sneakers.

Dewberry Beach was a small town, less touristy than Belmar or Point Pleasant. Beach access was private and there wasn't an arcade or a boardwalk to attract visitors, which is exactly how the residents preferred it. The houses in Dewberry Beach were a quirky jumble of sizes and styles—it wasn't unusual to see ramshackle beach cottages sharing space with older Victorian homes. The walk into town was a familiar one, past cedar-shingled bungalows with rustic gardens behind white picket fences, some occupied already with lawn chairs and barbeques pulled out and arranged in the yard, and a few still waiting for their families to come. One or two of the homes she walked past displayed permits for construction, still not made whole after the hurricane that had changed everything.

In early October of 2012, forecasters noticed a tropical depression gathering strength off the coast of Jamaica. For five days residents of every state along the east coast watched the storm's progression as it picked up speed. When it finally hit the coast of New Jersey, it was ruthless, bringing howling winds and savage, pounding rain. In Dewberry Beach, storm surges sucked most of the beach into the sea, flattening sand dunes that had stood for decades and were meant to protect the town. Floodwaters five feet deep smothered the entire town, from the beach to the inlet bridge. Residents who'd followed the evacuation orders watched live reports on television, horrified, as entire homes were sucked into the sea, leaving no trace of life. Days later, when the governor allowed coastal residents to return to their homes, they were stunned. The hurricane had changed the entire coastline, carving out inlets in places where none had existed before and splintering miles of established boardwalk as if it were nothing.

But New Jersey residents are always, in equal measure, resilient and tough. Those who were able to set about the task of rebuilding. Those who couldn't bear to sold what remained of their property and left. Her parents' home was spared all but the flooding, and they were still very grateful.

Stacy walked for another block before leaving the sidewalk entirely and moving onto the road. At the shore, life was casual and almost no one bothered with the sidewalks on the side streets here, a welcome change from the bustle of the area in Morristown where she and her family lived. Dewberry Beach had an easy summer rhythm that she loved—pancake breakfasts at the firehouse, crabbing at the inlet pier, late afternoon strolls through town. Maybe it would be good for the kids to experience this kind of unscheduled time.

There were only two main streets in Dewberry Beach: Ocean Avenue, which ran parallel to the shore, connecting one beach town to the next like pearls in a necklace, and Bridge Street, which ran smack down the center of town, beginning at the inlet bridge and ending at the beach stairs. The official business district was on either side of this second street, five blocks total, where residents shopped and conducted the affairs of the day. Four churches, each a different denomination, stood on the corners of the main streets, and scattered between them was a florist, a cheese shop, a greengrocer's, a deli, three small restaurants, an ice cream stand, and half a dozen gift shops that sold everything from postcards to floppy hats. And of course, the *grandes dames* of Dewberry Beach—Applegate's Hardware and Mueller's Bakery—stood regally in the center of town.

Tucked alongside Mueller's was a tiny slip of a store, not more than five feet wide—a Dewberry Beach institution for as long as Stacy could remember. Knowing her father's fondness for the morning newspapers, she started her search for him there instead of the boatyard. She waited for one lone car to pass before crossing the street. It would be some weeks yet before the streets were busy with minivans and SUVs carrying vacationers to their rented houses; for now, the town was quiet with residents still settling in.

The bell on the door jingled as Stacy opened it.

Inside, perched on a stool behind the counter, was Maeve Berdock. Maeve was a fixture at Dewberry Beach and had been running Ocean News since Stacy's father was a child. She knew every kid's name and was friendly with all their parents because most of them stopped by the newsstand for the city newspapers that Maeve stocked. When Stacy was a kid, it was customary for parents to give weekly allowance on Saturdays, but a week in summer was long and children were impatient so Maeve extended credit to any kid brave enough to ask. If you cleared your account by the next Saturday afternoon, she'd allow credit again. If you didn't, she'd speak to your parents when they came by on Sunday morning to pick up their newspapers, and by then you'd have a whole new set of problems. Most kids knew better than to stiff Maeve Berdock.

"Morning, Miz. Berdock. How are you?"

Maeve ground the stub of her cigarette into a glass ashtray. The air inside the shop was dim, lit only from the open front door and a few dim florescent lights overhead. She narrowed her eyes behind black-rimmed glasses and focused her gaze. "Stacy Bennett, is that you?"

"It is." Stacy walked the four steps from the front of the shop to the back, passing racks of newspapers and piles of candy bars as she went. "It's good to see you again."

"Honey, it's good to see you too, all grown up. How've you been?"

"I'm fine, Miz. Berdock." Stacy brought her fingertips to her belly. "Married now, with two children and one more on the way."

"I'm glad to see it." Maeve chortled. "You were always one of the quiet ones. So polite. Not like some of these other hooligans." She shifted her position on the stool. "Your mother was in here just a few days ago, in fact. Mentioned you and your brother would be coming to visit. Shoulda seen how happy that made her."

"My mother was here?" Stacy asked. It was usually her father who came for the papers.

"She was." Maeve gestured to a wall of comic books. "Came in specially to get comics for her grandchildren. Asked me what the kids read now'days and I told her. Was I right? Did they like them?"

Stacy didn't know anything about comic books. "I'm sure they will," she said vaguely. "We arrived last night so we're still settling in."

"Well, you got time then. Specially considering you're here for the summer," Maeve said. "So what brings you in today?"

"Well, I came to say hello and also to see if you've seen my father. He's out walking and I'm trying to catch up to him."

"Hasn't been here today, doll." Maeve tapped another cigarette out of the pack. "Try next door."

"Mueller's?"

"Yep."

Mueller's Bakery was the hub of the wheel that kept Dewberry Beach residents connected. On weekend mornings, men were the first to arrive; they sat at creaky metal bistro tables, ordered strong drip coffee and fresh crullers, and discussed the week's business. After them came women picking up the weekend's orders, bribing young children with sugar cookies for good behavior. Next came kids flush with the week's pocket money, anxious to spend it on sugary treats. Finally, just before closing, anyone looking for a good deal on day-olds.

Stacy pulled open the metal-framed glass door and stepped inside. The shop was busy, despite the early hour, and was filled with the scent of warm bread and coffee, with a soft hum of conversation threading the air, the occasional tap of silverware as it sliced a pastry, or a burst of laughter from a patron. Nothing about this place had changed since she was a kid. A black and white checkered floor led to a bank of curved glass cases. Displayed inside were trays of colorful Italian cookies, flaky Danish pastries, cupcakes, cannoli, brownies, and sugar cookies meant to be given away. On the back wall was a selection of bread: everything from challah for Shabbat to hard rolls for egg sandwiches, to French baguettes for party trays. To the side of all that, against the wall was a sideboard set with a coffee service, because the Mueller ladies had gotten tired of refilling coffee.

Her father rose from one of the tables and came to meet her. From the look of things he'd been there a while, chatting with friends. On the tabletop was a collection of plates dusted with powdered sugar and scattered with crumpled paper napkins, alongside sturdy coffee mugs half-filled and forgotten.

"Stacy?" His brow creased in confusion. "I didn't expect to see you here."

"I came to join you on your walk."

"How did you know I'd be at the bakery?"

"Mom told me."

"She told you I'd be at Mueller's?" His eyebrows lifted.

Stacy hesitated as the clues fell together with an almost audible thump. The abundance of vegetables at dinner the night before, the bottles of mineral water on the bar, the salads. The uneasy smile on her father's face.

"She said you'd be at the boatyard, but I went to the newsstand instead. Miz. Berdock said to try here." She let her father usher her out the door. On the sidewalk, she turned to face him. "You're not allowed in here, are you?"

Her father grimaced as they fell into step together. "Your mother and I have yet to agree about the extent of my recovery."

"So you're sneaking?"

"I'm choosing not to broadcast my visits," he corrected. "Sometimes it's easier to let your mother have her way. She means well, even if her methods are a bit heavy-handed."

"Is it dangerous for you to eat that stuff?"

"It's true that the doctors have encouraged a healthier diet, but my numbers are good and even the nutritionist says an occasional hard roll with real butter is fine."

"Then why are you hiding? Why don't you just stand up to her? Why is everyone so afraid of standing up to her?" Stacy fumed.

"It's more complicated than that, Stacy." They turned down the side street that led to the boatyard and walked in silence for a while. "Your mother and I spent summers here when we were kids, did you know that?"

Stacy was frustrated at the change of subject. Both she and Brad knew their parents met at Dewberry Beach when they were both about ten years old, running with the same pack of neighborhood kids every summer. They were friends for years and started dating the summer before Chase left for college. They married after his graduation.

"You know already that my summers were spent in the house we have now, because it used to belong to your grandparents. But your mother's experiences were very different. Her family spent their entire two-week summer vacation packed into one room of a cinder-block hotel on the edge of town. The other kids knew your mother was a renter's kid, and they weren't always kind to her or to her sisters." Chase drew a breath and slowly exhaled. "Kids can be so mean."

Stacy didn't know that. Details of her mother's childhood had always been sparse.

They slowed to look at the fenced front yard of the flower shop. The owners had mixed honeysuckle with climbing roses and woven both vines between the wooden slats of the fence. The effect of the delicate yellow flowers against the sturdy red roses was unexpected and striking.

"Isn't that pretty?" her father said. "I don't think I've ever noticed that before. Funny how clearer things become when you slow down."

After a moment, he continued the story as they walked toward the boatyard.

"Your mother's father was not a good man." Chase inhaled slowly. "He got mixed up in things he shouldn't have and left the family without a word of explanation when your mother was very young." He raised his hand to stay her objection, then continued his story. "We never told you because you didn't need to know. I'm telling you now because it might help you understand your mother. She holds tight to her family because she knows what it's like to have one of them suddenly taken away." He slowed his pace. "I was at work when I had my heart attack, you know that. What you don't know is that in the confusion, your mother was sent to the wrong hospital. When she arrived, they had no record of me, so of course, she thought the worst. It wasn't until hours later the hospital discovered their mistake and called to correct it."

"She thought you were dead?"

"She did. For almost a whole day."

"I didn't know that."

"So if it takes your mother a bit longer to recover from this, we need to understand why."

They carried on walking, feeling the morning sun on their skin and listening to the songbirds in the trees.

"It's been three years, Dad," Stacy said finally.

"I know."

Chapter 7

Whatever Chase had said to Stacy seemed to help. From her place at the kitchen window, Kaye saw them walk up the driveway, Stacy leaning into her father and Chase laughing at something she'd said. *Like peas in the same pod, those two.*

The rest of the day passed leisurely, as summer days at the shore house seemed to. Stacy retreated upstairs with a book while Ryan looked after the children. Chase settled into his den, with one of the newspapers Maeve held for him behind the counter at her shop. Around noon, Ryan and the kids wandered into the kitchen for lunch then ventured back out again, this time to the salt pond with a heel of bread for the ducks. Chase went to join them, ignoring Kaye's observation that he might be doing too much.

By early afternoon, Kaye had found a project herself, planting a flat of red geraniums into the side garden. She'd planned to hire landscapers to cultivate, plant, and mulch all the bedding gardens before Stacy and the kids arrived, but they had been slow to respond so Kaye took on the task herself.

Time passed quickly as she leaned into the rhythm of her work. She felt the warmth of the early summer sun as she listened to the cicadas coming to life and let her mind wander, hoping to find a solution to her troubles with Stacy. While it was true that she loved both of her children fiercely, she did not love them equally. From the moment she was born, Stacy seemed to know exactly what she wanted from her life and met all of its challenges with unapologetic independence. She took her first steps, made friends at school, medaled in track and field events, and excelled in academics, all without assistance. Even when it came time to apply to college, Stacy didn't ask for help though Kaye would have been pleased to provide it. Her daughter's focus seemed to be absolute, and to get in the way of it felt like stepping in front of a moving train—not good for either of them. So Kaye didn't. She held back, leaving Stacy alone to navigate her life while Kaye poured her energy into Brad. Her son had always been much more willing to share the details of his life with his mother—his first girlfriend, stories from school, dreams of travel. Kaye had been pleased to feel needed. And, to be fair, it was easier to be in her son's company, especially after that day at the beach when Stacy was little.

It had been one of the worst days of her life. The only way Kaye found to live with what she'd done was to imagine that Stacy was too little to remember that day. But now, it seemed, she did remember. Ryan's comment the night before about Stacy being afraid of the ocean had chilled Kaye to the bone.

When the last geranium was planted, Kaye stood to survey her work. Red geraniums had always signaled the beginning of summer for her. Her mother-in-law had planted her garden full of them and Kaye was happy to uphold the tradition.

Brushing the dirt from her knees, Kaye collected her gardening things and crossed the backyard to the shed. When she'd first put the house up for rent three years ago, the agent had insisted families would need access to the shed. Kaye had refused. As a compromise, she'd bought an oversized storage box for beach things and positioned it in the corner of the yard. Looking at the rusted padlock securing the shed now, she wondered if this was the summer to finally unlock it. Inside was her father-in-law's workshop, dusty and filled with tools—it had been an almost sacred space for him. Many weekends, he'd spend whole days there waiting for his son to join him, to work on a project together, but Chase never did. Chase's love was the world of business, and when he changed his given name from Cesidio Bennetti to Chase Bennett to better fit in with his Ivy League classmates, the rejection of his heritage caused a rift between father and son that never quite healed.

As she walked toward the house, Kaye wondered what would happen if Chase had joined his father in the work shed, just one time. Then, deciding nothing good would come from looking back, she went inside to start dinner.

Dinner was ready just as the afternoon light gave way to the softer blues of twilight. Kaye walked out onto the back deck to light the citronella candles scattered across the deck. She's been worried that Sophie might be allergic to mosquito bites as Stacy had been when she was that age, so the first thing Kaye did when she arrived was buy almost the entire stock of citronellas from Applegate's Hardware. There were three on the outdoor dining table, a half-dozen more along the deck railing, and a few larger ones stuck in the sand by the firepit just in case. She'd made sure there was fresh wood laid in the firepit, along with bags of marshmallows, clean sticks and packets of chocolate bars in the kitchen in case anyone wanted s'mores. The cushions on the Adirondack chairs had been freshly scrubbed, and the blankets draped over the arm would be warm if the night air cooled. She wanted to serve dinner on the deck as well, especially for the first night at the shore, but decided it was still too chilly. They'd move outside later, for coffee and dessert.

Back inside, Kaye checked on dinner and was pleased with what she saw. She'd set the table with new linens bought especially for the summer and flowers fresh from the market.

"The table looks nice, Mom." Stacy entered the dining room with Connor and lifted him into his booster seat. They'd come to an understanding of sorts, which Chase had no doubt orchestrated and which Kaye was grateful for.

"Thank you." Kaye added a garnish of julienned basil to the caprese salad. "I hope you're all hungry. There's plenty of everything, so have as much as you want."

"It looks delicious, Kaye." Ryan guided Sophie into her high chair. "I haven't had a good lobster roll since we left Boston."

"Are they from the Fish Shack?" Stacy asked.

"They are." Kaye turned to Ryan to explain. "When the kids were little, we'd pick up dinner from a shop by the inlet bridge for the first night—"

"And it was delicious," Stacy added.

Kaye glanced at her daughter and smiled. "It was, wasn't it? For whatever reason, we stopped going and I think it's a tradition that needs to be revived."

"Did I hear something about lobster rolls?" Chase came in from the den, reading glasses perched on his head. He looked tired. The trip to the duck pond, along with the walk this morning and a game of pirates with Sophie, had been too much for him.

"You did." Kaye pointed to the toaster over on the counter. "I think the brioche rolls are done. Would you take them out please?"

"I'll get them," Stacy offered as she slid past her father.

"What have we got here?" Chase glanced at his grandson. "Looks like you're all buckled in."

"That's his booster seat, Dad," Stacy answered.

"What's a booster seat?"

"He can't quite reach the table from the chair, so a booster seat lifts him up a bit."

"What's wrong with using a phone book?" Chase teased as he reached for a tear of brioche. "The Yellow Pages were good enough for both you kids."

"Not for you." Kaye nudged Chase's hand away and ignored the pointed look that followed. He knew bread was off limits.

Instead, she asked him to fill the glasses with ice and take charge of the drinks, and he reluctantly headed back to the kitchen. Ryan followed, volunteering to pull the corn from the pot and stack it onto a platter. Stacy clipped the tray onto Sophie's high chair and claimed the seat beside her.

This was it.

The chatter, the teasing, the overcrowded kitchen. This is what she'd wanted, what she'd imagined months before, this eruption of chaos of a house filled with family and everyone talking at once. She stood, soaking in every detail. Then it occurred to her: this was *almost* what she wanted but not quite.

The only thing missing was her son.

She pushed that thought away as quickly as it appeared, reminding herself that Brad was an adult and wasn't required to check his messages or telephone his mother. But she wished he would.

During dinner, Connor and Sophie chatted about the afternoon they'd spent feeding the ducks and asked when they could go to the beach.

"That reminds me," Kaye interrupted quickly. "Beach badges are in the wicker basket in the mudroom, next to the beach towels. You'll need them to get on the beach starting Monday.

"There's a corn-eating contest later this summer, if you're interested." Kaye continued, in a frantic gesture to change the subject from any mention of the beach. She pointed to the town's event calendar taped to the kitchen wall. "Also a kite festival later and a crab-crawl. Oh—and a corn-shucking contest too, and don't forget the Firefly Festival at the end of the summer."

"Good to know." Ryan reached for another ear of corn. "I can start my training right now. This corn is delicious. Everything is."

Kaye glanced at Stacy, then away. "Remember when Brad won the pond race that one year?"

"Of course I do." Stacy snorted and her expression cleared. "I wanted to race against him but they wouldn't let me." She rolled her eyes. "Something about age categories. Anyway, he won and taunted me with that stupid plastic medal. He wore it around his neck for a full week, then taped it to his bedroom door." Stacy shook her head. "I'm willing to bet he still has it."

Conversation for the rest of dinner touched on everything except the beach. They talked about the upcoming bike parade, especially for the kids, which friends planned on summering at Dewberry Beach this year, and guesses as to who might have children or grandchildren Sophie and Connor could play with.

"And don't forget, we have the welcome party soon."

"Are we still doing that?" Chase asked.

"Of course we are—it's tradition," Kaye replied firmly. "We don't attend summer parties without hosting at least one in return."

*

After they'd eaten, Ryan leaned back in his chair and groaned. "I haven't eaten this much since college. I can't believe I had two lobster rolls."

"And corn. So. Much. Corn," Stacy added. "I'd forgotten how good summer corn is."

"I hope you saved room for pie," Kaye announced as she rose to collect the plates.

Ryan groaned and Stacy laughed. "Rookie mistake, Ryan. Should have saved room. Mom always has pie."

The ding of an incoming text was unexpected because they were still seated. It had long been a family rule that there were no electronics allowed at the table during dinner.

"Oh, that's me." Stacy fished her phone from her pocket and unlocked the screen.

Stacy scanned the message and smiled with a light in her eyes that hadn't been there before.

"Mom, it's from Brad. He's coming. He's on the bridge."

How had Brad known to come? Kaye had left messages but none of them provided details of their summer plans. And none of them had been returned. Confused, she glanced around the room at her family. Stacy was tending to the children, cleaning them up and directing them outside. She would have said if Brad had returned her calls. Kaye looked at her husband, piling dishes up by the sink, his back to her. Then dismissed his involvement immediately. She wasn't sure Chase even knew Brad's phone number. Kaye's gaze swept to Ryan, transporting the last of the dinner dishes from the table. He met her gaze and gave the briefest of nods, then returned to his work.

Her son-in-law was a treasure.

After tidying the kitchen the rest of the family wandered outside. Kaye stayed behind to make up a plate for Brad. It was something she'd done for years because her son was never one to watch the clock. In kindergarten, he'd become so absorbed in the wooden blocks on the playmat that his teacher had to remind him that it was time to go home. And later, in high school, when sports practices ran late or he was out and forgot to call, she'd always made sure there was a plate of food waiting for him in the refrigerator.

She assembled the food on a platter, remembering what he especially liked. She decided on two lobster rolls, a side of caprese—with fat tomatoes and an extra splash of balsamic—and the last of the green beans. Unfortunately, that's all that was left. They'd eaten everything else. She covered the plate with plastic wrap and slipped it into the refrigerator.

Summer traffic from the bridge would be light this time of day and Kaye expected Brad before long. He could eat his dinner, and when he was finished, they'd have dessert as a family. She waited a while then glanced at the clock beginning to wonder what bridge Brad had meant when he texted his sister. Surely he'd be here by now?

She reached for the sponge to wipe down the counter again, when the door from the mudroom burst open and her son filled the frame. He stood, with wild auburn hair that needed a good cut and a shadow of stubble across his jaw, wearing a faded T-shirt under a rumpled flannel shirt, jeans that needed a good wash, and a collection of corded bracelets on his wrist.

"Hello? Anybody home?!" he called out, his cheeks dimpling as he smiled.

"I'm right here," Kaye replied as she tucked the sponge away. "No need to shout."

"Hey, Ma." Brad dropped his duffel, a thread-worn canvas thing that needed replacing. It landed with a thud on the mudroom floor as he went to hug his mother.

She was overjoyed to see him. The unanswered phone calls, the unreturned messages, all of it would be forgiven now that he'd come home. Her family was together, all of them under the same roof, and the summer stretched out before her waiting to be filled with new memories.

She eventually released him, then glanced at the luggage he'd brought with him, two more bags beside the one he'd dropped. Each bag was filthy, the canvas splattered with mud, the handles frayed at the edges. How had he managed to travel with such a ratty collection? She'd speak to him later about replacing all of it.

"You brought dirty laundry home for me to do, I see." She bit back a smile.

"Maybe a little." He lifted one shoulder and offered a lopsided grin. "I've been busy. Traveling."

"Have you?" Kaye arched her eyebrow. "Have you been traveling? So far away you couldn't return a single one of my phone calls?"

"I texted Stacy. Ask her."

"You texted your sister from the bridge. That hardly counts," Kaye pointed out. "I saved some dinner for you. It's in the refrigerator, same as always. Lobster rolls— though you don't deserve them, coming in late like this, without a word to anyone." As she walked past him she squeezed his shoulders, then let go. "Pick up a telephone and call me next time. No more of this texting business."

Stacy and Ryan came in from the deck when they heard Brad's voice.

"Brad, you little weasel, I thought I heard your voice. Why haven't you returned my messages?" Stacy shoved her brother before reaching up to wrap her arms around his neck and hug him. "I left a million of them."

"Woah," Brad said, as he pushed her gently away and looked at her stomach. "What happened to you?"

Stacy scoffed. "Seriously? I have to explain it to you?"

"See?" Kaye said, as she filled a glass with lemonade. "I'm not the only one who thinks you've been away too long."

"It's hard to get an internet connection on the trail, Ma. It's pretty isolated up there." Brad went to greet Ryan.

"Good to see you, man," Ryan said. "Glad you came."

Chase joined them and the energy in the room shifted. The light in Brad's eye dimmed as if he were awaiting judgment, which, Kaye supposed, he was.

"Hi, Dad."

"Good to see you, son." Chase's tone was formal, cool, as he extended his hand, and Kaye wanted to shake them both.

There had always been an underlying tension between Chase and Brad that went way beyond normal father-son dynamics. It was as if Chase couldn't bring himself to accept what he termed his son's "lack of direction." The truth was that Brad had more in common with his grandfather, Santos, than he did with Chase and Kaye wasn't sure what to do about it.

Quickly, Kaye brought the lemonade to the table and pulled out the chair. They had all summer to heal the rift between father and son. She didn't need to start now.

"Uncle Brad's here!" Connor called excitedly to his sister as he grabbed Brad's hand. "Come see, Uncle Brad. We have marshmallows. And sticks."

Brad laughed as he followed Connor out to the deck. "My two favorite things. Lead the way, little dude."

At the door, he stopped and called back to his sister. "I'll know if you touch those lobster rolls, so keep your hands off."

Stacy rolled her eyes at him. "Oh, please. Mom may have saved you sad little leftovers, but you missed out on corn. It was deee-licious."

Brad turned, lifting his gaze to Kaye for confirmation. He loved corn.

Kaye shrugged. "You should have called."

"We ate the last of it," Stacy pressed. "The farm stand won't have any more for the rest of the summer. You lost out, pal."

"Stop teasing your brother." Kaye turned toward the sink to hide her smile. "Honestly, you sound like children."

It was wonderful to have them home.

Connor led Brad outside and Ryan followed. To Kaye's disappointment, Chase returned to his den.

"Should I start the dishes, Mom?" Stacy asked.

"No, don't worry—I'll get them later," Kaye replied as she made her way to the washing machine in the mudroom. The duffels were filthy, the clothing inside undoubtedly worse, and since Brad was probably wearing the cleanest outfit he owned, it would be best if she got started. If she got the first load in now, at least he'd have something clean to wear tomorrow. The fact that he'd brought his laundry home for her to do made her happy. It didn't matter how old her son was; it was nice to know that she was still needed, even for something as basic as laundry.

Kaye made her way across the kitchen and froze.

Someone had entered her home. The woman stood in the mudroom as if she had every right to be there though Kaye didn't recognize her. She looked to be close to Brad's age, maybe a little younger. Her outfit was wildly inappropriate even for a tourist, which Kaye assumed she was. The woman's black bra was clearly visible underneath her thin crop top and her shorts too short and much too snug. A frayed hair-tie secured a mess of blonde hair piled on top of her head and it seemed as if every inch of her earlobe was studded with earrings or hoops.

After a moment, Kaye reasoned the girl must have come with Brad—a friend, maybe, who had given him a ride.

"Can I help you?" Kaye prompted. In the spirit of hospitality, Kaye would offer the girl a cold drink and a chance to use the powder room before she went on her way.

"I'm Iona," the girl replied, in a casual tone that assumed Kaye already knew who she was. She looked past Kaye and into the kitchen. "Where's Brad?"

Kaye blinked.

Behind her, she felt a stir of air as the screen door opened then slapped shut. Her son entered the kitchen, walked over to the girl, and draped his arm over her bare shoulders.

"Mom, this is Iona."

The girl leaned her body against Brad's in an irritatingly possessive way. She lifted her chin. "Hey."

Kaye released the fabric handle of her son's duffel; it landed on the floor in a shower of dirt.

Iona walked past them, into the house, into Kaye's kitchen. She opened the refrigerator and removed the plate meant for Brad. "Is that caprese salad?" She unwrapped the plastic and with grubby, unwashed hands, lifted a slice of tomato from the plate and popped it into her mouth. "This is good," she said, her mouth filled with crushed tomato. "Good balsamic too. You wouldn't believe how much of it is imitation these days." A drop of balsamic dripped down her chin and she swiped it away with the back of her hand.

Kaye tore a section of paper towel from the roll and pushed it toward the girl.

The screen door slapped again and Stacy walked into the house. "Mom, do you have any bug spray? The candles aren't..." Her voice faded and she looked at Brad for an explanation.

"Stacy, this is Iona."

"Hi. I'm Stacy, Brad's sister. It's nice to meet you." Stacy's smile seemed genuine but Kaye knew her daughter well enough to see what was behind it: protectiveness.

Ryan made his way inside too, followed by Sophie and Connor who wanted a story and needed a bath. Ryan introduced himself, seemingly oblivious to the tension sparking in the group of women. Chase came into the kitchen shortly afterward, welcoming Iona as he would any visitor, making Kaye ashamed of her own behavior. This girl was a guest in Kaye's home and should be treated like one.

"We have more stuff in the car. I'll just go get it." Brad picked up his car keys and headed toward the door.

"I'll give you a hand." Ryan followed Brad out the back door, their voices deep and echoing against the wood paneling of the mudroom. Stacy took Connor and Sophie upstairs and Chase retreated to his den once more.

That left the two of them alone, Kaye and Brad's friend.

"Can I offer you something to drink?" Kaye moved toward the cabinet for a glass. "Water?"

"Oh yeah, a mineral water would be great." The girl slid into one of the stools along the breakfast bar and slumped across the surface, oblivious to the smudges of dirt she left on the granite. "I'm so into mineral water lately. Can't get enough of it." She lifted her head. "What do you think that means?"

"We have a few bottles in the bar—I'll get one for you." Kaye set the glass on the counter and headed for the bar in the den.

By the time she returned, Iona had helped herself to a plate of crudités from the refrigerator and was crunching on a slice of red pepper. "Do you have any hummus?" Iona tilted her head to the side. "Brad and I have been practically *living* on hummus."

"I'm afraid we're all out." Kaye's patience was rapidly coming to an end. Hopefully, her stay would be short. Brad knew the rules for visitors.

"No biggie. I saw something else that looks just as good." Iona returned to the refrigerator and removed a jar of pesto Kaye had bought at the Italian market in Plainsboro before she left. It was Ryan's favorite, made with roasted pine nuts and aged cheese. She'd intended it to be a surprise for her son-in-law, a gift for his part in persuading Stacy to come. Before Kaye could stop her, Iona popped the seal and stuck her finger into the jar.

"This is pretty good," she said, as she licked her finger.

"I'm so glad you approve." Kaye's sarcasm was lost on the girl.

"Do you have any sourdough?"

"Bread?"

"Yes."

"I'm afraid not."

"I guess any kind of artisan bread is fine for now," Iona allowed as she stuck her finger back into the jar. "Brad can take me shopping in the morning and he'll buy what I like."

There was not enough air in the room for the deep breath Kaye needed to steady her nerves. She managed a tight smile as she crossed the kitchen to the bread box on the corner counter and slid open the lid. Behind the fresh loaves of sourdough and rye was a plastic-wrapped loaf of cheap white bread. The loaf was light and squishy, the sides collapsing as Kaye grabbed it and pulled it out. She placed it on the table in front of Iona.

Duck bread.

A doughy loaf of cheap bread for the grandchildren to feed to the ducks on the salt pond.

It wasn't her finest moment.

Then she imagined how horrified Chase's mother would be about Kaye's lack of hospitality and Kaye sobered. No matter how this girl appeared, she was Brad's guest and would be treated as one. She set the breakfast bar properly, with placemats, napkins, and silverware. She'd offer them both a proper meal. She set food out just as Ryan and Brad returned with the luggage, this set looking very different from the one before. These suitcases were newer, brightly colored, hard-sided and branded with a designer label Kaye recognized. Iona's, Kaye assumed, since she'd never known Brad to travel with much more than faded canvas duffels from L.L.Bean. Ryan set a matching backpack down on the floor beside the rest. It was decidedly feminine.

"You're just in time," Kaye called to them. She pointed to the powder room down the hall. "Brad, go wash your hands. I'll give you both some dinner."

Luckily, Iona decided to join him, giving Kaye a chance to catch her breath. And plan. It was unexpected, her son bringing this girl to the shore house, even though Kaye knew Iona wouldn't be staying for long. Brad and Stacy both understood that while friends were welcome to visit, only family stayed longer than a few days. Summer at the shore house was for family only.

Stacy returned from bathing Connor and Sophie. Her sleeves had been rolled to her elbows and wisps of hair had tumbled from her ponytail.

"Ryan, you're up," she called to her husband, who had slipped out to watch part of the ball game with Chase. "The kids want their dad."

"On it." They heard the stairs creak as Ryan went up. Stacy leaned against the doorframe and yawned.

Brad and Iona returned to the kitchen and settled in the places Kaye had set. But almost immediately, Iona dragged her stool across the floor to a position that was so close to Brad as to be almost on his lap.

Brad smiled at his mother. "Lobster roll night—the best part of being at the shore. I'm glad I didn't miss it."

"You didn't miss it," Kaye answered. "I told Betty I thought you were coming and she made them up special, with extra mayonnaise and celery salt, just the way you like them. I'm afraid there are only two left, but they're meaty and should tide you over until breakfast."

Stacy snarked from her place in the doorway, "If I'd known Mom was saving them for you, I'd have found a way to eat them. In fact," she said with a smile, "I think I'm hungry again. I should eat."

"Forget it." Brad bent over his plate to protect his dinner from his sister, swatting her away with his free hand. "Pregnant or not, I will take you out if you get in between me and Betty's lobster."

"Babe." Iona's voice cut through the hum of activity in the kitchen. "What about Oregon? Our agreement?"

"What agreement?" Stacy asked.

Iona pushed a tangle of hair from her face. "We've joined the Zero Footprint Movement. We posted about it on Insta—don't you follow us?"

"What does this have to do with lobster rolls?"

Iona's expression hardened. "Among other things, it means we're vegan." Iona slid the plate out of Brad's reach and went to the refrigerator to retrieve Ryan's jar of pesto.

"Vegan," Kaye echoed. "So, no meat or dairy?"

"That's right," Iona said, as she popped the lid and swiped the contents with her finger. "We have to be considerate of other living things."

"There's aged Romano in that pesto. That's what makes it taste so good." She turned to her son. "And you agree with this? You're vegan as well?"

Brad shrugged and the spark in his eyes faded. "Sure, I guess."

It was a small thing, not worth getting upset over, but Kaye couldn't help herself. She was annoyed that this girl, someone she'd never met, could hold such sway over her son. She wanted to shake some sense into him, force him to follow his own mind, but of course she couldn't. Her son was a grown man, not a child who could be reminded to make smart choices. She removed the plate and was encouraged when Brad's gaze remained on his beloved lobster rolls.

Iona must have noticed it too. She frowned and dropped her voice, as if she were speaking to a child. "Bae. We agreed."

When Brad exhaled, Kaye knew she'd lost.

"You're right: we did." Brad turned to Stacy. "You can have it."

Stacy shook her head. "It's fine. I don't want it."

During the exchange between her children, Kaye had kept her attention on Iona. She saw a glimmer of satisfaction flicker across Iona's face, then disappear just as quickly. As if she'd won.

What kind of game is this girl playing?

Kaye forced a smile, then left the room. Nothing good would come from engaging this girl, especially since Brad clearly had feelings for her. Kaye would just have to do her best to be cordial until Iona left.

When Kaye reentered the kitchen she saw that Iona had pulled her stool even closer to Brad's and sat with her leg hooked over his, feeding him pieces of raw cauliflower from the platter.

Iona's cell phone buzzed and she lifted it to look, a hint of a smile on her lips as her thumbs tapped the screen. "We're getting Insta-likes, babe. Our hike pictures from Oregon are blowing up, especially the one where we pledged to join the movement."

"What's an 'Insta-like'?"

"Social media, Mom," Brad answered. "Iona has an account and it's gaining followers."

"*We* have an account and *we* are gaining followers," Iona corrected. "We're going to be huge. You just wait and see."

"What's the picture?" Kaye looked over Stacy's shoulder as Iona tilted the phone screen.

The picture was one of Brad posing on a mountain path in a forest, looking completely at ease and utterly charming. He held himself with a confidence that came from a lifetime of playing sports in both high school and college. In the picture, the foreground was a maze of deep green ferns, soft moss, and polished river rock. Behind him, a jagged mountain range stretched across a spring sky, deep blue and clear. Brad stood with his arm draped around a trail marker, shades of dappled light from the pine trees above falling across his head and arms.

"The hiking one's the best yet, babe." Iona flicked through several pictures, all of them Brad. All of them versions of the same pose.

Kaye looked closer at the pictures, this time with a mother's eye. She ignored the exclamation-pointed comments, the heart emojis, and the likes from admirers, and concentrated on her son. What she saw was a plastic smile and a blank expression. And she was not pleased. The man in the picture looked nothing like the son she'd raised, the quiet boy who could lose himself in an afternoon playing quietly with building blocks and wooden trucks. And Iona looked as if she knew exactly what she was doing.

Between her two children, it had always been Brad who needed Kaye's guidance the most. Where Stacy was fiercely independent and frustratingly strong-willed, Brad was a follower who hadn't yet found his way. In high school, he played team sports—lacrosse in the fall and rugby in the spring. In college, he changed his major six times, and to this day Kaye wasn't entirely sure if he'd even earned a degree at all. After graduation, he picked up a backpack and took off to see the world, working odd jobs when he needed the money. He always seemed to be looking for something but never quite finding it.

Kaye filled a glass with filtered water. "Brad, would you please bring this to your father? He's in the den watching the game."

"Sure." Brad slid off the chair.

Stacy's gaze cut to her mother, then back to Brad. "I'll go with you."

After they left, Kaye took a moment to gather her thoughts. This would be tricky.

"So, Iona. How did you and Brad meet?" Kaye picked up a sponge and wiped the counter, though it didn't need to be done.

When the girl didn't answer, Kaye asked again.

Her attention had been on the screen. Iona held up her index finger. "Sorry, just one second—I have to reply to this comment."

Kaye returned the sponge to its holder, leaned against the counter, and waited.

Iona's movements were languid, as if she had all the time in the world, and it wasn't until the girl snorted at something on her screen that Kaye realized Iona's behavior was deliberate. Kaye was being made to wait on purpose.

So that's the way of it.

Iona finished her typing and slipped her phone back into her pocket. "I'm sorry, what was your question?" She tilted her head as she spoke.

Kaye would not be baited again. She offered a smile. "I asked how you know my son. How did you meet?"

"Oh, that. Brad was with a bunch of guys in New Mexico and I joined the group. When the guys went home, Brad and I hooked up." She pulled a fork from the drawer and walked toward the pie.

"That's not vegan."

"Excuse me?"

"The pie." Kaye pointed. "It's made with lard." She smiled, genuine this time. "The lard is what makes it good."

Iona shrugged. She turned, removing a bottle of iced tea from the shelf of the refrigerator door, popped the top, and sipped.

"And the pictures? Where did that idea come from?"

Iona looked at Kaye with a glint in her eye that Kaye did not expect to see. She swallowed another mouthful of tea, then set the bottle on the counter and straightened. "That was my idea actually. Brad and I like to travel, and the pictures pay for it, if they're curated and managed correctly." Iona reclaimed her place on the stool. "When we get enough of a following, we'll use our platform to bring awareness to causes that are trending. We can use our social-media platform to eventually crowd-fund our documentary. No one's thought of that yet. We'll be the first."

"Documentary?"

"Yeah." Iona sighed, clearly losing patience explaining a grand idea to someone who didn't share her vision.

"You're making a documentary?"

"That's the plan. Didn't Brad tell you?"

"No. He did not," Kaye replied.

After a few moments, Brad and Stacy wandered back into the kitchen from the den.

"Is your father okay?" Kaye asked.

"The game's still on but he's asleep," Stacy answered with another yawn. "I think I'm going up too. It's getting late."

Iona went to Brad and tucked herself under his arm. She leaned against him, practically purring. "I'm tired too, bae. I think we should go to bed."

"Okay," Brad agreed. "Mom, do you have anything I can wear? My stuff's dirty."

"I'll get something from your father's closet." Kaye squeezed her son's arm as she moved past him. "I'll be right back."

"I'll meet you upstairs." Iona tilted her head. "Which bedroom is ours?"

Kaye hesitated. "I thought Brad could stay in his old room and you can have the guest room at the back of the house. You'll like it back there. It's very comfortable, sunny and light in the morning."

"But—" Iona's eyes narrowed, then darted to Brad. "I thought we'd sleep together."

"Oh, I'm afraid not." Kaye interjected. "There are young children in the house, and you and my son are not married." She paused, just for moment. "I'm sure you understand."

Iona's eyes narrowed, in a look meant for Kaye alone. "We've been dating for *quite* a long time."

They stared at each other, like feral cats in a back alley, neither one willing to give in. But this was the hill Kaye was willing to die on. Her house. Her rules.

It was Brad who spoke first.

"Mom's right, Iona," he said. "Connor and Sophie wake me up in the morning when I'm here anyway. But you'll like the guest room. It's nice."

"That's fine. I'm sure it's great," Iona said, her tone even though her eyes snapped with fury. "I don't mind at all."

"Good. It's settled then." Kaye's tone was brisk. "I'll just get some sheets."

Once the dishes were done, the coffee set to brew in the morning, and the house was quiet, Kaye made her way upstairs to the master bedroom to get ready for bed.

"I don't like that girl," Kaye began as she drew back the bedspread.

"So you've said." Chase had been roused from his chair in the den and helped pull back his side of the bedspread. "Several times."

"Something about her doesn't sit right with me," she mused.

"That's because you've never liked any of your son's girlfriends."

Kaye stopped, stung at the accusation. "That's not true. I liked— what's her name, the one who came to Thanksgiving dinner his freshman year of college?"

Chase snorted as he untied his bathrobe and tossed it on the chair. "The one with the nose ring? You did not."

"The athlete then."

"You made her cry."

Kaye paused, indignation returning as she remembered the incident. "She broke the kitchen window with that baseball. Anyone with any sense at all would have known not to hit a baseball so close to the house."

Without a word, Chase settled into his side of the bed and reached for his book.

"I liked the bookish one. She was very intelligent," Kaye continued. "We had a nice conversation."

"Until she asked to borrow one of your novels," Chase countered absently as he found his place.

"Everyone knows I don't lend books." Kaye voice was sharper than she'd intended. She was stung by the implication that she'd made someone feel unwelcome. She slipped off her robe and settled into the bed, feeling the fresh cotton sheets against her skin. "I would have gladly *bought* that girl a copy of her own, but the one she wanted to take was signed by the author."

"A local author," Chase countered, as he bent the corner of the page and closed the cover of his book. "A woman with whom you have lunch frequently. How hard would it have been for you to ask her to sign another copy of her book?"

"Hmm." Arguing wasn't good for Chase's heart so she changed the subject. "I saw Nancy at the market the other day. She said she and George are here for the summer—the whole summer."

"Is that right?" Chase looked at her with interest. "I didn't think George would ever take that much time away from his job."

"She told me he'd retired," Kaye offered as she smoothed the bedspread. "She said he's much more relaxed now. You should look him up; maybe have lunch with him."

Chapter 8

Three doors down, at the front of the house, Ryan and Stacy were also getting ready for bed. Stacy snatched the white cotton spread off the bed and balled it up before tossing it onto the floor. Her cheeks were flushed, her breathing short and jagged. It occurred to Ryan that if Stacy had been a cartoon character, steam would have been shooting from her ears, but he knew better than to point that out just now.

"Can you *believe* that harpy?" She crossed the room to open a window.

"Who?" Ryan asked, though he knew perfectly well who Stacy was talking about.

"Iona. Brad's new girlfriend." She snorted, impatient as she pushed a strand of hair from her face. "Don't you think she's awful?"

Ryan had been married to Stacy long enough to know that she was fiercely protective of her brother, and also that Ryan's opinion of Brad's girlfriend didn't matter just now. If Stacy didn't like Iona, the best thing to do was steer clear of the skirmish.

"I don't know her well enough to judge. Why do you ask?"

"No reason." Stacy snapped open the adjacent window too. "It's hot in here, don't you think?"

"Maybe a little. You want me to turn on the window AC?"

"Well, I think she's pushy, that's all," Stacy continued, as if Ryan hadn't spoken. "Did you see her telling Brad what to do—he's not strong enough to stand up to someone like that." She pulled the decorative pillows from the bed and flung them toward the chair. One of them missed and bounced against the wall. She ignored it. Instead she straightened and planted her hand firmly on her hip. "And what's the deal with this Instagram account? She's using him."

"Maybe he's developed interests you don't know about." Ryan's cell phone dinged with an incoming message. He glanced at the sender and suppressed a groan. Todd again.

"I know Brad." Stacy shook her head. "He hasn't."

"He's been traveling for the better part of six months. Travel changes people, you know," Ryan said as he clicked on the text message.

The VC partners' meeting has been moved to tomorrow morning instead of next week. I need to present projections for next quarter. Urgent need for new schedule.

Ryan's body tensed as he skimmed the message. The data for the projections was stored on a company server, and Sean and Jeff both had the same access he did. Why did the job of mapping the data fall to him? He typed a snarky reply and hit send.

Maybe Sean could take a break from car shopping and take care of it? He knows where to find the numbers, same as I do.

Ryan watched his screen as the text was delivered, then the checkmark appearing beside it as the message was read. As he waited for

Todd to reply, it occurred to him that he could have chosen his words more carefully. His reply wasn't professional, but he was so tired of every task falling to him.

Sean says you're slides are better. he working on soemthing else.

Ryan flinched at Todd's sloppy text, wondering if the reply had been sent in anger. If Ryan's refusal had gone too far. In his opinion, Todd was too slick, pushy, and untrustworthy, and those were on his good days. Overall, he was not helpful, his background in technology non-existent and his experience with start-ups minimal.

Ryan composed a quick reply, designed to end the conversation.

Get Jeff to do it. I'm taking time with my family. I told you all this.

Ryan watched as the message was delivered and read. After a moment with no reply, he assumed the task of graphing the data would fall to someone else. Relieved, Ryan put his phone away and turned his attention back to Stacy.

His wife was glaring at him. "Really? You're texting while I'm talking to you about something this important?"

Ryan sighed and he rose from his place. As he crossed the room, he picked up the thread of their conversation. Brad. Brad's new girlfriend. "Maybe you should consider that Brad is a grown man and knows what he's doing. Even if he doesn't, maybe you could respect his choice and let him find his own way."

"She's bossy," Stacy declared. "She's bossy and I don't like her."

Ryan laughed and crossed the room toward his wife. "You're no shrinking violet yourself, you know."

"What is that supposed to mean?"

"You're a formidable woman, Stacy; both you and your mother are. The Bennett women are redwoods. Anyone who is not *at least* as strong won't stand a chance with either of you."

"I don't know what you're talking about," Stacy scoffed.

"I happen to like strong women," Ryan replied, as he reached for the light. "But I knew what I was getting into when I married you."

Chapter 9

The front door was open, so Kaye called in through the screen door. "Brenda, you home?"

She and Brenda Galbano had been friends for more than thirty years. The women met as new moms, chasing after toddlers on the beach, and in the years following, their kids had played together every summer. Eventually the Bennetts and the Galbanos had felt equally at home in both houses, coming and going as they pleased.

Brenda's house was small, one of the smaller cottages at Dewberry Beach, not much larger than one of the oversized garages attached to the new mansions near the shore. It was a perfectly square structure on a tree-shaded lot, the way the town used to be before builders began subdividing the lots to make room for more houses. The cottage was a single floor with two rooms in front and a large, homey kitchen in the back. On one side of the kitchen were two bedrooms—the master that Brenda had shared with her husband, Eddie, and one for the children. On the other side of the kitchen was Brenda's favorite room: her pottery studio. For their fifteenth anniversary, Eddie had surprised Brenda by converting a tumble-down screened-in porch into a fully functioning art room. It took him a month of weekends to finish because he insisted on doing all the work himself. He rolled the insulation, ran the electrical, and added wide windows so his wife would have a view of the bay.

"I'm here, in the back." Brenda's voice came from the back of the house. "C'mon in."

Kaye pushed the screen open and slipped off her shoes. She walked on the braided rug down the short hall from the front door to the kitchen.

Her friend stood in front of the white enamel farm sink in her studio and turned on the tap with her elbow. The water splashed over her hands, and rivers of clay ran down the drain.

"Brought you something," Kaye said as she set a lemon pound cake on the kitchen counter.

"Don't you have a house full of people? When have you had time to bake?" Brenda called from her place at the sink.

"I didn't bake this one. Mueller's did." Kaye pulled two mismatched plates from the cabinet.

"I don't understand." Brenda emerged from her studio in her denim work smock, her hands dotted with clay. "You make the best lemon pound cake. Why would you buy one?"

"I can't have it in the house because I don't want Chase being tempted by things he can't eat." Kaye lifted the coffee pot from the warmer and tested the side with her fingertips. It was cool to the touch. "Should I warm this up or make a new pot?"

"The timer probably switched it off." Brenda looked at the clay still coating her hands and frowned. "Go ahead and make a fresh pot. I'll be right back."

Kaye knew Brenda's kitchen as well as her own. The lighting was soft, with scarves gently draped over lampshades in the front rooms;

framed photographs of her and her husband and the kids lined the walls. The air smelled warm, like the vanilla candle Brenda kept flickering on the counter. Brenda's home was a true beach cottage, one of the few left in Dewberry Beach. She and her husband had furnished it with a comfortable mismatched collection of yard-sale finds, estate-sale pieces, and built-ins. People hired decorators to recreate the same mood that Brenda pulled together on instinct.

Kaye found the coffee and filters in the usual place and had the coffee brewing by the time Brenda came back, wiping her now-clean hands on a strip of faded blue beach towel.

"You look like you've been busy," Kaye remarked.

"Not as busy as I'd hoped." Brenda sighed. "I'm a bit off today."

Brenda made her living as an artist. When she was younger, her parents had planned for her to attend art school in London, to study with the best instructors the world had to offer. But Brenda had other ideas. She married Eddie on the afternoon of her high school graduation. They had a courthouse ceremony and her parents cut her off, thinking she'd return to them when she realized her mistake. Again, Brenda had other ideas. She earned a teaching certificate and became an art teacher at a public school, working on her art at night. She and Eddie bought a starter apartment in Queens, New York and she fixed it up. She and Eddie had lived there for years and were very happy. Her parents never spoke to her again.

Brenda retrieved two coffee mugs from the drainboard and set them on the table. She added a generous pour of cream to her coffee and set the pitcher aside, knowing Kaye preferred hers strong and black.

"Have a seat." She gestured to one of four wooden chairs positioned around her sturdy wooden kitchen table. "Are the kids here yet?"

"Yes." Kaye pulled out a chair.

"You don't sound pleased."

"Brad got in last night and brought someone with him."

"What do you mean 'someone'?"

"I guess you could call her a girlfriend."

"I didn't know he was dating anyone."

"I didn't either. And she's awful."

"How so?"

Kaye sighed. "They have some sort of picture account on the internet. She poses him like some kind of doll, then posts his picture on this account." Kaye waved her hand in the air. "And they're *vegan* now, of all things—my son. So he wouldn't even eat the lobster rolls I bought especially. I don't know how to feed them, or even if I want to." Kaye propped her elbows on the table and cradled her head in her palms. "It's awful."

"How long is she staying?"

"They haven't said, but they came in the same car."

"Oh, that's not good." Brenda snorted. "Have you set a summer calendar out where she can see it?"

Her eagerness made Kaye laugh. "Not yet, and I'm not sure if I can. Remember those people Chase invited down that one year? Them? They came for a 'weekend' and ended up staying for the month of July."

"I remember they were the reason you started the summer visit calendar in the first place." Brenda said. "'The shore house is for family.' You've said it so many times, I should embroider it on a T-shirt."

"But if Brad leaves then Stacy will too, and I don't want that" Kaye countered. "Not this year."

"Seems like an easy choice." Brenda shrugged. "If you want Brad to stay, then you learn to get along with someone you don't like. As Mrs. Ivey would say, life has presented a lesson for you."

"It gets worse."

"Tell me."

"Stacy hasn't taken the kids to the beach yet."

"They just got here. Give her a chance to settle in."

Kaye shook her head. "Ryan let it slip that she's afraid of the ocean."

"Oh dear." Brenda set her coffee cup on the table with a gentle thump. "So you haven't told her?"

"I didn't think I should. If I brought it up and she *hadn't* remembered, I'd be stirring up something that was best left alone."

"Clearly she remembers something or she wouldn't be afraid."

"Or she just doesn't like the ocean anymore."

"You know that's not it," Brenda scoffed as she rose to collect the plates. "You have to do this, Kaye. You have to tell her."

While Brenda made a second pot of coffee, Kaye sat in silence, listening to the familiar sounds of Brenda's kitchen and leaning into more than three decades of friendship. Brenda was right, of course—she usually was—but Kaye and her daughter had forged a bit of an uneasy truce as neither of them cared for Iona. Kaye didn't want to upset that.

Kaye glanced at her friend. "Enough about me. What's going on with you?"

Brenda scooped fresh coffee from a can, turned on the tap, and filled the machine with water then snapped it on.

"Nice try," she said as she scooped the coffee into the machine.

"What?"

"We're not finished with you yet." She flicked the switch and returned to her seat opposite Kaye.

"You have to tell Stacy what happened but you already know that. Tell her yourself before she finds out another way."

"But I don't want her to leave," Kaye protested. "I want both kids here. I need them here."

"Why? Why can't the summer be just for you and Chase?"

"Because I need him to forgive me."

"What kind of twisted logic is that?"

"It's true, Bren. I wasn't there when I should have been. I had no idea he was in trouble and I should have. I should have known."

"Listen to me." Brenda's gaze was sharp. "You're not afraid *because* it happened, Kaye. It *did* happen and you've already survived it. What keeps you up at night is the idea that it might happen again, and I'm here to tell you that kind of obsessing will make you crazy. There is nothing you could have done to prevent Chase's heart attack. Nothing. No sign you missed, no way you could have known it was going to happen before it did."

In the silence that followed, Kaye heard the vanilla candle on the countertop pop. The chirp of a bird outside the kitchen window. The laughter of children as they biked past the house.

"Mrs. Ivey would have known," Kaye said finally.

Brenda snorted into her coffee mug and the mood was lifted. "Maybe so."

"That's more than enough about me," Kaye decided. "Tell me what's got you in your studio this early."

Brenda's expression veiled and her gaze shifted to the trees outside. "I got an invitation from the Families Group. The twentieth anniversary is next year and they want to plan something."

"Oh, Brenda," Kaye breathed.

Eddie Galbano's dream was to be a firefighter. When he and Brenda were first married he worked construction during the day and volunteered at the firehouse while earning the accreditations he needed. Precious days off were spent at Dewberry Beach. The process took years but Eddie passed with honors and was offered his first-choice post assignment in Midtown Manhattan. To celebrate, the Galbanos bought a ramshackle cottage on the edge of Dewberry Beach and went about making it a home. Brenda and the girls made the trip down from their apartment in Queens on the last day of school, and for the rest of the summer, they met the commuter train from Grand Central Terminal to welcomed Eddie to the shore.

They loved Dewberry Beach so much, they made plans to live there permanently. At the end of the summer in 2001, Eddie put in for a transfer to the Dewberry Beach firehouse and it was accepted immediately. Brenda enrolled the kids in the nearby public school, and the family planned to make their permanent home at the shore as soon as Eddie worked his notice in Manhattan.

Two weeks later, on a bright morning in September, Eddie reported for his last day of active duty in Manhattan. Early that morning, his battalion received a call about a plane flying into the Twin Towers and at first it was treated as an accident, pilot error from the airfield in Teterboro. Eddie suited up with the rest of his crew and went to help. At the end of the day, the fire chief called for a final headcount and Eddie was one of the responders who didn't return. Heartbroken, Brenda quit her job, sold their apartment in Queens, and moved her family to Dewberry Beach because that's what she and Eddie had planned to do. Brenda had been living here full-time ever since.

"What are you going to do?" Kaye asked softy.

"I don't know."

"What do you *want* to do?"

"I don't know that either." Brenda's voice cracked. "You know, it's been twenty years. You'd think I'd be fine by now."

"No, I wouldn't." Kaye reached across the table for Brenda's hand. "I wouldn't expect fine. Eddie was an extraordinary man and we all miss him." After a moment, Kaye rose from her chair. "Show me what you've been working on."

The studio breathed life into Brenda. Kaye watched the transformation as her friend described the oxide wash she'd ordered from Japan and the silver clay she wanted to try. Afterwards, they moved outside where Kaye helped Brenda plant a flat of violets in a shady spot of the yard. When they were finished, Kaye gathered the empty pots and shovels and put them away. She held open the screen door as they walked back into the kitchen.

"Are you going to be okay?" Kaye asked.

"'Course I am." Brenda nodded. "We both are."

There was sense in what Brenda had said about the truth behind Stacy's fear of the ocean coming from Kaye and no one else. Maybe Kaye could explain in a way that she'd understand. But when she returned home in the early afternoon, the house was empty. A flutter of notes on the kitchen counter were the only indication that a family lived here.

From Brad:

Took Iona to the mall. Will eat there and maybe see a movie. Don't wait up.

From Stacy:

Ryan drove back home to work. He'll be back tomorrow. Dad and I took the kids to the duck pond with the last of the bread. Will get more on the way back.

And from Chase:

Doctor's appointment rescheduled from next week to August. Back later.

At least they were all under one roof.

Chapter 10

"It's crowded today." Chase looked through the windshield at the line of cars in the parking lot. "I didn't expect it to be."

"I suppose after the crab crawl, everyone decided to come here for breakfast," Kaye replied from her place in the passenger seat. "There's one." Kaye pointed to a car pulling out.

Chase pulled in then turned off the ignition. As they crossed the parking lot, the cicadas began to sing, signaling the beginning of another hot day at the shore.

"Our house party is next weekend—I hope it won't be this hot then," Kaye remarked.

"I'm sure it will be fine."

"They've decorated for the Fourth of July already." She gestured to swaths of bunting and miniature flags poking out from potted plants at the restaurant's entrance.

"Very nice," Chase murmured, though he hadn't noticed them. Could it be they'd been at the shore house a month already? Time seemed to have very little meaning without a job or a purpose to anchor him to the rhythm of the day.

"Here they come." Kaye brightened as she spotted Stacy and the kids moving toward them, and Chase's mood lifted too. After all, they were about to have breakfast at one of his very favorite restaurants.

Breakfast at the Parkway Diner had been part of the fabric of summers at Dewberry Beach since Chase was a kid. It was the kind of place that locals loved and renters remembered, with pancakes overflowing the edges of the plates they were served on, oniony home fries, fat omelets, and crisp, grill-toasted hard rolls. The coffee was hot and fresh and the refills frequent, by servers who were almost as old as the diner itself. The wait staff knew all the locals and got to know the renters, if they tipped well. Chase and his brother ad deferred all rewards for grades and achievements during the school year to the summer, so they could collect their prize in the form of a stack of chocolate-chip pancakes, extra whipped cream, and sometimes a waxy little candle pegged on the top. Chase hadn't thought about those pancakes in years.

His gaze skimmed the large dining room and he felt himself relax. The smell of warm bread and fresh coffee provided the background for a hum of quiet conversation and the delicate clink of silverware. *It never changes*, Chase thought. The Parkway Diner was always, reliably, the same.

They were led to a large table by the window, which was impressive considering how busy the restaurant had become. They were seated immediately, bypassing several groups who had arrived there ahead of them. Kaye could be quite persuasive when the situation required it and Chase wondered what she'd said to the hostess.

They table was set with a glass of ice water at each place, beaded with condensation dripping on the paper napkins below. In the middle of the table were coffee mugs filled with crayons for the children or anyone who needed to draw on the paper placemats. Chase held the chair for Kaye, then took his place beside her, snapping the paper seal on his rolled napkin and smoothing it on his lap. While his family settled in, his mind wandered back to the pancakes he and his brother enjoyed years ago and he wondered if they tasted the same now.

The hostess distributed plastic-covered menus, pausing beside Chase. "Mr. Bennett, it's good to see you again. We're happy you've recovered."

Kaye covered his hand with hers. "Thank you for the card, Millie. It meant a lot to us."

When the hostess left, Chase leaned toward his wife. "They sent a card?"

"About a week after you came home from the hospital; everyone signed it. Flowers too, I think."

"I didn't see a card."

Kaye looked at him, confused. "Did you want to?"

"Yes, of course. I would have liked to thank them."

She turned her attention back to her menu. "I thanked them for you. I wrote a nice note."

And that seemed to be the end of it.

Ryan flicked open his menu and settled back in his chair to read the contents. "What's good here?"

"Everything," Stacy replied as she glanced at her brother. They shared a look, an inside joke Chase didn't understand that ended with Stacy rolling her eyes. "Almost everything."

They'd been sitting for several minutes, menus down, when a waitress Chase vaguely recognized came to take their order. Dressed in a standard yellow uniform with the Parkway Diner logo embroidered over her pocket and a green plastic nametag pinned underneath, she made her way to the table. "The Bennetts are at my station." Her eyes crinkled when she smiled. "I'm glad you're back."

"Thank you, Shelly. It's nice to be back," Kaye replied.

Shelly. That's her name.

"You brought the whole family with you, I see?" Shelly's gaze swept the table.

"Yes," Kaye offered. "You know Stacy and Brad already. And I think you remember Ryan, Stacy's husband, and their children—our grandchildren—Sophie and Connor. And this is Iona, Brad's friend."

"Girlfriend," Iona corrected.

Kaye allowed a quick nod of acknowledgement. There would be a reckoning later between Kaye and that girl, and Chase almost looked forward to it. Not for the drama that would follow, but for the spark in his wife's eye as she reminded the girl of her place. There was a time, after his incident, when he had looked for the spark in his wife's eyes but couldn't find it. All he had seen was worry. And fear. He was afraid that his illness had been too much for her, that *he* had been too much of a burden.

Shelly shrugged as if the girl's title didn't matter in the slightest. She slipped her pad from her apron pocket and flipped to a new page. "Ladies first. What can I get you, Mrs. Bennett?"

Kaye ordered, then Stacy next to her, and Shelly continued around the table. Everyone knew what they wanted. Ryan and the kids ordered, then Brad, and then it was Iona's turn.

"What can I getcha?"

"I'm not sure exactly." Iona reached for her menu and opened it.

"Do you need more time?" Shelly shifted her weight and glanced at the tables in her area. They were filling up with customers who wanted attention.

"No," Iona said idly. "I have questions about the menu."

"Lemme hear 'em."

Iona paused, tilting her head as she scanned the menu's contents. "Are your eggs responsibly sourced?"

Kaye and Stacy exchanged a quick look. Ryan picked up a crayon and helped Connor work the maze on the placemat. Brad had no reaction at all, making Chase wonder how many times this type of thing had happened—his friend taking pleasure in behaving badly. It was a strange type of power play and Chase had seen it before at work. New hires flexing their muscles, eager to prove their worth. It didn't end well there and it wouldn't end well here, with Kaye. Iona was out of her league.

"Our eggs come from chickens. Whether the chickens are happy or not, I don't know. They don't tell me."

Iona flushed at the comment but pressed on. "Can you *at least* tell me if the hash browns are vegan?"

Shelly laughed, making no attempt to hide her disdain. "No, sweetie, they're not. Javier has bacon grease spread on that grill all day long and nothing that comes off it would be remotely considered vegan. But if it matters, I can tell you the whitefish is fresh this morning and I think that part of the grill was just cleaned. You might want to go with that."

"Vegans don't eat fish."

Shelly signaled to a nearby table that she'd be with them in a minute.

"Toast," Iona conceded. "Just toast. No butter."

Brad reached for her hand under the table, but she shook it off and pushed him away.

When it was time for Chase to order, he knew *exactly* what he wanted. If this summer marked a new start, he knew the perfect way to celebrate it. "I'll have chocolate-chip pancakes."

"You got it." Shelly chuckled as she jotted the order on her pad. "You want whipped cream or butter with that?"

"Both." Chase raised his chin as he pictured his breakfast plate, the same as when he was a kid: dripping with syrup and pooling with melted butter.

"Okay then." The waitress collected his menu and tucked it under her arm.

"Just a moment please." Kaye spoke, her tone cutting through the conversation at the table. She had everyone's attention.

"Yes?"

"I think we can do a little better than pancakes." As she opened her menu, Chase heard the crackle of the plastic cover and felt frustration bloom in his chest. Kaye had been ruthless in seeing that he followed the diet plan the nutritionist gave him, but his heart attack was three years ago and that diet wasn't meant to be a prison. Surely Kaye wouldn't do this in front of the entire family?

"Instead of pancakes, please bring my husband an egg-white omelet with vegetables only—no cheese—and a slice of whole wheat toast. No butter. And maybe a fruit cup on the side if the strawberries are ripe."

Kaye turned her attention to Chase and spoke to him in the same tone she used with Sophie. "Did you want fruit?"

"No," Chase said. His frustration turned to anger. "I do not."

This is where it ended. He would not accept a life of egg whites and weak, herbal tea. A life where his wife ordered for him, leaving him with no agency at all.

Kaye folded the menu and handed it back. "Okay, no fruit then."

"I mean 'no' to all of it." Chase spoke as politely as he could under the circumstances. "Shelly, please bring what I ordered."

But Kaye wouldn't let it go. "Maybe egg whites and a side of pancakes instead?"

"Kaye." His voice was stern, a tone he hadn't taken in years, and never with his wife. Despite seeing the color rise in her cheeks and feeling the attention of everyone at the table, he continued. "I am a grown man and if I want pancakes, then I will have them."

Kaye nodded and surrendered her menu without another word.

The victory seemed hollow to him. It was an odd hill to plant his flag on, this order of chocolate-chip pancakes. He knew his tone had embarrassed her, that his order would cause Kaye to fret about his heart and cholesterol levels, but it was his heart and his cholesterol, and he wasn't a child.

In the end it was for nothing. The pancakes were overly sweet and didn't taste anything like he remembered. That was the problem with chasing memories: they never stood still long enough to be caught.

When breakfast was over, he paid the check and everyone went their separate ways. Iona and Brad to the jetty for pictures to post. Ryan and Stacy home to put the kids up for a nap. Kaye didn't say anything at all and spent the afternoon in the garden.

Chapter 11

The Fourth of July was a big deal at Dewberry Beach, and if the holiday fell on a weekend, as it did this year, the celebration was even bigger. The festivities began with the Kids' Parade, early Saturday morning. Every kid in town decorated their bike with streamers and glitter ribbon and, following tradition, had filled their bike's basket with candy to toss to spectators lining the parade route. Getting Connor and Sophie ready for the parade had taken multiple trips to Applegate's to gather supplies. Stacy had helped them clip playing cards to the spokes of their bikes and add tassels to their helmets, like she and Brad did when they were kids. It had been a tiring week, but worth it. By 8 a.m. Stacy and her children were positioned at the starting line, helmets on, waiting for the mayor to ring the cowbell to launch the parade.

When the bell sounded, the crowd of kids surged forward. The older kids zipped ahead quickly, clearly trying to finish first. Parents of younger kids walked alongside, offering encouragement and placing a guiding hand on their handlebars to help them navigate the crowd. A few families had brought their dogs, accessorized with flag neckties, and kids too young for bikes were pulled in decorated wagons. In short, the Kids' Parade was a knot of barely contained chaos from the starting line at the cheese shop to the finish line at Mueller's, a distance of three blocks.

"Mommy, I'm done." Sophie pushed back on her pedal and stopped abruptly, dropping her bike.

They'd traveled half a block.

Stacy stopped and just missed getting nicked in the shin with a pedal from a kid behind them. She reached for her daughter's bike. "Sophie, you can't stop in the middle."

"But I'm hot." She pushed the edge of her helmet away from her eyes.

"I am too." Stacy tucked a strand of damp hair behind her ear. Though it was still early, it was hot—and crowded. In the rush to get the kids ready on time, Stacy had forgotten her sunglasses and a hat. She could feel the sun scorching the part in her hair and a trickle of perspiration slide down her back. "We're almost there," she lied.

"But I don't have any candy left," Sophie whined.

"That's because you gave it all away already. You're supposed to toss a little at a time." At the start of the race, Sophie had misunderstood the directions and dumped the basket's entire contents. Now, she had nothing to throw.

Sophie allowed her mother to guide her back on the bike, but she refused to pedal. As Stacy leaned over to grip the handlebars, the baby kicked sharply and Stacy winced.

"You okay, Mommy?"

"Yes, but you need to be a big girl and do this yourself." Sophie's training wheels were dangerously close to Stacy's heels. "Have you seen your brother?"

Sophie pointed to Connor, riding with his friend Miles. They had already reached the finish line, at Mueller's Bakery.

"Soph." Stacy straightened and pointed to Connor and his friend. "If you pedal—all by yourself—to the finish line, you'll get a donut, any kind you want."

Sophie glanced at the finish line and nodded, accepting the challenge. "Okay."

And just like that, Stacy had become a parent who bribed her child with food.

Stacy eventually caught up with Connor at the finish line. She gave the kids money and sent them into the bakery, then found a shady place to rest. The parade was supposed to be a family event, but one by one every other adult in the family had bowed out, leaving Stacy to manage the kids alone. She swatted a cloud of gnats away as she remembered their excuses: Iona's sudden mall emergency that required Brad to drive her, Ryan's work, the preparations for tomorrow's party that required both her parents' attention.

Apparently, everyone was allowed to have outside interests except for her.

Connor was the first to emerge from Mueller's, holding his sister's hand and half a donut, both of their faces dusted with powdered sugar. Stacy rose awkwardly to her feet. The baby wasn't due for another three months but navigating this humidity had become uncomfortable.

"You guys ready?"

"Can we go to the beach now, Mom? Miles and his brother said they'd teach me how to boogie board. Can we go?"

"I don't think so, buddy."

Connor's face fell. "But you haven't taken us one time yet."

"I haven't?"

Connor shook his head.

"We'll have to see then." Stacy guided them home.

Stacy would do almost anything for her children, except take them to the beach. The ocean, the waves in particular, filled her with a dread that took her breath away and made her heart race. Before she'd agreed to come to the shore house, she'd told Ryan that she wouldn't take the kids to the beach, no matter what. She said it had to do with the baby and her balance on the sand, but she'd lied. He'd agreed to beach duty, but he'd been busy with work and hadn't been available to go.

With any luck at all, Brad would be home and he could take them.

When they got home, the kids walked their bikes up the driveway. Stacy pointed to the shed in the back. "Park your bikes over there, then come inside."

She pushed open the screen door and called into the house. "Anyone home?" As the screen door slapped shut behind her, the breeze caught a note laid on the counter and it fluttered into the sink. It was from Ryan:

Wi-Fi is down. Went to a coffee shop in Point Pleasant to work. Back late.

She stared at the empty kitchen as she listened to the kids clamber up and down the stairs, and her shoulders sagged. They'd want their lunch, which she'd have to make. And since it seemed that she might be forced to take them to the beach after all, there would be towels to find, toys to pack, the cooler to load, and chairs to wrangle into the car.

She would not go to the beach. Fortunately, she didn't have to.

"Change of plans." She stood, pleased at her work-around. "Go upstairs and find your bathing suits. First one down, wearing your suit, with flip-flops and goggles in your bag, is the winner."

They raced upstairs and Stacy followed them, grateful that her kids were still at an age where bragging rights was prize enough. She found her own suit and tugged it on, then grabbed one of Ryan's shirts and slipped it on.

"Do we need sand toys?" Connor asked as he headed for the mudroom.

"Not today, buddy. We're going to the pool."

"The pool? But what about Miles? He's waiting for me at the ocean."

Stacy drew a breath and spun the lie. "You need a swim test before you go into the ocean. So we have to go to the pool first."

For as long as she could remember, Stacy had been afraid of the ocean. Even from the relative safety of the shore, waves seemed looming and monstrous, the force of the crash as they broke terrifying and inescapable. The thought of swimming in the ocean pulled the air from her lungs and left her dizzy with fear, though she had never understood why. She was a confident swimmer in the pool or on a calm lake; it was the ocean that made her panic.

So, no. She would not take her children to the beach. She couldn't.

With their suits on, they returned to the kitchen to gather a few things before they left. Stacy tucked her wallet and a couple of water bottles into a canvas tote for the drive over. The kids were in the mudroom looking for their flip-flops.

"What's going on here?" Stacy's father entered the kitchen. The sight of him so casually dressed, this time in a white T-shirt and Bermuda shorts was still something Stacy was getting used to.

"Grampy, Mommy won't take us to the beach and we really want to go." Sophie threw Stacy under the bus with ruthless precision.

"I'm sure she has a good reason," her father replied as he filled a glass with water. "She'll probably take you another day."

"She hasn't taken us at all!" Connor glanced at Stacy before ratting her out too. "Not one time."

Chase turned off the tap and looked over at Stacy. "You haven't taken them to the beach yet?"

"No, I haven't." She turned to her children and frowned. "But I *have* taken them to story time at the library every week since we arrived, *and* to the farmers' market, *and* to the playground, *and* to the inlet to look for crabs. These children are hardly suffering."

The admonishment was stern and directed at the kids, but the guilt behind it was Stacy's. *What kind of mother brings her children to the shore and refuses to go to the beach?*

Stacy approached her father at the sink and lowered her voice. "Would you mind taking them to the beach, Dad? Ryan's working and I could use the break."

"I'm sorry, but your mother has me on lockdown." Chase set his glass on the counter and frowned. "Why don't you set up the sprinkler and let them play in the backyard?"

"I do not have you on 'lockdown,'" Kaye countered as she entered the kitchen. "I asked for your help with the party. That's all." She faced Stacy with an expression she couldn't decipher. "Why don't you want to take the kids to the beach?"

"No reason," Stacy lied as the knot of guilt tightened in her chest. She turned and guided them into the car. They'd have fun at the pool.

It was the monotony and long days that got to her, Stacy decided as she helped Sophie into her car seat. She dearly loved her children, but some days were never-ending. It was overwhelming, the number of things she managed to do in a single day—making breakfast, packing lunches, gathering worksheets, signing permission slips, volunteering in the classroom, scheduling doctor and dentist appointments, driving to after-school activities, and finally dinner, bath, and bed. Only to wake up the next morning and do it all over again.

She'd thought a summer at the shore house would be different, but it wasn't. The truth was that Stacy sometimes envied Ryan his work. At the end of the day he had something to show for his efforts, something other than crumpled lunch bags and a pile of dirty laundry. It wasn't that she didn't care for her children; she did. But was it so horrible to want something for herself too? She remembered when she began her days with purpose, a passion for her career, and she missed it. But she'd made her choice—looking back was pointless.

"Done." Stacy smiled as she snapped the seat belt.

She closed the door and took a deep breath as she rounded the car, the summer air warm on her skin as she listened to the cicadas humming in the trees. Her mood lifted as she imagined about how nice it would be to spend a hot day at the pool.

It was a short drive from their house to the swim club, and she drove with the air conditioner blasting and the vents aimed directly at her face. The water would feel wonderful.

The parking lot was almost empty when they arrived, and Stacy easily found a parking space near the entrance. From there it was a short trip up the stairs to the pool deck.

"You're going to love the pool, Connor," she said. "I think you might even be old enough to learn to dive. If you want, I can find someone to teach you, then you'll have something to show your friend Miles."

Stacy turned to Sophie. "Upstairs, they'll have floating pool toys for you, and there'll be other kids to play with. You guys can lounge on rafts just like movie stars."

Stacy herself was looking forward to reading another chapter of her much-loved copy of *A Winter to Remember*. Without interruption. Yes, an afternoon at the pool was just what they needed.

"I'm hungry, Mommy," Sophie said.

This time Stacy's smile was genuine. "That's okay, Soph, because they have a magical place called a snack bar. You tell the man at the window whatever you want to eat. He'll make it and bring it to you."

Sophie looked skeptical. "Anything?"

"Anything."

"What about a hot dog?" Connor asked.

"With extra-extra ketchup, just the way you like it." Stacy held Sophie's hand, her excitement growing as they climbed the stairs. "And after lunch you can have ice cream—whatever kind you like. And there will be kids to play with, and games. You'll love it."

They reached the top of the stairs and stopped.

Today, especially, Stacy assumed the swim club would be busy, but it wasn't. She blinked, expecting to see a bank of lounge chairs draped with fluffy pool towels, picnic tables set for lunch and shaded from the sun by wide canvas umbrellas. She looked for attendants dressed in crisp white polos and khaki shorts, supervising happy children splashing in the water.

But there was none of that.

Instead, the entire pool deck was vacant. Umbrellas were tied shut and the lifeguard chair was vacant. The window to the snack bar had been rolled closed and padlocked. A line of orange cones barred entrance to the grill room restaurant. Worst of all, the pool was only half-filled with water; a hose attached to a compressor seemed to be pulling water from it instead of adding to it.

Stacy stared, dumbstruck by what she saw. Where was everyone?

A maintenance worker dressed in khaki pants and a blue polo shirt approached with an apologetic frown. "Pool's closed. Sorry."

"Closed?" Stacy repeated dumbly. "For how long?"

He shrugged. "At least a week."

"But it's July. Why would you close the pool in July?"

"The lifeguards found a crack in the foundation of the pool the other day. We have to drain it and call someone in to patch it. Takes a day or two to dry, then we'll fill it back again. Whole thing'll take a week. Maybe more."

Connor squeezed her hand to get her attention. Stacy looked down to see an expression of delight on his face. "Can we go to the beach now, Mommy? Can we, Mom, can we?"

She pretended to consider the idea. "I'm not sure. We'll see if Daddy's home. First, both of you need to eat lunch. Then we have to find the badges and pack the car. That's a lot to do. I'm not sure we have the time. Maybe you can go tomorrow, with Daddy or Uncle Brad."

"But Miles is there *right now*," Connor whined. "You said we could go to the beach after I passed my swim test, but now I can't get one."

"A swim test?" The maintenance man gave him a puzzled look. "Don't need a swim test for the ocean, little dude. Just a beach badge."

They turned back and went home. Both kids were furious about not being allowed on the beach, and the short drive home was peppered with demands and questions. Stacy did her best to answer calmly but by the time she pulled into the driveway, her head ached and her patience was frayed. She let them out of the car, sighing as she watched them run into the house. After gathering the bags from the back, she made her way inside too.

"Anybody home?" she called as she dropped the keys on the side table by the door.

"We're in here." Ryan was seated at the breakfast bar, casually munching on an apple.

"I thought you were working all day," If Ryan found himself with a free afternoon, the least he could have done was offer to take his turn with the kids.

"I finished sooner than I thought." Ryan took a final bite, then rose from his stool.

"The pool is closed, Daddy. They're taking the water out," Sophie said as she ran to her father's side and reached for his hand. "So we didn't go swimming."

"Good grief, Stace. What happened to you?" Brad entered the kitchen, utterly relaxed. He appeared freshly showered and was wearing a loose pair of board shorts and a baggy T-shirt. He glanced at her again before crossing to the refrigerator and peering inside. "You look terrible."

"Nothing. Nothing's wrong." Stacy retorted as she dropped the bags and kicked them to the side. She'd been chasing both children all day long, while her husband sat at home without a care in the world. She'd had enough. "I'm going upstairs to read. You need to take the kids to the beach."

"Okay." Ryan shrugged as he tossed his apple core in the trash. "When?"

"Now."

"What's going on?" Brad swigged from an open carton of orange juice, then slid it back on the shelf.

"I'm taking the kids to the beach apparently," Ryan replied. "You want to come?"

Brad shrugged. "Yeah, sure."

"They need lunch first," Stacy said.

"Okay," Ryan said warily as he glanced at her. "We'll stop at that little stand by the beach stairs for grilled cheese. You want to come with us?"

"No," Stacy snapped as she crossed the kitchen. "I'm going upstairs to take a nap."

"You want to meet us at the beach later?" she heard Ryan ask, but she ignored him.

From the hallway, she heard Brad answer for her. "Dude, she never goes to the beach. Didn't you know that?"

Stacy dragged herself up the stairs and down the hallway to her bedroom, feeling utterly exhausted, as if she were swimming against a current. She pushed open the door and dropped her book on the nightstand, too tired to even read, then flicked the dial on the window air conditioner to maximum and made her way to the bed. Stretching out, she listened to the hum of the compressor and felt goosebumps rise on her skin as the cool air blew across it.

The humidity and the activities of the day had drained her. She felt herself drift off to sleep, wondering how long she could keep this up, entertaining the kids without actually taking them to the beach. If they insisted, she'd insist on going home, to their apartment in Morristown.

That was her last conscious thought before sleep overtook her.

She woke sometime later, breathless and disoriented. The blanket twisted around her legs like a noose, pillows tossed onto the floor, sheets damp and wrinkled.

She'd had the dream again.

She pushed herself upright, steadying herself against feelings of panic and waves of nausea that had always followed. Like she'd done so many times before, she collected the shards remaining after she woke, hoping to piece them together in a way that made sense.

But it never did. None of it ever made sense.

In her dream, she stood on the beach, ocean waves breaking gently against her ankles. She had the sense that she was younger, a child maybe, holding on to someone's hand as she gazed across the ocean to the horizon. At first she stood safely on shore, whitecaps breaking far out to sea. Then the water began to rise and the waves grew taller and stronger, breaking against her body as they continued to the shore. Salty water churned around her, the waves unforgiving as they tumbled over themselves, gathering strength. When the water reached her chest, she tried to run back to the safety of the shore but couldn't because her feet didn't touch the ground. All around her was water and she was terrified. It rose to her throat and sucked the air from her lungs. In an instant, she was pulled under. Swept into the current, she tumbled over and over in a prison of sand and ocean water.

Just when she thought she'd never draw breath, the wave that had trapped her crashed against the sand and broke open, allowing her a single moment to catch her breath before it receded, clawing her back into the ocean.

She always woke then, as she had just now, heart racing and gasping for breath.

Slowly, she became aware of her surroundings. Home, safe in her room. After a moment, her breathing slowed, and she loosened the sheets from her legs and pushed them away. She swung her feet to the floor and stood. Crossing the hardwood floor, she turned off the air conditioner and opened the window, drawing in great breaths of fresh air. She listened to the blood roar in her ears and felt her heart thump in her chest, waiting for it to return to normal.

What kind of mother brings her kids to the shore but won't take them to the beach?

The kind of mother who's afraid of the ocean.

Stacy eventually made her way to the bathroom to splash cold water on her face. Her reflection in the mirror was grim; dark circles and puffy eyes suggested she had been crying in her sleep again. The tap water was cold against her hot skin. She dried her face on a soft towel, brushed her teeth, and headed downstairs. The wooden stairs creaked in the quiet of the house as Stacy descended. Her head was still stuffy with sleep, fragments of the dream still embedded in her mind.

As she got close to the kitchen, she heard the tinny sound of talk radio. The air was threaded with the scent of chopped onions and melted butter sizzling on the stove. Her mother was at the cutting board, slicing a stack of celery ribs. Behind her, a pot of potatoes bubbled on the stove.

"Hi, Mom."

"Oh, honey." Stacy's mother lowered her knife and frowned. "You look terrible."

"Great." Stacy opened the refrigerator and pulled out a bottle of iced tea. She twisted the top and turned back to her mother. "Where is everyone?"

"Let's see." Her mother tidied the stack of celery and resumed her work. "Your brother and Ryan are out with the kids. Dad's in his den, supposedly watching the game but I think he's asleep. And Iona has driven herself to the mall to buy a juicer. She juices now and apparently, there's 'nothing to juice in my house.'"

"Juicing?" Stacy sipped her tea, feeling the liquid cool her throat. "That's new. I thought she was vegan. Somebody should tell her to pick a lane."

"Don't be nasty or she'll smudge the house again."

"She'll what?"

Stacy's mother gathered the chopped celery from the board and tossed it into a nearby bowl. "Earlier this morning, I found her burning a bundle of dried leaves and fanning the smoke with a white feather. Apparently the 'energy'—or something—is off in this house and needs to be addressed, and that was the only way to do it."

"What was she burning?"

"Sage. And the smell was horrible. Your father thought it was drugs."

Stacy snorted. "What did you say?"

Kaye paused. "Keep in mind that girl's been working my last nerve since she walked through the door."

"I've noticed."

"Well, I stopped her, of course. What else could I do? I told her that our family has occupied this house longer than she's been alive and we've never had an 'energy' problem until she came. So she went crying to your brother."

"So you decided to make soup?" Stacy eyed the collection of vegetables spread across the counter.

"No. The potatoes and onions are for potato salad, for tomorrow's party." Her mother sighed as she put down the knife, her energy apparently spent. "The rest of this forest is for that girl. *Some* of the vegetables we have on hand are suitable for juicing, but not all. She said she'll 'text me a list' for the rest."

Stacy pointed to a plastic bag of carrots. "Brad hates carrots. He says they make his tongue itch."

Kaye drew a breath so deep that Stacy could see her mother's body expand. "I guess he likes them now."

Stacy finished her tea and tossed the empty bottle in the recycle bin. "Are the kids still at the beach?"

"No, in the end Ryan and your brother took them to feed the ducks instead." Kaye scraped the last pile off the cutting board and rinsed it.

Stacy groaned, exasperated at Ryan's easy way out. "I take them to the duck pond all the time. There's nothing new in that. I *asked* Ryan specifically to take them to the beach because I can't."

"You can't?" her mother echoed as her gaze sharpened. "Why can't you take them to the beach?"

"Never mind. It doesn't matter." Nothing would be gained from sparring with her mother, so Stacy swerved the subject.

Thankfully, her mother cooperated. "Do you mind walking into town for me? I need a few things from the greengrocer's, things I couldn't find at the farmers' market."

"Trouble with the tomato guy again?"

"How do you know about the tomato guy?" Kaye wiped her hands on the tea towel. "That happened last year and neither of us were here for it."

"Small town, Mom." Stacy shrugged. "It's still big news."

"There's a list of things I need on the counter over there," Kaye directed. "Take some money out my wallet."

Stacy laughed, in spite of her mood. "Mom. I'm not twelve anymore. I have my own money."

"Sometimes I forget."

"What about dessert for the party?" Stacy asked. "You want me to get pies from Mueller's?"

Kaye shook her head. "No, no pie. Nothing sweet or carby. Your father can't have that stuff anymore. Not until his cholesterol drops another fifteen points."

It was an odd restriction and one Stacy wasn't sure her father was following. She knew for a fact that he had visited the seafood shack more than once because she'd seen him eating fried clams from a paper bag. She'd also seen her father at the bakery, enjoying a toasted hard roll with butter.

"Are the doctors concerned about Dad's cholesterol?" Stacy wasn't sure whether to rat him out or keep his secret.

"No, not his doctors. Me. I saw his numbers on the May labs and I think there's room for improvement. I'm sure we can do better."

"Dad's okay with you opening his mail and checking his numbers?"

"Of course he's okay with it." Kaye lifted the pot of potatoes from the stove and brought them to the sink. "Why wouldn't he be?"

*

After Stacy left, Kaye finished the potato salad and was able to start two more dishes, purposefully cleaning as she went. The kitchen at the shore house was relatively small, and with a house full of people it was important to keep the clutter at bay. When the house belonged to Chase's parents, the kitchen had always been spotless, and Kaye tried to keep it that way. She knew how much her mother-in-law had loved the shore house and felt keeping it orderly was a way to honor her memory.

With the kitchen tidy, Kaye stretched a bit of plastic wrap across the serving bowl and made her way to the spare refrigerator in the garage, where she kept the rest of the party things. She stood in front of the refrigerator for a moment, surveying the contents. It had taken almost two full days of cooking, but everything she'd planned to make seemed ready to go. The caterers would bring the rest. There was a bit of time left in the day—maybe time enough to start a marinated fruit salad? Chase would like that, especially if he wasn't allowed to have dessert. Satisfied that things were finally ready for the party, she closed the door and headed back inside the house.

She entered her kitchen and froze in her tracks.

In the few minutes she'd been gone, the kitchen had been destroyed. In the middle of the room was the remains of an enormous cardboard box, the top and sides ripped open and tossed aside. Scattered across the floor was splintered Styrofoam and ripped plastic bags. The kitchen counter that Kaye had wiped clean just moments before was now home to piles of vegetable peelings and puddles of green liquid. The sink was already crowded with drinking glasses and the water was running, splashing onto the floor. And there was an alarming smell of burning plastic in the air.

"Oh, hi, Mrs. Bennett." Iona. Of course Iona.

"Back from the mall, I see." Kaye crossed the kitchen to turn off the faucet.

Iona stood before the juicer, stuffed the chute with handfuls of carrots. When she flicked the switch, the sound of the motor set Kaye's teeth on edge.

After what seemed like an eternity, Iona filled another glass with a few inches of green ooze and drank it. "Have you seen Brad?"

"I think he went to the duck pond."

Iona set the glass on the counter. Kaye watched a thread of pulp slide down the side of the glass and puddle on the counter.

"I'll get all this later, 'kay?" Iona gestured to the mess in the kitchen as she grabbed Brad's car keys and headed for the door. "It's just that we need to get on the beach while the light is still good." She paused to look back, tilting her head and pursing her lips. "Do you remember what he was wearing?"

"Who, Brad? Shorts, I think. Why?"

"Oh, good. Our followers like to see him in shorts. It's all about giving 'em what they like, y'know?"

Kaye stiffened. "Brad's okay with the pictures you take?"

"I don't know. I guess so." Iona shrugged. "I never asked."

"Seems like maybe you should," Kaye muttered as she removed the dishes from the sink and filled it with soapy water.

After washing the dishes Iona had left, Kaye put away the remaining vegetables and collected the packing material from the floor. Any normal person would have tended to their own mess, but Iona hadn't, and that basic lack of manners was one of the things Kaye strongly disliked about the girl. Admittedly, the list was long, but Kaye had tried to ignore most of it, for Brad's sake. She stuffed the rest of the garbage back in the juicer box with a little more force than necessary, while reminding herself that her son was an adult and this girl, however vapid and annoying, was his choice. Kaye would have to learn to live with it.

When she was satisfied with the state of her kitchen, Kaye folded the tea towel and returned it to its place. Then she opened the refrigerator, intending to get to work on Chase's fruit salad.

"Where is everything?" she muttered to herself as she stepped back to survey the contents. Was it possible that she'd only imagined buying it all? No, she distinctly remembered being shocked at the price of blackberries at the market but buying them anyway because Sophie liked them.

"Did you say something?" Chase wandered into the kitchen and grabbed a glass from the cabinet.

"I had a big container of fruit in here—peaches, plums, cherries, and cantaloupe—and now it's missing."

"Did you check the party fridge?"

"I was just out there," Kaye murmured.

Chase pointed to the cardboard box on the floor. "Were they juiced?"

"No. I would have known because I just did the dishes." Kaye closed the refrigerator and planted her hands firmly on her hips. "I can't imagine what happened to it."

Chase opened the freezer for ice. "Uh-oh."

"What?" Kaye moved closer.

There, stuffed onto a shelf in the freezer, was a plastic bag filled with fruit meant for the party. Kaye pulled it out; bits of frost falling to the floor. Inside, it was a mess. Nothing had been washed or trimmed; an entire cantaloupe was pushed against the delicate blackberries, crushing the fruit.

Kaye slowly and deliberately closed the door. She walked across the kitchen to retrieve her car keys from the hook, teeth clenched all the while. "I'll be back."

Kaye was aware that the last time she'd had coffee with Brenda, she'd been warned to lower her expectations. Brenda said that Iona was young and still finding her way. That she'd come around eventually. And although Kaye didn't entirely agree, she said she'd try if only to keep the peace in the house. Now she could honestly report that her expectations could not be any lower.

Chapter 12

If Stacy hadn't stopped to toss her water bottle away, she would have missed it.

The little shop was tucked into a quiet side street, beyond the main shops of Dewberry Beach. The entrance was enticing, decorated with thick terracotta pots planted with beach grass, their feathery flowers waving in the breeze. Tucked here and there were little tin buckets filled to overflowing with deep red geraniums and tiny dots of blue nasturtiums peeping from underneath. The sign over the shop's entrance read "Beach Reads" in bright white letters painted on an ocean blue background. She moved closer and smiled. The display window had been staged to look like a summer day at the beach. Hardcover books had been placed atop thick beach towels, and a few paperbacks had been placed casually on the seat of a beach chair with the pages open, as if the reader intended to return any minute.

The bell overhead rang gently as she pushed the door open, the cool air in the shop a welcome break from the muggy day. One of Stacy's favorite things in the world was an undiscovered bookstore; even better if the shop had a used book section, as this one did. Stacy imagined a world of stories she hadn't read, characters she hadn't met, places she hadn't seen. The inside of a bookstore felt like magic to her, as if the best adventure was here, waiting.

"Welcome to Beach Reads," an older woman with a kind, open face greeted her. "Can I help you find something?"

"I'm not sure yet, but thank you," Stacy replied. "I'd love to look around a little."

"Of course. Be my guest." The woman gestured toward the shelves. "Along the front wall is fiction—new releases mostly; older things along the far wall. On this table is local interest—good if you want to know more about Dewberry Beach history. And on the back wall are memoirs and poetry. I'm just setting up so there's more in the back. Let me know if I can find something for you."

A title on the front wall caught Stacy's eye, but it was a cover she didn't recognize. "Is that *A Winter to Remember*? The same book that was released a few years ago? The cover looks different."

"You're right, it is new." The woman nodded. "The publishers have re-released the first book. The second book in the series, *A Promise of Spring*, is scheduled to come out soon and I guess they hope to refresh readers' memories since it's been so long. But even as a re-release *Winter* is doing well, finding a whole new audience they say. It's a wonderful novel. Have you read it?"

"I have, and I loved it." Stacy picked up the book, weighty in her hands. Turning it over, she looked at the author's picture. Billy Jacob, leaning against a brick wall, arms crossed over his chest, with just the tiniest smirk on his face as if he were sharing a secret with the reader. The picture had turned out well, very well in fact. Despite the trouble behind the scenes. "When does the second book come out?"

"Well, that's the mystery. The publishers say in the fall, but they won't give an exact date." The woman shrugged. "I suppose it doesn't matter to me all that much because I'm a small shop. I hear the bigger sellers are anxious to schedule author events, but without a firm release date, they can't."

Stacy shook her head. Billy Jacob had the most talent of any writer she'd ever met, but he had been impossible to work with. So many hours of her life spent working with that man—arguing, pleading, threatening...

Oddly enough, she missed it.

After browsing for the better part of an hour, Stacy left with two bags of books, mostly filled with things she thought Connor or Sophie might like, but also with a new copy of *A Winter to Remember*. This new release contained an excerpt of the second book and she was curious, along with everyone else, to see what direction the story had taken.

Stacy headed home with her bags of books, which seemed to grow heavier in the late afternoon sun. She paused as the baby kicked, then shifted the weight of the bags to her other hip. Four more blocks.

"Mommy!" Sophie ran toward her, her face shining with joy as she thumped her body against Stacy's legs.

"Hi, Princess." She brushed Sophie's cheek with her fingers.

Stacy spied her husband trailing behind and overloaded with packages of his own. "I see you've found Applegate's."

"That store is amazing. It has *everything*." Ryan lifted a bag that appeared to contain several tin buckets and a small bag of sand. "Stuff I didn't even know we needed until the guy helped us."

"We got sparklers for Bibi's party," Connor said. "Daddy said *I* can have one, but Sophie can't."

"I said Sophie needs help with hers," Ryan corrected. "Not that she can't have one."

Stacy peered into another bag. "Is that a fire extinguisher?"

Oversized and hopelessly old-fashioned, the unit had a cracked rubber tube attached limply to the side of the canister. Stacy ran her finger across the top, leaving a clear trail in the dust.

Ryan nodded. "The guy said I needed it. For the sparklers."

Stacy bit back a smile. "Aaron's been trying to get rid of those things for years and is probably thrilled to have finally sold one. Are you sure it even has a charge?"

Ryan scowled. "Of course it does. He assured me it was new."

Stacy traded bags, adding her purse to lighten her load. She wouldn't need money at Applegate's. Her family had kept a house account there for years. "If you take my books home, I'll take it back and have the charge tested."

As they jostled bags, Ryan eyed the books. "You found a bookstore?"

"I did." Stacy's smile widened; her mood lifted. "New this summer."

"Did you find anything good?"

"Stuff for the kids mostly. I found a pirate chapter book for Sophie, something to get her interested in reading, and magic books for Connor."

"That's great." Ryan peered inside. "Mind if I look?"

"Sure."

He flipped through the stack of books, then hesitated. "*A Winter to Remember*? Don't you have a million copies of this book already?"

"I have two copies, including this one, so a bit less than a million," Stacy pointed out. "The publishers are re-releasing it with a sample of book two in the back. My copy at home doesn't have that."

"Do you miss it?" Ryan asked suddenly.

"Do I miss what?" The question was unexpected.

"Your job in publishing. Do you miss it?"

"I have a different life now." Which was technically the truth, but it didn't answer the question so Stacy tried again. "I miss it the same way you miss college, and the fun you had with Jeff and Sean before things got complicated."

"They're not—"

"They are," Stacy interrupted. "I hear you on the phone with Sean and with Todd. I see how hard you work, and you don't seem to enjoy any of it anymore. Not the way you used to."

"I didn't realize you'd noticed."

"I have." She leaned into him.

They continued walking, each lost in their own thoughts, parting ways when they reached the corner of their street. Ryan took the kids back to the house and Stacy continued for another block, on to Applegate's. In truth, she hadn't realized just how much Ryan disliked his job until she saw it on his face, a moment before.

Somehow, it seemed, they'd both lost their way.

When she reached Applegate's Hardware store, she pushed the wooden door open and stepped inside. Applegate's musty smell and crowded shelves had always reminded her of her grandfather's workshop, mysterious to everyone but her grandfather and her brother. Applegate's was organized in a way that made sense only to employees; the walls lined with tools, the shelves stuffed with buckets of odd bits of hardware. When the store first opened in her grandfather's time, it was designed to serve a working community of craftsmen, woodworkers, cabinetmakers, and shipbuilders. Even now, it remained true to its roots. No wonder Ryan has been mesmerized; inside was a jumble of everything.

The shop floor was empty, so Stacy called out to the back office. "Hello? Anyone here?"

"Be right with you." There was the sound of wooden pallets scraping across the cement floor as Aaron made his way over. He eyes widened behind a pair of thick eyeglasses and he reached out to clasp her hand. "Stacy Bennett, what a surprise. My, oh my. I haven't seen you in a very long time." He was exactly as she remembered: a tuft of wispy gray hair on his head and a neatly pressed collared shirt secured with a maroon bowtie. A canvas apron was tied around his waist, the red Applegate's logo emblazoned on the front pocket, with a ballpoint and a carpenter's pencil poking out the top.

"How are you, Mr. Mahoney?" Stacy set her bag on the floor.

"I'm well, Miss Bennett. Very well." He smiled at her. "Your family came in just a few moments ago—your husband and your children. They are delightful. I must say, you are a lucky woman."

"Thank you."

"Your little girl is adorable; she looks just like you did at her age." Mr. Mahoney shook his head as he smiled. "I remember your grandfather coming in with you on Saturday mornings during the summer. You'd bring an empty tin bucket for me to load up with nails and you'd carry it all the way home, even as little as you were."

Stacy laughed. "I was Grandpa's helper. If I did a good job, he'd take me to Mueller's for a cruller on the way home. I'm surprised you remember."

"'Course I do." He puffed out his chest. "It's my job. Your husband told me the whole family's down for the summer. Your mother must be so happy."

"I think so," Stacy agreed. "It's been fun."

"I heard about your father," Mr. Mahoney continued. "I made sure Father Nova mentioned his name at mass all during that winter. I'm glad to hear that he's recovered. Please give him my best."

"I will," Stacy answered as her heart warmed. "Thank you."

Where else but Dewberry Beach would the hardware store man know so much about Stacy's family? It meant something that her father's name was mentioned at mass and that Mr. Mahoney remembered when she came in with her grandfather. There was a history here, one that spanned generations.

"So, what can I do for you today, young lady?"

She nudged the bag with the fire extinguisher out of sight. "I'm not sure that Ryan bought enough sparklers, for the party tomorrow. Do you happen to have any more?"

"I do." He snapped to attention, then navigated a cluttered path to a metal rack. "How many boxes would you like?"

"Three please. No, wait—four. And another bag of sand, I think, just to be safe."

"You can't be too careful." Mr. Mahoney's blue eyes twinkled. "Shall I put the charge on your account?"

"Please." Stacy waited while he bagged the purchase, wondering how she'd carry an eight-pound bag of sand home, in addition to the other things. "I'll see you at my mother's party tomorrow?"

"Wouldn't miss it for the world." The bag crinkled as he rolled it closed. "She makes the best potato salad I've ever eaten."

As the wooden door shut behind her, Stacy chuckled. Mr. Mahoney was a Dewberry Beach treasure, the best salesman she'd ever encountered.

Chapter 13

"Have you heard from your brother?" Kaye asked Stacy as she removed the place settings she'd laid out earlier for Iona and Brad.

"I texted him," Stacy replied. "He said not to hold dinner for him and Iona."

It was probably just as well. Kaye hadn't mentally recovered from the mess Iona had left in the kitchen and wasn't looking forward to seeing her again today.

"Ryan's bringing the chicken in from the grill." Stacy set the salad bowl on the table.

"Would you call your father, please? He's in the den."

The caterers would arrive early the following morning, so Kaye had decided that a simple supper would be best, just grilled chicken and salad. It looked as though she'd made the right choice. Glancing around the table, everyone seemed tired from a full day in the sun. Conversation between adults was subdued and both children fell asleep before the meal was over.

"We should take the kids to bed." Stacy pushed away from the table and went to Sophie's chair.

Ryan rose to collect Connor, lifting him from his chair and laying him over his shoulder. "I'm going to turn in too. I'm tired."

"I think I'll go up as well, Mom," Stacy echoed. "Unless you want me to help with the dishes?"

"No, you go ahead." Kaye waved them both away. "There's not much to do here. I'll see you all in the morning."

Chase also decided an early bedtime sounded like a good idea, so it was left to Kaye to straighten the kitchen and close the house for the night, but she didn't mind. She'd come to appreciate the stillness of a quiet house. With the dishes done, Kaye gathered her notes for tomorrow's party and settled in to wait for her son to come home.

Kaye heard the car door slam sometime later. Glancing out the window, she saw them approaching the house, both of them stone-faced and angry.

They were arguing as they entered the house—she could hear Brad's rumbling voice and Iona's hissed replies. Although she tried, she couldn't understand what they were saying, and she wasn't entirely sure she wanted to know. She would have felt obligated to defend her son and that would lead to nothing good.

Best to let them work it out themselves.

As they stopped in the mudroom, their voices rose and fell as they snapped at each other. Kaye left the kitchen and crept up the back stairs to her room. Unfortunately, the master bedroom was directly above the kitchen, which was where Brad and Iona chose to settle their differences. Chase slept through it, oddly enough, but Kaye did not. She listened, like a Cold War spy, straining to hear and not at all proud of her curiosity.

She heard her name mentioned more than once—by that girl. And although Kaye couldn't understand the words, Iona's tone made the context very clear.

After a few more minutes, she heard a bedroom door slam.

And then silence.

In the early hours of the following morning, Kaye was woken by the sound of the side door of the house slamming shut. She rose from her bed and crossed the room to the window where she watched Iona drag her suitcases down the driveway and toward the train station.

So, that was the end of it.

Of course Kaye was happy to see that girl leave. She wasn't right for Brad. She was pushy and opinionated, socially immature and entitled. Worst of all, the pictures she took of Brad and put up for everyone to see, and comment on, were exploitative.

Brad was fortunate to be rid of her. They all were.

When Iona was out of sight, Kaye returned to her bed. Later, she'd tell Chase what had happened, reminding him that she had nothing to do with Iona leaving. And then she'd wait for him to apologize for his earlier comments.

A family of redwoods indeed.

Chapter 14

Ryan descended the deck stairs and made his way across the backyard, the dewy grass cool on his bare feet. The sun was barely above the horizon and he was up and outside. Just moments before he'd been woken abruptly, handed a cup of coffee, and given a mission. Then he'd been firmly pushed out the back door to complete it. Still mostly asleep, he paused in the yard to sip his coffee and gather his thoughts.

They'd told him Brad was upset and would most likely be in the very corner of the yard, near the firepit. So after another fortifying sip of coffee, that's where Ryan headed.

But Brad wasn't where they said he'd be. Instead, Ryan found a zip-hoodie tossed across the back of one of the Adirondack chairs that circled the firepit and a small cooler with half a dozen empty dark glass bottles tossed carelessly to the side. He opened the cooler to inspect the contents. Inside were three or four dark bottles buried in a bath of melting ice cubes and cold water.

This was not good. Brad didn't usually drink. Maybe Stacy and Kaye were right to worry.

Ryan snapped the lid shut and stood. To his left was the grassy field the family sometimes used as a shortcut to the boatyard. Maybe

Brad had gone for a walk to clear his head? Ryan looked closer but dismissed the idea because the dew looked undisturbed, without visible footprints across it. So, he hadn't gone that way. Ryan turned to the right and started walking. Within a few minutes, he found Brad, fully dressed in jeans and a rumpled T-shirt, in front of the padlocked door of his grandfather's work shed.

"Hey, man," Ryan said.

"Hey."

Ryan's assessment would have been easier if Brad had turned. Ryan would have at least been able to look into his eyes to see how bloodshot they were. Break-ups were always hard.

"Look, I'm not trying to tell you what to do," Ryan said finally, rubbing the back of his neck as he searched for the right words. "But is that really a good idea? The party's tonight."

Brad turned. "Is what a good idea?"

Ryan gestured to the unopened dark glass bottle tucked into Brad's front pocket.

Brad rolled his eyes as he slipped the bottle from his pocket and handed it to Ryan.

Ryan read the label and laughed. "Dude, this is *root beer*."

"What did you think it was?"

"Beer-beer," Ryan said as he twisted the cap off. "That's why they sent me. They think you're out here drinking, drowning your sorrows."

Brad snorted. "It's a little early for that."

"It's barely past six." Ryan took a sip, then a swallow. The sweetness brought back memories. "Oh my gosh, this is delicious."

"I know." Brad's smile was wide. "Root beer has always been my favorite drink, but Iona would never let me have it. She said too much soda would make me look bloated in the Instagram pictures." He shrugged. "Mom bought a case for the party, so after Iona left, I took a bunch and came outside with a cooler of ice."

"You been out here all night?"

"Yeah." Brad turned his attention back to his work, spraying the rusted padlock and twisting the mechanism. "I had some thinking to do."

"You good now?"

"Yeah."

Ryan knew that there would be questions later from Stacy and her mother, which he would be unable to answer. But for now, he thought he'd done a fine job of talking to his brother-in-law.

Several root beers later, Ryan and Brad were still standing in front of the shed, determined to open it, despite the rusted padlock barring their way. When the stick they were using to pry the lock open broke, they switched to knocking the join with a rock. It took a few tries, but finally the padlock opened, sending a shower of rust flakes to the grass below.

Ryan looked at the lock, broken in Brad's hand. "How long has that thing been on there?"

"Too long." Brad pushed the door open and Ryan followed him inside.

"Holy cow." Ryan's voice was barely a whisper. "Talk about a 'man-cave.'"

As Ryan walked toward the dusty workbench, shafts of sunlight showed dust motes floating in the air. Neatly placed on the workbench's surface were dozens of glass jam jars of various sizes, filled with washers, bolts, and nails. Hanging from a pegboard fastened on the side was a collection of tools, carefully arranged by size, many of the handles worn smooth with use. Stored in the rafters above were odd-sized pieces of wood, two boat oars, and an old wooden crab trap. A push mower stood next to the side door, the blades dulled and rusty.

"Did all this stuff belong to your grandfather?"

"Yeah, it did," Brad answered, a swell of pride in his voice. "Gramps liked to work with his hands." He pointed to a dusty stool on the far side of the workbench. "He used to let me sit right there and watch him work."

"He sounds like a great guy."

"He was." Brad picked up a broom and swept a veil of cobwebs from the window. "You would have liked him."

"What's under there?" Ryan pointed to a faded blue tarp partly hidden beneath some twisted aluminum chairs and a deflated canvas raft.

"Oh, that." Brad pulled the chairs off and set them aside while Ryan removed the raft. Underneath was a lemon-yellow Volkswagen Thing, with black vinyl seats and a faded graduation tassel hanging from the rear-view mirror. "That's the beach car."

"Wow." Ryan whistled under his breath as he approached the car. "Vintage." He ran his hand along the edge of the hood. It needed care but it was still in good condition. "Is it yours?"

"I wish." Brad snorted. "It's Stacy's. We shouldn't even be looking at it."

"Really?" Ryan murmured. "We've been together for ten years. You'd think something this awesome would have come up. When did she get it?"

"She saw an ad for it somewhere—or maybe it was a posted flyer—I don't remember exactly. It was the summer of her junior year in high school and she'd just learned to drive. She nagged my parents for *months* until they finally agreed to match whatever money she saved."

"She can be persistent." Ryan knelt down to look at the underside. He brushed his hand against the tire. "Must have been fun to drive."

"She never drove it."

Ryan look up in surprise. "What?"

"The car never passed inspection. Transmission was busted, I think. Or the exhaust. I don't know. Anyway, she didn't have the money to fix it and Mom and Dad wouldn't lend it to her. When she went off to college, she left it here."

Brad turned back to his grandfather's workbench and Ryan stepped outside to give him a moment alone. He found a place to sit and wondered what else he didn't know about his wife.

"That should do it."

"You finished?" Ryan straightened. Brad hadn't been inside long.

"To be honest, I'm not sure if Dad would want me in there so I just straightened up a bit."

Brad found a dry spot on the grass and they sat in silence for a moment, listening to the sounds of the neighborhood waking up and beginning a new day: the thud of a newspaper hitting a driveway, the hum of cicadas in the trees, the hiss of a sprinkler in a neighbor's yard.

"This must have been a great place to grow up," Ryan said finally.

"It really was," Brad agreed. "Especially coming down when Gramps was here. He's what made the summers fun for me. I didn't have to try so hard around him, you know?" He reached for a twig and rolled it between his fingers. "Don't get me wrong, Dad did the best he could, but there was always the expectation I had to be more like him. I'm not, and I think that disappoints him." Abruptly, Brad scoffed, snapping the twig between his fingers. "Don't mind me. I'm tired and I think that's just the root beer talking."

"It's hard being a parent," Ryan offered. "I make more mistakes than you can imagine, with both my kids. In the end, you just cross your fingers and hope they turn out okay."

Brad shrugged.

"What time do you think it is?" he asked.

"No idea." Ryan realized he'd left his cell phone inside, on the charger by his bed, and it surprised him that he wasn't at all concerned. As Ryan finished his root beer, he let his mind wander. A lawnmower's engine sputtered to life three houses over and a group of children called to each other as they rode by the house on their bikes. When he and Stacy were first dating, she described her childhood at the shore house in such an idyllic way that he assumed time had softened her memories. But he could see it now. Here, families got together for weekend cookouts, for bike parades, for evening walks. The beach was four blocks to the east, the pool and the boatyard three blocks in the other direction, and in the evenings an ice-cream truck still drove the streets, stopping for any kid waving a dollar.

What a great place to live.

"How did you know what you wanted to do?" Brad spoke, pulling Ryan from his thoughts. "As a job, I mean." He pulled a few blades of grass from the ground. "How did you know computers would be your thing? And how did you know you wanted your own company?"

"Me?" The question caught Ryan by surprise. "I don't think any of it was intentional. I saw a puzzle that looked cool and I wanted to see how far I could take it. My roommates eventually saw what I was doing and asked to be a part of it."

"What about your company? Stacy says it's going public next year. That's got to be great for you, right?"

Ryan shrugged as he reached for another root beer. "Not as much as you might think."

"What do you mean?"

Ryan leaned back and sighed. "The fun stuff was all at the beginning—the problem to solve, the right code to address it—seemed like anything was possible then. Now a money guy is in charge and it's not fun anymore."

"So why don't you leave?"

The question was obvious, the answer was what Ryan had been struggling to find for the past few months. He supposed that even with Todd the work had been bearable until Jeff disappeared. After that, the balance of power shifted to Sean and Todd, and the company he had started became unrecognizable. Now, Ryan stayed because leaving would feel like giving up and he wasn't one to surrender.

"Too many people depending on me," he said finally.

"It's the money," Brad agreed. "I get it."

"Something like that."

It wasn't the money. Brad had misunderstood but Ryan let it go. That wasn't the reason Ryan stayed. The partnership agreement allowed any of the three founders to leave the company, granting them an immediate payout for stock and bonuses. Even if Ryan left before the company went public, he wouldn't lose much. He stayed because he started the company and he refused to have it taken from him.

The sound of approaching footsteps from the yard next door caught their attention.

"Excuse me, boys." Mrs. Ivey emerged from the path between the houses, startling them both.

"Hello, Mrs. Ivey." Brad shifted in his chair, resisting the impulse to snap to attention. When Brad was younger, Mrs. Ivey would sit on her front porch, watching him and his summer friends ride bikes or play in the street. Every kid knew to expect a phone call home if they misbehaved and Mrs. Ivey saw it. That was years ago, but Brad still felt the need to be on his best behavior with her. "This is my brother-in-law, Ryan. I don't think you've met before."

"We've waved to each other a few times, but I don't think we've been properly introduced. How do you do, Ryan?" She straightened, planting her hands firmly on her hips. "I wonder if you boys wouldn't mind doing me a small favor?"

"Of course, if we can."

"Lovely. Please follow me." She turned and made her way along the path to her house.

Ryan and Brad quickly followed, stopping at the front of Mrs. Ivey's house, shocked at what they saw.

Brad's first thought was vandalism. There were at least a dozen plastic bags of cedar bark scattered across her yard, disastrous for her lawn. The heavy plastic would absorb the summer's heat and redirect it to the grass underneath, suffocating it and turning it yellow in only a few hours. In addition, there was damage to the plants in the front beds—Brad could see that several bags had been tossed against Mrs. Ivey's hydrangeas, splintering the plant's woody stems to the ground.

"What happened? Did you see who did this?"

"I did see, yes. In fact, I watched them do it." Mrs. Ivey frowned as she gestured to her yard. "I hired that no-good city landscaper two months ago to mulch my flower beds. I told them that my hydrangeas were drooping in the sun and needed attention. I booked them and even paid them upfront like they wanted. But they didn't come. Last week, I called again to remind them I was still waiting for their work crew, and this time I'm afraid I was a bit short with them." Her frown deepened as her blue eyes snapped with fury. "This was their response. You can see that my yard is ruined."

"You hired them two months ago?" Brad asked, as he lifted the corner of a bag. Underneath, the grass had already begun to turn yellow.

"Yes, I did. I see now that may have been a mistake."

"How long have these bags been on your lawn?" Ryan asked, picking up one of them and moving it to the driveway. It left a trail of mulch in its wake.

"Since Wednesday—four days." Her expression hardened. "And I've been on the telephone with them every morning since, trying to get them to come out and finish the job. They've been unforgivably rude."

Ryan deposited the bag on the driveway then went back to get another. "What did they say when you called them?"

"The girl said the entire crew is on another job. My friend Betty Marple has spotted their work trucks at the new construction just past the jetty. Been there for a month, at least."

"It doesn't take any more effort to stack these bags neatly on the driveway than it does to throw them on the grass." Brad wiped his forehead with the hem of his T-shirt. "I don't know why they wouldn't."

"Because they're not from around here." Mrs. Ivey pursed her lips, clearly agitated at what she must have viewed as a shoddy work ethic. "They came down with those New York City builders and if you ask me, they should go right back."

It only took a few minutes to move the bags from the lawn to the driveway, and when they were finished, Mrs. Ivey beamed at them. "Oh, thank you, boys. I was at my wits' end, I'll tell you that. I couldn't possibly have moved those darned things myself."

From his place on the driveway, Brad glanced at Ryan and lifted his chin. Ryan nodded in agreement.

"Tell you what, Mrs. Ivey," Brad said. "Spreading this mulch in your flower beds won't take long at all. Why don't we do that for you?"

"You wouldn't mind?"

"Not at all." Brad brushed bark chips from his arms. "I'll just go back to Grandpa's shed and find some tools."

"Oh, I have everything you boys need right here." She pointed to a pile near the front steps containing work gloves, a couple of rakes, and a utility knife to open the plastic bags.

"Would you like to borrow something to wear, Ryan?" Mrs. Ivey offered. "I might be able to find something in Mr. Ivey's old closet."

Ryan looked at what he'd been wearing to drag the mulch bags across the yard—a ratty college T-shirt, PJ bottoms and bare feet. He laughed. "That's okay. I don't mind getting a little dirty. In fact, I'm kind of looking forward to it."

They pulled on the work gloves, grabbed the rakes, and got to work.

It took the better part of the morning. Mrs. Ivey interrupted them twice; once with a tray of lemonade and oatmeal cookies as a snack, and once more to offer a check as payment for their work. They refused the check but accepted the food and sat in the shade to eat it when the work was done.

"I used to do some landscaping," Ryan said. "During the summers, to earn money for college."

"You worked your way through school? I didn't know that," Brad said.

"Yeah, I did. My parents have seven children and we had to find our own way. We always had a place to live and food to eat, but anything else we had to work for."

Ryan remembered those summers fondly. The work was hard sometimes, outside in every kind of weather, but at the end of the day he could see the work he'd done, the progress he'd made. That didn't always happen with the work he did now. Today, the simple repetition of slitting open a bag, emptying the contents, and raking it across a flower bed was immensely satisfying.

"Are you sure I can't give you boys anything for your trouble?" Mrs. Ivey had come to collect the tray. "You've both worked so hard."

"No, thank you," Brad said as he stood. "We were glad to help."

"Well then. Thank you both. I'll see you later this afternoon at your mother's party. I've got a pie in the oven."

They found their way back to the path between the houses. Ryan paused. "I don't know about you, but I forgot all about the party."

"We better get back before they send someone to look for us."

Chapter 15

The commotion in the kitchen was getting on his nerves. Distracted by clattering pots and loud voices, Chase had read the same sentence so many times it no longer made sense, and his patience had come to an end. Tossing his newspaper aside, he rose from his chair and snapped off the radio. This morning, as he had in years past, Chase had retreated to the quiet of his den while Kaye saw to the details of her party, knowing that his contribution would come later, at the grill. This year, however, Kaye had hired a caterer, eager to make a good impression. She'd arrived early with a team of assistants who took over the kitchen and yard and created such a racket that it made it impossible for him to relax. Heaving a sigh, he left his den and ventured into the kitchen.

"Hi, Dad." Stacy stood in front of a fully stocked refrigerator, pushing items aside to make room for the foil-covered bowl in her hand. "Mom says if you want coffee, you can have one cup of decaf and that I'm supposed to make you some."

"There's coffee in the pot," Chase grumbled. "What's wrong with that?"

"It's caffeinated. It's for the caterers."

The kitchen itself was an unrecognizable mess. Every inch of counterspace had been stacked with aluminum trays, shopping bags filled with party decorations lined the far wall, and pots bubbled on the stove, but worst of all was the constant smacking of the screen door as workers filed in and out of the kitchen.

"Where's your mother?"

"Outside, I think."

Chase shouldered his way around a worker carrying an armload of serving platters and made his way outside. He found Kaye leaning against a table, supervising a crew of workers. He slowed, surprised at her slouched posture and the worn expression on her face, and it occurred to him how tired she must be. They'd hosted their Fourth of July party for so many years that he assumed she enjoyed organizing all of it. He hadn't considered that this year, with a house full of people to tend to, the party might be too much for her.

"You need any help?" Chase approached, interrupting a conversation with a worker. *Why hasn't anyone offered Kaye a chair?*

Kaye straightened and reached for his arm. "In fact, I do. It seems that whoever bought the tiki torches forgot to buy the oil that fuels them. I was going to send Ryan but he's busy setting up the soccer field, and I can't find Brad anywhere. Do you mind going to Applegate's to pick some up? Aaron should know what we need. I can call ahead if you want."

"Sure. I'll go right now." Chase covered her hand with his and guided her to a deck chair, annoyed that these caterers hadn't noticed Kaye needed to rest. He lowered his voice so only Kaye would hear. "These people work for you. Sit down and make them come to you."

A few minutes later, Chase walked out the front door and headed to Applegate's, happy to do his part.

*

Chase returned home from his errand to find the catering trucks had been moved away from the house and a line of cars parked along the curb. Apparently, the first guests had already arrived. He shifted the paper bag to his other arm and increased his pace. He'd been away longer than he'd planned, chatting with Aaron about the state of the world, and while Kaye might understand, she wouldn't appreciate him arriving at her party dressed as he was. It would only take him a moment to shower and change his clothes.

A few yards from his front door, Mrs. Ivey called to him from her front porch. "Chase, wait a moment, will you?" She made her way down the stairs slowly, carrying a pie plate covered in a red-checked tea towel.

"Hello, Mrs. Ivey." He crossed her yard to meet her. "Can I carry that for you?"

"Of course you can't," she scoffed, accepting his arm but holding tight to her plate. "You keep treating me as if I'm an old lady, I might start believing it myself. I'm glad I ran into you. I was hoping for a moment alone to speak with you."

Chase slowed his pace to match hers. "Oh, really? Is something wrong?"

"No, nothing like that." She stopped and turned to face him, her blue eyes holding his gaze. "You know your mother was one of my best friends, and it has been my great pleasure to have lived next door to your family for almost the whole of my life. Since before you were born, in fact."

Chase nodded respectfully, though he didn't understand where the conversation was going.

"And you know that my policy has always been to keep my opinions to myself."

Chase snorted.

She narrowed her eyes, but the smile below softened the impact. "This will be difficult for you to hear, but what I have to say is important and I want you to listen." She paused for just a moment. "You remember your father had planned for you to go into business together as soon as you graduated high school?"

"I do, but—"

"But you didn't because that wasn't the right path for you." As she finished her thought, she frowned briefly, a reminder not to interrupt her again. "And you were right to do so. You are much more suited for a career in finance than you would have been going into business with your father. Though no one thought so at the time and it was difficult for your father to accept your decision."

Chase took advantage of the pause that followed. "I know it was, but I don't understand why you're bringing this up so many years later."

She squeezed his arm. "Your son is so much like your father that when I look at Brad, I see Santos. I see your son trying to find his way, just like you did. Chase, you need to let him, just like your father let you."

Chase bristled at the suggestion but said nothing. He *had* allowed Brad to "find his way," as Mrs. Ivey put it. Brad had taken much longer to settle into college than his sister did. In college, when Brad changed his major from business to history, Chase made no objection, even though the decision delayed Brad's graduation by at least two full years. And when Kaye let it slip that Brad had abandoned history to study something else, Chase still said nothing. If that wasn't allowing the boy to find his way, then he didn't know what was.

"You see that trellis?" Mrs. Ivey pointed to the side yard of her house. Chase nodded.

"Your father made that for me when you were a boy because he thought I should have a beautiful place for my mother's climbing rose to grow." She smiled and leaned against him. "Your boys spread mulch for me this morning, as a favor, because I asked them to. Then Brad came over again to fix some water damage on my trellis and redirect the vines, all on his own because he could see it needed doing."

"He's a good kid."

"He is, and I'm not sure you understand that as well as you should."

As they made their way toward the Bennett house, Chase's thoughts turned to his children. They both had attended elite private schools. They understood he expected excellence from them. He required them both to participate fully in all their school had to offer—academics, sports, and extracurriculars. It was Chase's way of giving them something he never had. When Chase was a boy, he had attended a series of unremarkable public schools where trying your best was good enough, and simply graduating was an achievement worth celebrating. Chase had worked hard to better himself and he wanted his children to have better opportunities, but while Stacy had embraced the rules and thrived, Brad always seemed to need an extra push. But that was okay with Chase. Wasn't that what fathers were for?

Of course Chase had allowed his son to find his way. Mrs. Ivey was mistaken.

After escorting Mrs. Ivey to the front door, Chase slipped to shower and change for the party. It had always been his job at Kaye's cookouts to flip the burgers and turn the hot dogs, and he enjoyed it. In fact, it was his idea one year to add a toppings bar on a side table near the grill for anyone who wanted to add caramelized onions or extra cheese to their burger as it cooked. He hoped someone had remembered to set that up this year too.

Freshly shaved, and with his hair still damp from his shower, Chase made his way down the stairs, enjoying the scent of a freshly ignited charcoal fire coming from outside. Someone had started the grill for him and now it was time for him to assume the duties. He knew Kaye would have remembered to hang his big apron on the hook by the grill. She was good with details like that.

He left the house by the side door, bypassing the chaos in the kitchen and most of the guests in the yard. Despite his eagerness to get to his grill station, he paused for a moment to take it all in. His wife knew how to throw a great party, but this year she had transformed their yard into something remarkable. The grassy field next door had been set with orange cones and soccer nets, and a group of children had already gathered to play. Chase could hear their shouts and laughter from where he stood. Tables of food were arranged beneath the shady tree—a buffet of cold salads on ice, steamed clams in warming trays, corn on the cob, and new potatoes sprinkled with what looked like parsley. Desserts were laid out on another, smaller table, with ice-cream churns nearby. Old-fashioned, galvanized washtubs had been filled with ice and stocked with soda cans, and juice pouches were placed strategically around the yard and field. Chase was glad to see that Kaye had hired a bartender to serve, if only to spare herself the busy work of stocking and replenishing an open bar.

The decorations, too, were exceptional, with colors in keeping with the Fourth of July holiday weekend. Blue tablecloths stretched across the buffet, and on bistro tables in the back of the yard. Red and white paper lanterns hung from tree branches overhead, and patriotic bunting was strung along the deck's railing. It really was something to see.

Chase made his way around the corner of the house to the grill station in the side yard, hoping Kaye would forgive him for being late.

He reached the side yard and stopped. There, behind the grill, wearing his chef's hat and his apron, was one of the caterers, cooking and serving hamburgers to his guests.

His irritation cooled when it occurred to him that Kaye had needed *someone* to cook in his absence, and it made sense to choose a caterer. Feeling slightly better, Chase continued toward the grill, intending to assume his duties.

"I'll take over now, thank you." Chase reached for the spatula.

"Chase, there you are." Kaye rounded the corner. She threaded her arm through his and gently guided him toward the party. "There are people we haven't seen in years and I'd like you to say hello please."

"Can't I say hello when they come for their burgers?" He stopped, annoyed that she was managing him as if he were a child. Something else was going on here and he didn't like it. "What is it?"

Kaye pursed her lips. "You might as well know now that I've hired the caterer to cook too, because I thought standing at the grill would be too much for you."

"You *what*?" He stiffened, feeling the color rise to his face. "Without discussing it with me?"

"It's done, Chase." Kaye met his glare with one of her own. "Now please come greet our guests."

Party manners prevented him from saying too much more, but he and Kaye would have a discussion after their guests left. For now, he needed a bit of distance between himself and his former job at the grill. And between him and his wife.

He broke free and strode across the lawn.

*

With each step, his irritation waned and he began to reproach himself for being childish. Kaye had gone to some trouble to arrange this party and she'd done an exceptional job. The weather was glorious, a few puffy white clouds gliding across a deep blue summer sky, with an occasional breeze from the bay rustling the oak leaves above them. Weather was always the most unpredictable part of an outdoor summer party, but somehow Kaye had found a way to control that too.

He slowed his pace and took it all in.

The atmosphere was welcoming. There was a soft buzz of conversation over the yard, peppered with an occasional burst of laughter as summer families became reacquainted. At the bar, he heard the sound of ice clinking against a glass. Further on, he noticed the sizzle of fat against hot coals as the burgers cooked, and the smell of charcoal wafting in the breeze. Not being in charge of the grill was a bitter pill to swallow, but if it made Kaye happy, then what did it really matter?

He glanced back toward the grill station and found his wife watching him. He lifted his chin and smiled, and she smiled back. Apology offered and accepted. All was right with the world.

"Chase Bennett, great party." A man broke away from a group of people who looked oddly out of place, as if they'd dressed for the idea of a summer party at the shore instead of the actual party. The man striding toward him gave the appearance of being casually dressed, but his Top-Siders were a little too new, the crease on his khakis a little too sharp, the cuffs on his Oxford shirtsleeves a little too precisely folded. He looked as though he were dressed for a job interview and it was odd. Chase glanced at the women in the group, impeccably turned out in black sleeveless silk, dark sunglasses and stacks of gold jewelry, and found it hard to believe any of them would be Kaye's friends. "My wife and I were just saying how much we've enjoyed the little parties here. We don't have anything like it back in Manhattan."

"Thank you, though I can't take the credit." Chase accepted the man's hand and shook it. His hands were soft, his grip a bit too eager. As a partner in a financial firm, Chase had gotten used to slick junior executives looking for a shortcut on the way up, as this man appeared to be doing. Though he hadn't said it yet, this man wanted something.

"Rick Maxwell, nice to see you. My wife and yours go way back, I believe." As he adjusted his sunglasses, Chase noticed a glint of sunlight reflecting off his gold Ivy League class ring and wondered if the gesture was purposeful. "Your reputation for deal-making precedes you, and I wonder if you'd mind me bending your ear for a second? I'd like your professional opinion on a business investment I'm considering."

Shop talk was actively discouraged at Dewberry Beach parties because the summer was meant for families and community events. Kaye, in particular, was known to break up a huddle and redirect the men's attention back to their children and their wives. So Chase knew for a fact that she wouldn't appreciate this. But curiosity got the best of him. It had been so long since he'd spoken about his work in a serious way to anyone. Chase glanced at Kaye, chatting with a group of women, and decided they were safe for the moment.

"Okay, but I'm not sure I'm the best person to help." Chase lifted his shoulder in a gentle shrug, then watched Rick's expression. Men who were overeager were usually reckless.

"Oh, it'll only take a minute," Rick pressed. "It's more of an idea really. I'm sure you can help."

"As you may have heard, I've retired from the consulting business. I can refer you to a colleague if you need more specific direction?"

Rick cleared his throat. "Yes, well. I'm not sure the consultants I met with properly understood the scope of my project."

So that was it. Chase bit back a smile. This man had already met with someone and either they didn't like his idea, or he didn't like their advice. As Chase wondered which one was true, it occurred to him that he did, in fact, know this man.

"You're Ginny's husband," Chase said suddenly.

"Yes. As I said."

The correction annoyed Chase.

Rick cleared his throat again and steered the conversation back. "Do you mind if we speak somewhere privately? I've got a file of papers in my car that I can show you."

Chase shook his head. "I'm sorry, but as I said, in general terms only. I'm afraid I'm not as current on the industry as I once was."

"Sure. Of course." Rick nodded reluctantly. He glanced back at his friends with a nervous energy that made Chase glad he had turned him down.

"If you'll excuse me, I was on my way to the field to watch my grandson play soccer. It was nice to see you again," Chase said smoothly.

It was an excuse, to watch his grandson's soccer game; the first thing he thought of to escape the conversation with Rick. But now that Rick and his friends seemed to be watching him, Chase had no choice but to follow through. The soccer game on the grassy field was a pickup version, the kind Chase used to play when he was a kid. It struck him as odd that parents would be interested enough to watch. His own parents had never watched his sports games. As Chase approached the field, he spotted Ryan on the sidelines, looking genuinely thrilled to watch the children play.

"Hi, Chase." Ryan fished a cold bottle of water from a nearby tub of ice. "Can I offer you some water? It's getting hot out here."

It was getting warm. Chase hadn't noticed it before now.

"Thank you." He twisted the top and sipped.

They stood in companionable silence for a moment, sipping their drinks and watching the children run. At first it seemed like a knot of children moving up and down the field, kicking up the occasional puff of dust. One of the older kids kicked the ball toward Connor in goal, a strike that should have gone in but hit the frame instead.

"You know," Ryan said, "I didn't think Connor actually liked soccer all that much, but maybe he does. Maybe he was just in the wrong position. He seems to like being goalie."

Chase chuckled. "Look closer."

Ryan scanned the field. "What am I supposed to see?"

"Someone switched the balls." Chase pointed to the metal-framed goal. "That's a kid-size goal and they're playing with a regulation ball, which, I imagine, makes it harder to score. Even if the goal was untended, they probably wouldn't score."

"That's cheating." Ryan blinked.

"That's finding a weakness in the game and exploiting it," Chase corrected. "Funny thing is that in my business, that sort of thing would be admired, and I would have done it too. Even as distasteful as I find it now."

Ryan shrugged, generous as ever. "Sometimes you have to do things you don't want to do, especially if people are depending on you."

"I'm not sure that's true." Chase's gaze wandered to his father's workshop. "Sometimes a life well lived is measured in friends and family, not success in business."

Chase noticed Ryan's wary expression and dismissed it. "I'm fine. Just an old man with too much time on his hands and a few too many regrets."

Brad came jogging up. "Dad, Mom wants you."

"I guess that's my signal to leave. Ryan, I'll see you later." Chase finished the rest of his water and dropped the bottle into the blue bin. He turned to follow Brad. "What does she want?"

"Some kid ran into the screen door."

Chase paused, not understanding.

"Mom wants you to look at it."

"How bad is the damage?" It seemed the obvious question to ask, though the answer would tell him nothing. Chase was completely unqualified to fix anything in the house. Kaye usually arranged repairmen.

"It's splintered off the hinges. Mom wants you to fix it before the flies come in."

They'd need tools. Chase led the way to the work shed, though he had no idea what to do once he got there. Hopefully, someone had remembered to remove the padlock.

As they approached the shed, Chase noticed that the outside windows had been scrubbed clean and the shutters had been straightened and rehung. Someone, Kaye probably, had arranged for someone to repair to the sagging window box so she could fill it with the plants she liked. In this case deep-red geraniums and delicate trailing ivy. Whoever she booked did a good job even removing the rusty padlock and refinishing the door handle to make the shed appear more inviting. If he remembered correctly, there was a dusty toolbox on an overturned

crate under the workbench, though he couldn't remember the contents. Hopefully the tools inside would be useful.

He pushed the wooden doors open and stepped inside his father's old
work shed. His breath caught as a flood of unexpected emotions washed
over him, and all at once he was ten years old again. They'd had a fight
in this shed, he and his father, last time he was here. A stupid one, never
resolved, one that fractured their relationship for the rest of their lives
and Chase remembered it as clearly as if it had happened yesterday. It
was a summer day and his father had called him to this place intending
to teach him something—hand-planing, Chase recalled. But Chase was
on his way somewhere else and had been annoyed at the interruption
to his day. He'd behaved terribly then, was petulant during his father's
instruction and dismissive of the work his father loved. In the end,
Chase had been allowed to go on his way and was never called into the
workshop again. Now, the regret of what he'd done then, how his attitude
must have hurt his father, settled into his chest and his body buckled.

If only.

"Dad?"

Chase looked up, almost expecting to see his father.

"You okay, Dad?" It was Brad, his son, so grown up, so fast. "You
need to sit down?"

"What happened in here?"

"I straightened up a little, but I thought it was okay," Brad added
quickly. Chase flinched at his son's tone, as if Brad were afraid of him.

"You did this?"

"I didn't think you'd mind…"

"You did a good job," Chase replied, walking toward the workbench.
He ran his fingertips across the surface. "Gramps would have been
proud."

"You think so?"

"I do." Chase turned. "And I'm proud of you too."

Brad stiffened, as if rooted to his spot, though his eyes widened. Chase closed the distance between them and wrapped his arms around his son. To his shame, he couldn't remember the last time he had hugged him. His eyes prickled with tears and he blinked them away.

After a long moment, he released his son. "My father was the most honorable man I've ever known, though it took me years to understand why. You remind me of him, and I should have told you long before this."

"Why don't you sit down, Dad?" Brad attempted to guide him to Santos's stool, but Chase shook him off.

"No, you sit there. You belong here more than I do. I think you should have it." Chase lifted a child-sized hammer from the peg board. It still looked new. He turned it over in his palm and read the inscription: *For Cesidio, my son.*

"I changed my name. Did you know that?" This time Chase let the memories come. "I was christened Cesidio Bennetti after I was born, named after my father's father. I hated that name and changed it to Chase Bennett the minute I left for college." He scoffed at his own arrogance. "I thought my new name would make me one of the Ivy League boys I idolized. My mother was furious when she found out, but my father said nothing. I think he couldn't. I think it broke his heart. He never mentioned it, but he also never called me by name again." Chase replaced the hammer on the peg board and turned to his son. "I think that was probably the end of any relationship I could have had with my father. He stopped trying after that, but I didn't notice until it was too late. I don't want that for us." He paused to gather his composure. "I believe I owe you an apology."

Brad shifted uneasily. "No, Dad. We're good."

"Nevertheless, I'd like to," Chase continued, grateful to Mrs. Ivey for planting the seed and to Rick for showing Chase the kind of man he'd groomed Brad to become. "You are a good man with a kind heart. I should have recognized that years ago, and I'm sorry I haven't—until now, son."

Brad hesitated but didn't turn, and in that moment, Chase knew. Did he really expect a single comment to erase years of misunderstanding?

He turned to leave.

"Hey, Dad?" Brad called him back.

"Yeah?" Chase's voice cracked. He cleared his throat. "What is it?"

Brad looked up from his work and for a moment, Chase saw his five-year-old son asking him to stay home from work on a Saturday morning and play catch with him instead.

So much time missed.

"Mom could use more room for beach towels in the mudroom. Thinking about maybe making a bench or something." He lifted his shoulder in a gentle shrug. "If you want to help…"

"I'd love to." Chase stepped closer to the workbench. "What have you got so far?"

They sat in compatible silence for a while. Chase claimed a space on a nearby stool, watching his son ticking off measurements along a board and noticing he held the flat carpenter's pencil in his left hand with the same grip his grandfather had used.

A sharp knock at the door shattered the silence of the room.

Ryan peered into the shed from the doorway. "Kaye sent me to find you guys. She said it's time for sparklers and that attendance is required."

"Okay." Brad reached up to flick off the desk light, plunging the workshop unexpectedly into shadow. Chase glanced at the light outside;

dusk had fallen already. Hours had passed, unnoticed, while Chase watched his son utterly focused on his work. Just like his grandfather.

Brad stood. "You coming, Dad?"

"Yes, I am."

Outside evening settled in, the summer air cooled, and the party atmosphere changed. As Chase and his son made their way up the path from the workshop to the deck, Chase noticed the citronella candles had been lit; their light danced and flickered on the tabletops. The fading light had activated tealights inside hurricane lanterns scattered around the yard, and strings of miniature lights threaded among the tree branches overhead bathed the yard in a warm glow.

As in years past, the badminton game in the grassy field next door would be the last game to end, despite the darkness. Chase heard the soft plunk of the birdie hitting a racket, followed by bursts of laughter as the players tracked the game by flashlight. Chase and Brad passed a group of older kids gathered around the firepit, toasting marshmallows on long sticks and flicking bits of graham crackers at each other.

The crowd had thinned, as it usually did about this time, with parents taking the youngest children home for baths and bed. Those who remained chatted softly, with their sleeping children curled on their laps.

They found Ryan on a corner of the back deck, pouring sand into a collection of tin buckets. Stacy stood nearby, two more empty buckets in her hands.

"Should we keep a closer eye on those kids back there?" Stacy gestured to the firepit.

"We just passed them," Chase offered. "They seemed to be behaving themselves for the moment."

Stacy frowned, considering. "I think I'd feel better if they had a sand bucket." She lifted one that Ryan had just filled. "Do you mind if I take this?"

"You want the fire extinguisher too?" Ryan asked, pointing to an ancient barrel-shaped fire extinguisher leaning against the base of a tree. "It might work, you never know."

"I'm sure they'll love it," Brad offered, biting back a smile as he bent to retrieve the extinguisher.

With his children busy and Kaye chatting to Brenda on the deck, Chase took the opportunity to find a seat. Though he would never admit it to Kaye, the day's activities had tired him.

By chance, he spied his granddaughter asleep on one of the Adirondack chairs by the side garden, and he went to join her. On his way across the yard, he pulled a fleece throw from a stack and carried it with him. Sophie didn't wake when he lifted her from the chair, or even when he settled her on his lap and tucked the blanket around her. As he brushed the hair from his granddaughter's face, he noticed how much Sophie looked like her mother. Strange that he hadn't ever noticed the resemblance before.

Sophie's feet were bare; she'd pulled off her shoes and socks like Stacy used to when she was that age. He grasped Sophie's little foot in his palm to warm it, then directed his attention to the grassy field to watch the kids line up for sparklers.

Strictly speaking, sparklers were considered a fire hazard and weren't allowed within Dewberry Beach town limits, but they'd been part of the shore parties for decades and residents had always been reluctant to give up their traditions. Applegate's Hardware stocked cases of them all summer long, in full view of anyone shopping. In addition, both the fire captain and the chief of police were at the party so Chase assumed they'd be okay.

He watched a swarm of older kids survey the field, sweeping the ground with flashlights, looking for sharp sticks or rocks, tripping hazards for a child running with a sparkler.

Chase tucked Sophie's bare foot under the blanket as he listened to Ryan issue instructions to a group of children eager to get started.

"Before we light your sparklers," Ryan began, "you have to agree to the rules. The ends are very hot so no jabbing anyone, no sword fights, no playing chicken. When the sparks fizzle out, come back and stick the end in the sand here." He tapped the coffee can. "Then you can have another. We have plenty."

Do we ever. Chase chuckled to himself. At least a dozen boxes were stacked on the tabletop, more than enough for the entire population of Dewberry Beach.

Ryan flicked his lighter and held the flame to the tips of the sparklers. Almost at once, a shower of orange and yellow sparks burst from the metal ends. Kids ran across the field, drawing shapes in the darkness and shrieking with laughter.

As he listened to them play, Chase scanned the party for his wife. He found her eventually standing near the buffet table chatting with their friends, George and Nancy Goldsmith. Something about her posture made him pause and look closer. Though they'd been married more than thirty-five years, he'd known her far longer and he recognized her expression now. She was about to refuse an invitation and he could guess which one. A few days earlier, Chase happened to run into George at Mueller's Bakery and George mentioned a big trip they were planning. It seems that Nancy had always wanted to visit Austria during the holidays, to shop the famous Christmas markets. They had room on the trip for another couple and he'd invited Chase and Kaye to join them. Chase had replied that he'd love to but needed to speak with Kaye first in case there were medical appointments to reschedule.

Now, it appeared that she'd already decided.

He felt his body stiffen as he watched Kaye shake her head and he could almost read her lips as she refused the invitation. If he rose now, he would probably wake his granddaughter and almost certainly embarrass himself if he went over there, so he did nothing. He sat and watched the conversation conclude, helpless to intervene. Kaye laughed and he wondered what excuse she was offering, which of his symptoms she was describing in such detail that no one would dare think to question her. Then he felt the anger ignite in his body.

Enough was enough.

Hours later, after the last of the guests had said their goodbyes, Chase retreated to his bedroom where he sat in an armchair waiting for his wife to finish with the caterers. He'd opened the window that faced the bay, inviting in the salty breeze but nothing stirred and the air in the room felt close and uncomfortable. The conversation he would have with his wife would not be pleasant. But it was long overdue.

He heard her come down the hallway, watched the doorknob turn, and waited for her to enter the room.

"Here you are," she said breezily. "I thought you'd gone to bed already."

"Not quite yet."

"That was a nice party, don't you think?" Kaye moved toward the bed and turned down the quilt, smoothing the creases as she went. "We had a good turnout this year and people seemed to have fun."

Chase's response was again noncommittal, but Kaye didn't seem to notice.

"You don't think hiring a caterer was too much, do you?" She nudged a decorative pillow aside. "Brenda says that's the only kind of party the city people throw now—fully catered. I do think it misses the point of a neighborhood cookout though, don't you?"

"Kaye." Chase's voice was firm, a tone he didn't often take with his wife. "We have to talk."

"About what?" Kaye straightened suddenly. "The scene you made at the grill? With the caterer?" She gave him a pointed look. "I think that was completely unnecessary. You knew I'd hired help and I thought you'd appreciate being free of that tedious job."

"As it happens, I like tending the grill. You took that away from me without even asking."

"Well." She shrugged, turning away as if it didn't matter. "It's over now."

"It's not over," Chase corrected. "We need to talk about it. Not just the grill either. Kaye, you've been managing my entire life—my walks, my food, my sleep, and my medication—as if I were a child, and I don't like it."

To his surprise, Kaye rounded on him, gripping the pillow so tightly that her knuckles were white. "I do *not* treat you like a child."

"You do," Chase insisted as he rose from his chair. As he paced the room, he counted off the incidents he could remember on his fingers. "You have forced me to walk every morning since we arrived, whether I want to or not. You open mail from my doctors, even though what's inside is solely my business. At the Parkway Diner, you changed my order—in front of the whole family."

"That's enough!" Kaye's tone was sharp as she dropped the pillow. "I'm doing everything I can to keep you safe and you don't even notice. You act as if the past three years didn't happen."

In fact, Chase did know how difficult his illness and recovery had been on her, and he regretted putting her through that. But now was not the time to reassure or to comfort her. If he did, the opportunity would be lost and the restrictions on his life would never ease. He couldn't let that happen. He couldn't live that way anymore.

He tried another tactic. He paused and gave his wife a deliberate look. "What did you and Nancy Goldsmith talk about?"

Kaye blinked in surprise and her face told him all he needed to know. He closed his eyes and felt his shoulders sag. His assumption was right, and he hadn't realized until just this minute how much he wanted to be wrong.

"Nothing really," Kaye finally answered. "Just chatting."

"That's not the truth."

"Fine." Kaye's expression hardened. She raised her chin and glared at him. "Nancy wanted us to join them in Austria in December. They're planning a river cruise down the Rhine to visit the Christmas markets. I told them no. I told them that you weren't up to a long trip because it's true: you're not."

"That's not for you to decide."

"Well, I did." Kaye shook her head. "Austria is too far away. Too far from your doctors."

To prevent harsh words he couldn't take back, Chase grabbed his pajamas from the hook and went into the bathroom to change. Though he loved his wife dearly, living with her could be a challenge. Lately she'd become bossy and unyielding, controlling and sharp, but she hadn't always been like this. He understood her need to control things. The incident in the ocean when Stacy was little had broken Kaye. She blamed herself. Chase should have helped her then, should have talked about it or taken her to see someone, but he never did.

He emerged from the bathroom a few moments later, dressed for bed. Kaye was in bed already, pretending to read a book.

"You talk about finding a new normal," Chase said, his tone unchanged as he stood by the bed. "My normal cannot be restricted to egg-white omelets and mineral water, and you cannot expect me to stay close to home waiting to grow older."

With her attention still on the book, Kaye frowned but didn't interrupt.

He sat on the bed and reached for Kaye's book. As she looked up, he saw the fear in her expression and wondered if it wouldn't be kinder to just do what she wanted. She'd already been through so much. Then, just as quickly, he dismissed the idea. He couldn't live that way. "I can't sit at home just to make you feel better. And you shouldn't stay at home watching me." He offered a tentative smile. "Maybe we should start thinking about doing things together."

"You want to go to the Christmas markets? With the Goldsmiths?" Kaye asked, and he heard the apprehension in her voice. This was hard for her, this letting go, but if he pressed, she would do it.

He scoffed. "Not with those two. Are you kidding? They'd drive me nuts."

He heard her chuckle as he reached over and flicked off the light. He'd made his point.

Chapter 16

The ping of incoming messages on his cell phone sounded like scattershot, and the noise pulled Ryan from sleep. Bleary-eyed, he slipped the phone from the charger. He scanned the first message and then the second. Then the first one again because he couldn't believe what he'd read. With his heart pounding, Ryan scrolled to the top of the list and read every email twice, certain that he was mistaken. And when it became clear to him that he wasn't, his shock turned to anger.

It seemed that Todd had fired Ryan's entire department.

Ryan rose from bed, grabbed his laptop and his phone, and made his way downstairs. He dialed Todd's number twice before it dawned on him that the timing of these messages was purposeful. The email firing Ryan's employees had been sent in the middle of the night, on a holiday weekend. Todd would have sent the mail, then shut off his phone while he waited for tempers to cool. It was a coward's way out, one that Todd had taken before, but this time it wouldn't work. The fate of twenty-nine employees rested in the balance, and the thought of Todd sleeping peacefully after pulling something like this just made Ryan angrier.

Because it was unlikely that Todd would return his calls, Ryan decided to escalate matters. Opening his laptop, he scanned his contacts for someone with more authority than Todd but came up with nothing. He hadn't noticed until now, but his entire list of contacts from the Seattle company consisted of Todd and an administrative assistant whose job it was to schedule video meetings. He'd reached a dead end.

Changing tactics, Ryan opened a search engine and typed in the name of Todd's company. The search returned professional associations, Seattle city listings, newspaper announcements, and Ryan sifted through them all but found nothing, no executive contacts he could reach out to. Heaving a sigh of frustration, he closed his laptop and picked up his cell phone. He called Sean, then Jeff, and left messages for both when they didn't answer.

"Didn't you make coffee?" Stacy, puffy-eyed and still in her bathrobe, held up the empty carafe and frowned at him. "You know the rule: first one up makes the pot."

She pushed the carafe back in place with more force than seemed necessary, and Ryan's temper flared. He'd been up for hours, dealing with a real emergency. The least she could do was make a fresh pot herself.

"If the pot is empty, it's obvious that I didn't make any," he snapped.

"What's wrong with you?"

"Nothing. Forget it." It would take too long to explain, and he didn't have time to argue about who should have made coffee.

She stiffened but didn't reply. Turning toward the sink, she turned on the tap and filled the machine with water. "Are you still going to take the kids to the beach today?" Her tone matched his. "You promised, and they're looking forward to it."

"I don't know. I might have to fly out to Seattle." Ryan raked his fingers through his hair. "Something's come up."

Stacy froze, a bag of ground coffee in her hand. "Today?"

"Yes. Today." Ryan spat each word out, annoyed with her for making him explain. "Something's come up," he repeated. "Something important."

"Has it really?" Stacy met his glare and matched it with one of her own. "Well, 'something's come up' here too. You promised to spend the day with Connor and he's counting on you."

Ryan didn't want the morning to go this way. Last night's party was a reminder of how easy their relationship used to be, before Todd and the partnership. Before everything imploded. He couldn't explain his feeling of obligation to the people he'd hired, and he hoped Stacy would understand eventually.

Brad entered the kitchen and went to the refrigerator.

"Look…" Stacy drew a breath. "I was up most of the night with the kids. You didn't know because I wanted you to enjoy the day with them." She scooped the coffee into the filter. "Sophie was awake until just after eleven because she wanted to talk about the party. The sparklers. Playdates. And a new friend she made." She flicked the switch on the coffee maker, then reached for a mug on the drainboard. "When I finally got her to sleep, Connor woke up a few hours later—at four thirty. He was so excited for his day at the beach with his dad."

Ryan opened his mouth to speak but she silenced him with a single look.

"You promised your son, and I won't let you break it. Work will always be there. Your children won't be." She pushed the mug aside and turned to leave the kitchen. "I'm going back to bed. The kids are your responsibility today."

After she left, Brad looked at him, his eyes wide. "Dude."

"Yeah," Ryan sighed as he closed his laptop.

*

Hours later, Stacy woke from her nap naturally, surprised at how long she'd been allowed to sleep without interruption. She listened for sounds of her children or her husband but the house was still. Outside, she heard oak leaves rustle in a gentle breeze, then saw the white eyelet curtains on the bedroom window flutter as the breeze made its way inside, and finally, she breathed in the salty air as the breeze surrounded her. She yawned and stretched as she turned over to look out the open window. Cicadas hummed in the trees and someone bounced a ball in the street. The sun was high overhead, casting the world outside in bright possibilities.

Then she remembered the spat she'd had with Ryan earlier that morning and her good mood dissolved. At the previous night's party, Ryan was fun and engaging and the kids loved having their father's attention. She did too if she was honest. But the previous night seemed to be an exception. This morning, Ryan's attention was once again focused on his work.

Impulsively, she decided to find her husband and talk to him. Pushing aside the sheets, she rose from bed and splashed water on her face. Her maternity shorts still fit, though they were getting snug and she'd need new ones soon. She raided Ryan's side of the closet for another oversized shirt and made her way downstairs, rolling up the sleeves as she went. She was surprised to find the kitchen empty, the coffee pot washed and put away, the dishes done, the countertops cleared.

"Hello?" she called out. "Anyone home?"

No answer. She wandered the rest of the house, just to make sure. Her father's den was vacant and there was no one in the yard outside. Though both cars were in the driveway, that didn't really mean much;

Dewberry Beach was a walking town. Any other day, Stacy would have loved to have a day to herself. She would have settled into a deck chair with a good book, a floppy hat, a glass of lemonade. But today she couldn't. She wouldn't have been able to enjoy herself with things as unsettled as they were between her and Ryan.

She returned to the kitchen and spied a note she must have missed before. Written in Brad's hand, it was secured to the refrigerator door with a plastic fruit magnet.

Doofus,
    Went crabbing by the boatyard bridge. When you're done with your hissy fit, come over.
    Your fav brother.

The boatyard bridge was close, just a few blocks away on the west side of town. Narrow and creaky, it was hidden behind a thick bank of cattails and little more than a shortcut between the marina and the swim club. The locals knew about it, of course, and sometimes cast their line from it but fish caught there tended to be too small to keep. It was also where their grandfather taught them to crab.

She tucked a bottle of water in her pocket and grabbed a zipped cooler from the mudroom. She'd make a quick stop at the bakery for sandwiches and cookies in case they were hungry. On her way out, she found her flip-flops and grabbed her sunglasses from the counter. Outside, the late-morning sun was bright and hot, the air thick and humid. There would be a thunderstorm later, one of the best things about summer afternoons. Her mood lifting, she slipped on her sunglasses and started down the street, waving to Mrs. Ivey as she walked by.

At the bakery, she pulled a paper number from the dispenser and waited. When her turn came, she ordered lunch for everyone and bought a large black coffee and an almond croissant to enjoy outside while she waited for the food. The server added the charge to their account because, although Stacy had remembered her sunglasses, she'd forgotten her wallet.

The first sip of coffee was blissful; no one made coffee like the ladies at Mueller's. Wandering outside, Stacy found a table in the shade. The metal chair scraped across the cement patio as she pulled it from the table and sat down. She felt the breeze shift, this time bringing the scent of freshly baking bread. Settling into her chair, Stacy closed her eyes and breathed it in.

"Stacy Bennett? Well, look at you. You're enormous."

Stacy's eyes snapped open. A man she didn't immediately recognize pulled out the opposite chair and sat. Definitely not a local but too absurdly dressed to be a tourist. His white linen shorts were tailored and sharply creased. His Hawaiian shirt was printed with pictures of thrashing swordfish, and a matching fabric band circled his wide-brimmed straw hat.

She was about to tell him to go away when she saw a mischievous smile curl his lips and felt a slam of recognition.

"*Billy Jacob?*" she spluttered as she leaned forward. "What in the world are you doing here?"

"Looking for you." The author of *A Winter to Remember* fished a pair of sunglasses from his shirt pocket and slipped them on. "Bright out here, isn't it?"

"Me?" Stacy repeated stupidly. "Why are you looking for me?"

"As it happens, I've come to ask for your help," Billy said airily as he twisted the brim on his straw hat. He reminded her of a little boy playing dress-up with the clothes newly found in his father's closet.

"My help with what?"

"Oh, is that *freshly brewed*?" Billy breathed as he reached for her cup. "All I have in that tragic little excuse for a hotel is a rusted tea kettle and packets of *instant coffee*." He grimaced before he sipped, then he swallowed and sighed. "This is delicious."

"Billy."

"Yes?"

"Give me back my coffee."

"Fine." He pushed it toward her with exaggerated effort, though not before sneaking another sip.

It occurred to her that she was being rude so she tried again, this time softening her tone. "Congratulations on your success."

"Thank you," he answered absently as he glanced toward the bakery. "Do they have table service here?"

"Not outside. You have to go in."

He sighed and leaned against his chair, apparently put off by the effort.

To ask again why he came to Dewberry Beach to look for her would have been pointless. Billy Jacob would explain when he was ready. And because she was curious, she'd wait. But only until her food was ready.

"I've heard you're allowing fan fiction now, based on the world you created. Is that true?"

"Yes, it is."

"And a movie?"

"They've sold the option."

"You must be very excited."

He shrugged. "I guess."

This game was getting tiring. Stacy remembered why she and Billy hadn't maintained their friendship after his book was published. Why they were never really friends in the first place. She admired his talent. He was a brilliant author but also petulant and difficult when things didn't go his way. Managing his moods used to be her job, but it wasn't anymore.

Thankfully her order came then, so she rose from her chair and offered a genuine smile. "It was nice to see you, Billy. I hope you have a good visit here and I wish you great success with your second book."

"Wait. Where are you going?" He straightened, surprised at her departure. "I *said* I need your help."

"You did," she replied. "But you haven't mentioned it again so I didn't think it was important."

"I need your help"—he leaned across the table and whispered—"with the second book."

"What about the second book?"

"Sit down and I'll tell you." He gestured for her to sit back down.

Curiosity got the best of her, so she did. If the new book was to be released in the fall, it had already been written and edited. Billy must want her help with copy or proofreading, but she wasn't a proofreader and didn't have the patience for copy. There was nothing she could think of that he needed from her.

After a moment, Billy reached across the table for her hand, his voice barely a whisper. "The book. It isn't written yet."

"What?" Stacy gasped. "Are you kidding me?"

He shook his head as he leaned back. "I wish I were."

People were starting to stare and she doubted he wanted this conversation to be overheard.

"Come with me." She handed him her coffee, gathered up her food order, and guided him away from the bakery, down the first residential street she came to. When they reached a safe distance, she turned and faced him. "What do you mean, 'it's not written'?"

He shrugged, tipping the brim of his hat to cover his eyes.

"Take that ridiculous thing off your head, Billy. You look like Truman Capote." Stacy reached for his hat and snatched it away. "Now tell me what happened. All of it."

"I don't know. The story didn't flow, I guess, so I stopped writing. The other editors didn't *get* me like you did."

"They've scheduled a release date." Stacy remembered the posters she'd seen at the little book store in town. "Do they know you haven't written it yet? Someone at Revere has to know."

"You see the problem? It's not entirely my fault," Billy corrected, sipping the coffee with such indifference that she wanted to grab it back.

"Who's your editor?"

"Emmerson."

"Paul Emmerson? He must know."

"He knows a bit. I insisted on your help polishing the draft before I showed it to him, and he very reluctantly allowed it. To be fair, I'm not sure he would have had he known how far behind I really am."

"Polishing?" Stacy was trying to make sense of what he'd said. A conversation with Billy was always exhausting, a mental jigsaw puzzle you had to keep working until the pieces fitted together and the picture was recognizable. "So you *do* have a draft? You just told me it's not written."

"All these questions are making my head ache." Billy sighed, his body slouching dramatically. "I've told you everything."

They began walking again, Stacy processing the fragments of what she'd heard, and Billy loudly sipping her coffee.

"How did you find me down here?" she asked finally.

"Oh, please." Billy scoffed. "That part was easy." He reached into her bag and helped himself to a section from her croissant. "So, will you do it?"

"Do what?" Stacy snatched the bag back.

"Help me with the second book."

"But it's not written."

"Not yet, but it will be. And it will be magnificent." He brightened. "We work well together, you and I."

That part was true: they did produce an amazing novel.

A Winter to Remember would forever be her favorite book, and she'd always be proud of her part in bringing it to life. But the work behind the scenes was brutal, much of it falling on Stacy alone. Many times during the process Billy would declare his story "wasn't working" and would flounce off without warning. Sometimes he'd be gone for days at a time, unreachable by email or telephone. Because she was new at her job and didn't know any better, she'd cover for him in staff meetings. She'd lie to her coworkers about the book's progress, approve cover art and back copy without having an actual story to sell.

The stress had been overwhelming.

Billy never appreciated her efforts or even seemed to care that she'd put her job on the line for him. She couldn't do that again no matter how talented he was or how eagerly the world awaited his new book. She had other priorities now; a family to consider.

Stacy stopped in her tracks and gaped at him. "We don't though," she said. "We don't work well together at all. In fact, you're a nightmare. It's all coming back to me now: you're awful, Billy."

"I absolutely am not," Billy sputtered.

"You are," Stacy insisted. "I couldn't wait to start my maternity leave after working with you."

"Things are different now."

"How so?"

"Because I need you now."

"I don't think so, Billy. But I thank you for asking." She touched her belly as the baby moved. "As you so politely pointed out earlier, I'm expecting a baby and I won't be able to give you much time."

"I don't need much time," Billy pressed. "Just give me until the end of summer—Labor Day."

"That's six weeks from now."

"I know. That's all I need." He looked at her so earnestly that she was tempted to give in.

"I believe you're sincere now, but what happens when things get tough? When the story 'stops speaking to you'? Or when you insist on a weekend 'to clear your head'?" she replied. "You don't like deadlines, Billy. You've missed every one I've ever given—"

"That's not true. Not the important ones." He slowed and raised his forefinger. "The important ones I don't miss."

"You're scattered, temperamental, demanding, and easily distracted…" Stacy was pressing the point because she wanted him to understand her answer was a very firm no.

"How can you *say* that?" he gasped, pretending to be affronted.

"Seriously, Billy?" Stacy gaped at him.

"You don't understand." He paused to throw both hands in the air. "I'm a *creative*. You have to make allowances for my process."

As fun as it was to tease Billy—and it was—she had to put an end to it. Her job at Revere had been rewarding and she missed it. But as tempting as it might be to pick it up again she just couldn't. Her life was different now. Her family was her priority: Connor, Sophie, and the new baby. It had been her decision to start a family and it was her responsibility to care for them. The life she had did not include the craziness of working with Billy Jacob.

As painful as it might be, her decision had to be final.

They stood at the end of the street, under a canopy of leaves. She offered him the bag she'd snatched away earlier. "*A Winter to Remember* is an amazing book and you should be genuinely proud of it." She reached for his arm. "You need to remember that you're the one who wrote it—not me. And you can do it again. I'm flattered you asked but I'm afraid the answer's no."

"But I have an outline!" Billy's expression clouded. "A *detailed* outline."

"The same outline we worked on six years ago, before I left?"

"Yes."

"What have you written since then?"

Billy looked away and Stacy's heart sank. "You haven't written anything, have you? Why not, Billy? It's been six years."

"Technically five. No, four," he amended as he took his hat from her and waved a cloud of gnats from his face. "I had a lot of publicity to do after the release of the first book."

"You still had time enough to at least start."

He shrugged as if he had no idea where the time went. The expression on his face reminded Stacy of Connor's—remorseful at being called out for not doing chores. But Connor was six years old and Billy should know better. "I've been busy. Kyle and I bought a brownstone and fixed it up. It's beautiful—you should see it. Lots of light, hardwood floors, original fixtures—"

"Does Emmerson know you have little more than an outline?"

Billy shook his head. "Not entirely, but he must suspect. I can tell he's losing patience—his email manner has been very terse."

"Sorry, Billy." Stacy continued walking. "I can't help. There's too much work to do."

Billy swept the air with both his hands. The coffee sloshed in the cup. "I know people."

Stacy turned, puzzled.

"If you help me with this book, I can introduce you to people and tell them how vital you are to my work. You could go freelance after book two is published and you'd have authors *lining up* to work with you. Your pick of projects. Your pick of authors. All on your own time."

She hesitated. It was a very tempting offer. An introduction and a reference from Billy Jacob would set her up to work with any author or publishing house she wanted. And she really did miss the work.

Just then, Stacy felt the baby kick, a reminder of what was important. She shifted her weight and pressed her palm to her belly. Her life was different now; it revolved around her growing family and wasn't hers to direct.

Not anymore.

She shook her head again and watched his expression crumble. "The best I can offer is to talk to Emmerson for you, maybe smooth things out. I know him and he might understand if you're honest with him." She squeezed his hand. "It was nice to see you, Billy. Good luck with everything."

She turned and went to find her family.

Following the curve of the footpath to the boatyard bridge, Stacy came to a clearing, a manicured patch of grass on the bank of the inlet. Years ago, someone had dragged a huge piece of driftwood from the beach and carved a bench from it. The wood had aged to a soft gray patina, and it was positioned to take in the best views of the water. Sometimes, on an early morning walk with her father, they would come across someone sitting on the bench, sipping coffee and watching the tide come in or the seagulls dive and soar overhead. Stacy paused for a moment to look across the water, the maze of floating docks hugging the shore of the bay. As the breeze from the bay stirred the air, the leaves rustled, and the air smelled of the sea.

As she continued past the swath of cattails on the shore, she spotted her family on the bridge. Ryan untangled the cords of a knotted crab net while Sophie threw rocks into the water.

"Don't do that, Sophie," Ryan said, his voice controlled. "The crabs don't like it when you throw rocks. It scares them away."

"Like this, buddy." A bit further down, she saw Brad pulling up a crab line the way their grandfather had taught them, hand over hand, moving so carefully that the water didn't even ripple. "You have to go slowly or they'll swim away."

"Mommy!" Connor's eyes lit up at the sight of her. He dropped the string, abandoning the lesson, and ran to her.

Sophie followed closely behind, a little less willing to forgive her absence. "Where have you been?" she demanded.

"I took a nap." Stacy cupped her daughter's chin with her fingers. "You should try it sometime."

Scattered across the bridge was a collection of crab nets and new tin buckets. A dozen black flies buzzed around a trio of fish heads they'd used for bait. The Fish Shack by the inlet offered free packets of fish parts wrapped in newspaper to any kid who asked. Their grandfather had always insisted that a fish head was the best bait. He tied it to the end of a length of twine and held it near a dock piling to entice the crabs. But Stacy's family didn't seem to be having much luck today; a nest of twine lay tangled nearby and the biggest bucket, the one for storing the crabs before throwing them back, was empty.

"Didn't catch anything?" Stacy asked. She caught Ryan's eye and offered a tentative smile. He returned it with a nod of his head, and she felt her smile widen. She'd apologize later—they both would—but for now it was enough to know that tensions had thawed.

"Nothing." Brad cut the fish head loose from the crab line and watched it sink into the water. "Absolutely nothing. I have a new appreciation for Gramps's patience though."

"Are we done now?" Sophie asked.

"Yes, I guess we are." Ryan reached for the knot of twine and tossed it into a bucket.

"Hurray!" Connor ran toward the bait wrapped in paper. Before anyone could stop him, he kicked the fish heads, wrapper and all, into the water.

Brad picked up a stick and managed to snag the paper out of the water as Stacy moved closer to Ryan.

"I'm sorry I was snappy with you this morning." She stooped to help him gather the buckets. "I haven't had much sleep. But you haven't either."

"Not lately," Ryan agreed as he kissed her forehead. "I guess we were both grumpy."

"You guys go on ahead," Brad said. "Mrs. Ivey asked me to talk to one of her friends about a garden bed, and she lives down that block." He passed the crab nets to Ryan.

Stacy handed him one of the bags of food she'd brought and they parted ways; Ryan and Stacy walking back to the house together, both kids running ahead.

"How's work?" Stacy asked.

"Not good, but I don't want to talk about it." Ryan sighed. "Not right now."

"Okay."

They watched Sophie and Connor chase each other down the street and across front lawns.

"Where do they get so much energy?" Ryan marveled.

Stacy laughed. "They can play outside after lunch. I'll watch them and you can go take a nap."

"Deal," Ryan said as he reached for her hand.

And just like that, all was right with the world.

Chapter 17

The hot shower helped clear Ryan's head, but not entirely. With the exception of a few days here and there, he hadn't felt like himself for quite some time. He swiped the corner of his towel across the foggy mirror, barely recognizing his own image. It was more than just the dark circles and ragged expression; there was a dull throbbing at the base of his neck that never quite stopped. And he couldn't remember the last time he'd had a full night's sleep. He'd muscled through all of it, of course, because he was supposed to. That was his job. He and Stacy had negotiated their roles a long time ago: Stacy looked after their growing family and he provided for them.

The partnership with the venture capitalists had been difficult, to say the least. Ryan's hope had been that the job would get easier once the company went public as planned. Todd had assured them that months leading up to the IPO were always the worst and that things would settle afterwards, and for months, Ryan had held on to that single thought like a life ring.

But Todd had lied.

Todd had fired Ryan's entire team and neither he nor Sean had returned his calls to explain why.

Ryan toweled his hair dry and tossed the wet towel into the laundry basket. Then he slipped into a clean pair of shorts and T-shirt and crossed the room to lie down on the bed. He closed his eyes, listening to the homey sounds of his family downstairs, and allowed himself to drift off to sleep.

His cell phone rang and he pulled it from the charger. He glanced at the screen, planning to ignore anyone except Todd.

It was Jeff.

Ryan sat up and unlocked the screen to answer the call. "Jeff?"

"Yeah, it's me."

So many questions swirled in his head that Ryan didn't know where to start. Maybe where Jeff had been for the past four months, or why he was calling now?

"You still there?" The voice had a hint of a Midwest drawl—distinctly Jeff.

At seventeen years old, Jeff had been offered a full scholarship at MIT and assigned as the third roommate in a room with Ryan and Sean. A skinny, naive high-school junior from a small town in Oklahoma, Jeff arrived in Boston with a change of clothes, a battered laptop, and not a single clue how to navigate the adult world. They'd taught him to use the washer and dryer in the basement, but Jeff was the one who'd rigged it to accept metal washers from Home Depot as payment for a cycle. For an entire semester the whole dorm floor had washed their clothes for free. Jeff proved to be a gifted engineer, seeing connections that no one else could. He initially loved the puzzle, but Ryan saw that Jeff's heart wasn't into building the solution into a business. It wasn't unusual for Jeff to check out when tensions flared, but he'd never been gone this long before.

"Yeah, I'm here," Ryan answered, concern for his friend his first thought. "Where have you been? Are you okay?"

"Yeah. I'm okay now. Things are good."

"Where've you been, Jeff?" Ryan asked, unable to hold back his frustration. "Do you have any idea what kind of mess the company is in? Todd fired my whole department but won't answer my calls. I'm really close to hopping on a plane and flying out to Seattle."

"I'm guessing Sean hasn't been around either?"

"He didn't disappear without a trace like you did, but yeah, he hasn't," Ryan sniped. "Left all his work to me."

"I'm sorry, man."

"I've been trying to reach you for weeks and couldn't find you. Why are you calling me now?"

"Todd found me. He wanted to talk to you."

"Todd? Why does he want to talk to me? More importantly, why didn't he call me himself? I've left a million messages he hasn't returned."

"He asked me to call you. He wants to negotiate with you for your department's immediate rehire, but he thinks that once you hear the conditions, you'll tell him to jump in the lake." Jeff laughed, a deep baritone that reminded Ryan of the time they'd hid under the stairs to watch a very confused crew of maintenance people retrieve and examine washers from the coin box.

"Should I?"

"Tell him to jump in a lake? I did."

Despite himself, Ryan laughed at the image of little Jeff telling off a twerp like Todd. "Is that why you took off?"

"Yeah. I'm sorry about that, man." Jeff sobered. "The job stopped being fun a long time ago. And if it's not fun, what's the point?"

"Where did you go?"

"I've been traveling. Nothing big, just bought me a junker car, loaded it up, and started driving. 'Fore I knew it, I'm pulling up to my brother's place in Iowa and that's where I stayed."

Ryan switched his cell phone to his other ear, annoyed that Jeff and Sean could detach from responsibility so easily. "So what are the conditions Todd thinks I'll hate?"

"There's a start-up out of UMD that's gaining market share pretty quickly. Todd says he already told you that. What you don't know is that the UMD boys have implemented most of our features faster than we could have. They're on track to release a final build months before we do. This new release will essentially destroy the company's valuation. Shut it down completely." Jeff drew a deep breath and exhaled slowly. "The UMD team has put together a better user interface and their overall costs are lower."

"That means—" Ryan pressed his back against the headboard to steady himself. "Everything we've worked for, wiped out. Just like that."

"Not necessarily." The phone muffled for a moment and Ryan heard a door close on Jeff's end. "I'm supposed to tell you that the only way to beat the UMD guys to market is to tighten our schedule, hire contractors, and move the dates up. That's the condition Todd has set: he'll let you hire them all back if you agree to another three months of crunch work."

"I'm not sure I can," Ryan said.

"I don't think you should," Jeff said simply. "I'm not even sure why you're still working, to be honest. Thought f'sure you'd be gone by now."

"It's the team. They're counting on me."

Jeff just laughed. "That's what you're worried about? You know your people are really good at what they do. That's why you hired them in the first place. They'll be fine."

"It's more than just that." Ryan perched on the edge of the bed. "They've worked brutal hours for the payoff when the IPO hits in the spring. Only I'm starting to think there won't ever *be* a payoff, even if we meet this new schedule. I don't trust Todd to tell us the truth about anything." Ryan closed his eyes. "I just wish I knew for sure. I just wish we had all the facts, and everyone could decide for themselves if they want to cut loose or come back to work."

Jeff didn't answer immediately. After a moment, Ryan heard what sounded like staccato tapping on a keyboard.

"Done." Jeff smacked the keyboard a final time.

"What do you mean 'done'? What did you do?"

"Told 'em," Jeff replied. "You're right to believe Todd's not telling you the truth, but I know where Todd and the Seattle boys keep the real information. Projections and market reports, memos and email that tell the full story; everything they keep to themselves."

"Why didn't you tell me?"

"I thought you knew. Sean does," Jeff said. "Anyway, that's not an issue now."

"What did you do?"

Jeff chuckled, a deep and rumbling sound that carried through the phone lines. "I changed the privacy settings. I made all the docs public and sent a company-wide email with the links."

"But… that's proprietary information. Todd could sue you for sharing it."

"He's got bigger fish to fry now," Jeff countered. "Look—Todd and the others had you dancing like a marionette, using the loyalty you feel toward your employees to get you to do whatever they want. I just ended the secrecy, that's all. Leveled the playing field you might call it."

"Jeff—"

But Jeff cut him off. "Look. You hired smart people. They know the business. Now they have a clear picture of the competition. And forget offering them a guaranteed payoff. Anyone who works in start-ups sure as heck knows there ain't any such thing."

"You might be right…" Ryan admitted.

"'Course I am." Ryan heard the creak of a chair as Jeff shifted. "You'd see it yourself if you weren't so overloaded."

It felt as if the weight on Ryan's shoulders began to lift—not all of it and not completely, but at least he could breathe.

"You gotta be ready for the blowback, 'cause it's gonna happen, mark my words. Specially with Sean."

"I heard he just put fifty grand down on a Tesla," Ryan said.

"Yeah. What a jerk." Jeff chuckled. "Maybe don't tell him what we did. Let him read the email, along with everyone else."

Then, Ryan did what he hadn't done in years: turned off his phone and went back to sleep.

Everything else could wait.

That night, Ryan slept through dinner.

He woke the next morning later than usual, surprised to find a lightness that had been missing for months. When Jeff decided to make key documents public, he'd given every employee a clear picture of the amount of work ahead of them, and let them decide whether they wanted to stay with the company or not. Even more than that, Jeff's abrupt departure from the company he helped start had put things in perspective for Ryan, reminding him what was important.

Leaving his cell phone on the charger, Ryan headed for the shower. No doubt there were dozens of urgent texts and emails waiting for him after what Jeff had done, but they could wait. When he was finished, he stepped into the fog of a steamy bathroom, the basics of a plan in his mind. He would take Stacy to that restaurant she liked, while Kaye watched the kids. They'd talk.

He wandered downstairs and entered an empty kitchen. A note was taped to the coffee maker, a mug nearby.

Took the kids to the farmers' market with Mom. Back after lunch.

Stacy had prepared the machine so that all he had to do was flick the switch, so he did. Impulsively, he decided to take the morning off. When his coffee was ready, he poured himself a cup and went outside to watch the day unfold.

*

"Let's use the front door," Stacy suggested to her mother. They'd brought back quite a haul from the farmers' market. "The door is already open, and it'll be faster than going around to the back."

"I think you're right," Kaye replied as she walked the path through the front yard. She slowed and pointed to a trio of hydrangeas, which appeared to be staked and freshly mulched. "Did you do that?"

Stacy shook her head. "That looks like Brad's work to me. Looks like he went to the big nursery."

"Hmm." Her mother continued on her way and Stacy followed.

In the kitchen, they were met with a scattering of breakfast dishes and an empty coffee pot. Stacy set the bags on the table before collecting the dishes and taking them to the sink.

Her mother eyed the stack of dishes. "I keep telling your father we need a dishwasher. It's too much work to hand-wash after every meal." She removed a basket of strawberries from the refrigerator and put them on a tray.

"I dunno." Stacy filled the sink with warm sudsy water. "It's kind of nice." As she started her work, she noticed a pastry box from Mueller's had been left on the counter, a pair of her mother's "good" coffee cups beside it. "Are you expecting company?"

"Yes, a little later today," her mother replied, as she slid the vegetables into the refrigerator drawer. "I have a project I'm working on."

Her mother didn't seem eager to explain, so Stacy returned to her task, reaching for the sponge and letting her mind wander. Although her answer to Billy's request for help hadn't changed, she couldn't seem to let it go. If what he said was true—and Billy was many things, but he wasn't a liar—then the book Revere expected to publish was still little more than an outline. *A Winter to Remember* was hefty, more than five hundred pages, and Revere would expect the second book to be comparable. Even if Billy worked every hour of every day between now and the end of summer, she couldn't see him finishing in time. No one could.

The sound of the doorbell startled her, mostly because it was unusual for anyone in Dewberry Beach to use the front door. This was a come-around-the-back neighborhood and as the summer progressed, most visitors stopped knocking altogether.

"He's early." Kaye glanced toward the front of the house.

"Who is?"

"Can you get the door please? I'm not quite finished here."

"Sure." Stacy stacked the dish she'd washed on the drainboard and made her way to the front door, drying her hands on her shorts as she walked.

She opened the door and rolled her eyes.

Billy Jacob stood in the doorway, grinning. "Stacy Bennett, how nice to see you again." His linen blazer, wrinkled Oxford shirt, and tailored shorts made him look very much like a young Mark Twain.

"What are you doing here?" Stacy eyed his battered leather work bag and his scuffed sneakers. "I'm sorry, Billy, but my answer hasn't changed."

"Oh, I'm not here for you." Billy looked past her and into the house.

"Mr. Jacob! Thank you for coming." Kaye came to the door.

Billy's gaze flickered back to Stacy, his eyes twinkling with mischief. Then he turned his attention to her mother. "I'm happy to help."

"Mr. Jacob, this is my daughter Stacy," Kaye said. "Stacy, Mr. Jacob has agreed to help us plan a library fundraiser. And—" She turned to him for verification. "He might be coming to my book club next week?"

He nodded. "Happy to."

Stacy addressed her mother as Billy entered the house. "Mom, I didn't know you'd joined a book club."

"Your father and I both did. Well, that's not actually true," Kaye corrected. "I'm starting one and I'm trying to get your father to come to meetings. But the main thing is the fundraiser. Billy's endorsement will mean quite a lot for us and we appreciate his time."

"How generous of him," Stacy said in a tone her mother clearly missed.

"It really is," Kaye said, as she guided Billy to the living room. "Now, if you'll just come through here, there are several places we can work. Unless you'd like to sit outside on the deck. You tell me which seems most comfortable to you."

After they left, Stacy went to find her father. Surely he didn't know about this book club idea? She found him in his den but not in his recliner, reading the newspaper or listening to the ball game as she'd expected. Instead, he stood behind his desk, gathering papers and slipping them into a leather folder. And he was dressed in work clothes, which Stacy found strange.

She knocked on the doorframe, then leaned in when he glanced up. "You going somewhere, Dad?"

"Nowhere important." He fastened the clasp and tucked the folder under his arm. "Just to get a bite to eat at the club. I'm meeting a few people over there."

Stacy eyed the folder. "Does Mom know?"

"I believe she's occupied with a guest at the moment." He moved toward the door, then stopped. "I would appreciate it if you told your mother that I've gone for a walk." Chase's expression flickered. "So she doesn't worry."

"Sure, Dad." Stacy moved aside to let him pass. "Call me if you want a ride back."

After her father slipped out, Stacy wandered upstairs to check on the kids. They'd been surprisingly quiet, which could be either very good or disastrous. She peeked into their room and saw them coloring in the new art pads Kaye had brought back from the farmers' market. No sense in disturbing them.

Downstairs, she found Billy and her mother by the front door.

"I'm sorry, Kaye, but I don't have time for coffee and pastries after all. I should get back—this is a working vacation for me. I'm sure you understand." He caught Stacy's attention and smiled. "It was nice to meet you, Stacy."

She watched Billy leave without so much as a backward glance. Impulsively, she rushed into the kitchen for her cell phone, then yelled to her mother. "The kids are upstairs playing in their rooms, Mom. I'll be right back and I have my cell if you need me."

*

She caught sight of him a block later.

"Billy!" she called out.

He turned and waited for her to catch up. She expected a comment about how slow she walked now, but his face was solemn, his expression unreadable.

"Why are you still in town, Billy?" Stacy asked as she fell into step beside him. "It can't be because you're interested in the library fundraiser. You didn't even know about it when we spoke the other day."

"Maybe I needed a vacation?" Billy lifted his shoulder. "All this fresh sea air and sunshine is good for the muse, don't you think?"

"Enough." Stacy stopped and turned to him. "You came to my *house*, Billy. That's creepy. Is this some sort of weird stalker thing? Because if it is, it ends now. I told you I'm not helping and that's the end of it."

To her surprise, Billy sobered immediately. His expression was one she'd rarely seen on his face: earnestness. She'd expected more resistance, more drama. "You're right, Stacy, and I'm sorry. I met your mother by chance at the cheese shop and we got chatting. It was her idea for me to come to your house, not mine, although it did seem like a really good opportunity to get your attention one last time."

"Why do you need to get my attention? My answer was final."

"I'm afraid I didn't tell you the truth when we spoke the other day." Billy pressed his lips together, frowning. "Really, things are much worse than I let on. Would you just listen—please—to the whole truth? If you decide not to help after that, I'll accept your decision and be on my way."

"I'll listen, but I don't have long. I have to get back to watch the kids." She led him to a small garden beside a tiny white church. The garden was in full bloom, with tall sunflowers reaching for the sun and slender vines of deep blue clematis woven around the slats of the white picket fence that edged the property. There was a bench, and they sat for a moment in silence, listening to the hum of fat honeybees as they gathered nectar.

Billy reached to pluck a blade of grass from the lawn. "*A Winter to Remember* was written in a week." Flecks of green floated to the ground as he shredded it between his fingers. "There had been a massive snowstorm in New York that year, and the city was shut down for days and days. My roommates at the time were out of town so there was no one to talk to and the whole experience was very unnerving. Electricity and cable were out, so I had nothing to do." He glanced at her. "You may not know this, but I suffer panic attacks. I started to feel the walls closing in on me and I got desperate. I began to make up a story about a traveling bard. When the sun set that first day, the city was completely dark, not a single light anywhere. I honestly thought I was going to die." He drew a ragged breath as he reached for another blade of grass. "Of course, there was nowhere to go; everything was shut tight. But needs must, so I got a pen and paper and told myself a story. By the time I was finished, a week had passed almost unnoticed. The power company had restored the lights and the streets were returning to normal."

"I never knew that," Stacy said. "I never knew that's how you wrote your book."

"I never told anyone." Billy dropped the last shred of grass into the breeze and clasped his hands together. "Who would take a novel seriously if they knew it had been written in a week?"

"It's a brilliant story, Billy. Doesn't matter how long it took to write."

Billy turned his attention to a bumblebee crossing the head of a sunflower. "The difference between now and then is that I *want* to continue the story, but I can't. It won't come out." He pressed his palm together as he swallowed. "I even enrolled in one of those fancy writing retreats last spring. You know, where they put you in a cabin and bring you food?" He snorted. "Nothing."

"Does Emmerson know any of this?" Stacy asked gently.

"No."

"Could you tell him? Maybe he'd understand."

Billy shook his head. "When I got home from the retreat, there was a registered letter waiting for me, from Revere. It said they planned to release me from my contract, effective September fifth of this year."

"That's why you said Labor Day?"

"I thought if I showed them a few pages—something—I might get more time."

"Do you have the letter with you?"

Billy nodded. "Back in my room."

"Take a picture of it and text it to me. I used to share an office with Emmerson, back when we were both junior editors. Maybe I can talk to him for you."

"I knew you'd help."

"I only agreed to talk to him. I don't know how he'll respond."

"I understand."

"And you can't come to my house anymore, Billy. That's weird."

"What about the fundraiser? And your mother's book club?"

She shot him a look.

"Right. I'll reschedule."

Chapter 18

It started as a simple morning walk to clear his head, but Ryan ended up staying out for most of the day.

After a while, he found himself at the inlet bridge and stayed to watch the fishing trawlers start their day. He bought a bag of fried clams and ate them sitting on the jetty, staring at the waves breaking against the seawall. It occurred to him, not for the first time, how idyllic this little beach town was, and he understood why Stacy and her family loved their summers here. On his way back home, he stopped at Applegate's to buy new crab nets for the kids, and a pair of sunglasses for Stacy because she was always losing hers.

He sent a quick text telling Stacy where he was so she wouldn't worry, but otherwise kept his phone on silent.

The house was empty when he arrived mid-afternoon. Notes tacked to the refrigerator put everyone out until dinnertime: Kaye had taken the kids to see a friend's art studio, Chase was at the club, Stacy was out for a walk, and Brad had gone to work on Mrs. Ivey's friend's garden.

It was time to make his decision. He opened his laptop and wrote a formal email. He made sure it was time and date-stamped, then sent it on to Todd. He immediately forwarded a copy of the email he'd just sent to his attorney in Morristown.

Then he waited.

It didn't take long before his phone and his inbox filled with messages, all marked urgent. Ryan counted fifteen voicemails from Sean, eleven texts from Todd, and even one from someone he supposed was Todd's boss. They'd taken his company and fired his employees, and Ryan couldn't imagine any message or text that would explain it.

He sorted through the messages, deleting the message from Todd's boss without reading it. The man had never contacted him before, and Ryan had no interest in what he had to say now. Todd was a weasel, always had been. On that principle alone, Ryan deleted all of Todd's messages too. Next was a voicemail from Sean. Ryan hesitated. They'd been a team, the three of them, best friends. That counted for something, even now.

Ryan crossed the bedroom to open the window and pushed aside the lace curtains to allow the breeze in. The air from outside would make the room hotter, but he liked the smell of the ocean, so he let it be. He pulled a chair to the window and settled in, then he tapped Sean's number.

Sean answered on the first ring, screeching into the phone, which seemed a bit excessive. "Ryan, where have you *been*? Did you *see* the documents Jeff made public last night? Everyone here is *livid*. That stuff was *proprietary*."

"Good afternoon to you too, Sean," Ryan said as he gazed out the window. The sky had darkened a bit and the oak leaves in the tree out front rustled in the breeze. Another coastal thunderstorm was brewing.

"Are you listening to me?"

"No, sorry. I wasn't. What did you say?"

"I *said*: we can save this. The partners are in Boston now, taking pitches from other companies. Not optimal to talk to them now, but Todd's with them and he can make them listen. He needs you to address the tech side. The algorithm is yours, so you know it best."

"It is, isn't it?"

"What?" Sean hissed.

"I agreed with you. You're right: the algorithm is mine."

"Ryan, I don't think you fully understand the urgency of this. You have to find a way to get up there—you have to leave now."

"Get up where?" In the distance, Ryan thought he heard the bells on the ice-cream truck making its rounds in the neighborhood. He wondered if he could buy a Bomb Pop; he used to love them as a kid.

"Haven't you been listening to me?" Sean's voice was tight. Ryan pictured him red-faced and clenching his fist, like a toddler throwing a tantrum. The image made him smile. "Did you hear what I just said? Jeff shared documents he had no business sharing. His actions set off a chain reaction that affects everything. We should have cut off Jeff's access a long time ago, I told Todd that."

"What do you mean, cut off his access?" Ryan shifted in his chair. This was what he was waiting to hear, exactly how involved Sean was in shifting control of the company. "Jeff is a partner, why would you cut him off?"

"That's not important right now." Sean sniffed and cleared his throat.

Ryan pushed back. "It *is* important."

"It isn't," Sean retorted. "Ryan. We have to focus. The most important thing is for you to get to Boston. If you leave now, you can be there by late tonight. I've sent info about the guys at UMD. I need you to read it and update our company work schedule so we stay ahead of them."

"Was it you that fired my team or was that Todd?"

Sean sighed. "Okay, fine. You want to do this before you leave, we will. The decision was made by both of us and I see now that it might not have been the best idea. You can hire them back—all of them. I don't care. Just come up and talk to the VCs about your algorithm. Make them see that what we have is better than what the UMD crew came up with."

"You were only in it for the payout at the end, weren't you? You never had any interest in what the program could do. You only wanted money." Ryan knew it, but the words were still painful to say.

Sean's silence told him everything he needed to know.

"Okay, well I guess that's it then. I should go now."

"To Boston?" Sean sounded so relieved that Ryan almost laughed.

"No. I won't be going to Boston. I'm going outside to watch the thunderstorm. Maybe catch the ice-cream man before the rain hits." Ryan drew the curtain and rose from his chair. "You should know that I'll be exercising my options, and since Jeff already did, the company's yours. Congratulations." He paused and allowed himself a smile. "One more thing. I'm taking my patent with me and I plan to defend it vigorously. So I guess what I mean to say is that you can have *what's left* of the company. I hope you and Todd and all of them will be very happy."

"How can you do this?" Sean growled. "We're friends."

"*Were* friends," Ryan corrected. "We're not anymore."

Ryan hung up the phone and turned off the ringer.

*

Later that evening, with the dishes done and the kids in bed, Stacy, Ryan, and Brad sat around the firepit, chatting and tossing twigs into the flames. The passing thunderstorm had cooled the air and dampened the ground, sending them back inside for long sleeves and camp blankets. Their summer at the shore was more than half over; they'd be gone by the end of next month, back to their lives in Morristown. Carpool and ballet lessons, soccer and playdates; Stacy wasn't looking forward to any of it.

"You missed the excitement earlier," she began. "Mom invited Billy Jacob to the house. She wanted him to speak at her book club next week."

"The author whose book you worked on?" Ryan watched the flames. "That seems like a pretty big get for a local book club."

"It is."

Brad poked the logs with a stick and watched a column of embers rise. "A dinky local book club can't be the reason Billy Jacob came here. What would a big author like him be doing in Dewberry Beach?"

"He came for me actually." Stacy straightened as she felt both her brother and her husband turn to look at her. "He's asked for my help on his second book."

"Wow. My sister the Big Deal." Brad's teasing was good-natured, but Stacy ignored him. It was Ryan's reaction she wanted.

"And do you want to?" Ryan asked.

"I think I do, but I told him no."

"Why?"

"It's a big job and I won't be able to focus if I'm distracted watching the kids. And that's not what this summer was for anyway."

"What about me? I could help watch the kids so you can work," Brad offered.

"I appreciate that, but I need more than 'help.'" Stacy shifted her gaze into the flames, not realizing how much she wanted to work with Billy until just that moment. "I need someone to take over—all the time, every day—and I can't expect you to do that. You're busy with other stuff."

"Well, you're in luck." Ryan shifted in his chair. "It just so happens that I've just been awarded some extra time."

He told them about Sean wresting control of the company they'd all started, about Jeff leaving but not being permitted to tell anyone, about Todd firing his team in an effort to get them all to work harder, and about the proprietary papers that Jeff had made public, changing the dynamics of the entire company. Finally, Ryan told them that he'd quit his job but kept ownership of the algorithm that started it all.

"Dude," Brad whispered. "This is what you've been doing all summer?"

Stacy reached for his hand. "Why didn't you tell me things had gotten this bad?"

"It happened pretty quickly," Ryan scoffed. "And I didn't expect it to turn out the way it did."

"What are you going to do?"

"I don't know." Ryan turned to Stacy. "We have my payout from the partnership agreement—that should last a while. In the meantime, I'll make some phone calls to line up a few interviews. So don't worry."

The fire popped and a spark shot into the darkness.

"I'm not worried," Stacy said. "We have savings and we'll be okay. But you've been working so much lately that maybe you should use this time to unwind?"

"Nah, I don't need it." Ryan shook his head. "I'm fine."

"You're not fine." Stacy squeezed his hand. "Sean and Jeff have been your best friends for as long as I've known you. What they did to the company you all started must have affected you. I wish you'd told me sooner. Maybe I could have helped."

"Maybe Jeff and Sean are on drugs." Brad tossed a rock into the flames and watched the embers spark. "People get weird about money and drugs."

After a moment, Ryan spoke again.

"I think you should do it." He drew a breath and faced Stacy. "Maybe you're right about me taking some time off. I'll start by watching the kids so you can work with Billy."

"You mean it?" Stacy felt her heart thump in her chest. "Entertaining those kids is more work than you think."

"Sure." Ryan gestured to Brad. "Brad and I can double-team them. We got this."

Chapter 19

The first thing to do, of course, was talk to Emmerson to sort the truth from Billy's perceptions. Though Stacy left several messages, it took a couple of weeks for him to call her back. In the meantime, she thought about beginning work on the story while they waited, but Stacy wasn't sure Emmerson would agree with the plan and she didn't want to get Billy's hopes up.

So, they waited.

When Emmerson finally returned her call, her proposal to reinstate Billy's contract was met with disbelief.

"Let me get this straight: the book was never written?"

"He had an outline."

"But nothing more?"

"No." Stacy drew a deep breath. "But he came to me for help, doesn't that count for something?"

"I don't know why you think it would." Emmerson sniffed. "The boy lied about his manuscript. I won't ever trust him again."

"Then trust me," Stacy blurted.

"What?"

"Trust me," Stacy repeated. "We'll have the book to you by deadline. I promise."

"I don't know, Stacy," he drawled in his soft Memphis accent. "The boy's got talent, no doubt about it… cutting him loose wasn't an easy decision."

"Then reverse it." Stacy leaned back in her father's desk chair. "*Winter* has made a lot of money for you, Emmerson. The second edition is in the charts again, and there's talk about a movie and a video game. Seems to me that the whole world is waiting for the new book. Don't you want to be the one who publishes it?"

Emmerson chuckled. "You sound like an agent."

"I'm just trying to show you how important this book is."

"It's not a question of importance, Stacy. We've come to the point where we just don't believe we can get a story out of him. We've extended his deadline twice; did he tell you that? There are editors here who have threatened to quit rather than work with him—in any capacity."

"I can do it. I can get a story out of him."

"Just out of curiosity, what's your plan to make this happen?"

"We work well together," Stacy lied. "We've done it before and we can do it now. Provided you extend Billy's contract and hire me as a freelance editor to work with him on *A Promise of Spring*."

"I don't mean this disrespectfully, but you haven't worked in the industry in six years. Things have changed," Emmerson pointed out. "I'm not saying you can't pick it back up again, because you can. But Billy is not the author to test the waters on, and this is not the book to dive into."

"He wants to write the book and I want to help him."

In the silence that followed, Stacy could almost hear Emmerson rubbing his forehead and that was always a good sign. Finally, she heard a deep intake of breath.

"Okay. I think you're in over your head but it's your life and we have nothing to lose." The phone muffled as she heard him address someone in his office. "Tell him I'll be right with him."

Stacy held her breath as she waited.

He returned to their conversation. "Tell you what I'm going to do. Since you don't seem to mind jumping back into the crazy pond, I'll give you two until August fourteenth to deliver a polished draft. That will give me time to read it and decide what to do with it. And by polished, I mean action on the page and a plot a reader can follow. Not an outline, not author notes. I want movement. I want dialogue. I want setting. You still up for the challenge?"

An August fourteenth delivery was three weeks less than she'd hoped for. It meant three weeks instead of six to produce what Emmerson wanted.

She drew a breath and forced a smile. "Absolutely."

Emmerson laughed. "Well, I think you're crazy but if this is the way you want to spend the rest of your summer, who am I to tell you no? I'll have Tara write up a new contract and email it to you. And as for your fee, what do you say to our normal freelancer rates, plus a bonus on publication?"

"That's more than fair. Thank you, Emmerson."

"I still think you're biting off more than you can chew, but the bigger part of me really hopes you can pull it off." The phone muffled again as Emmerson rose from his chair. "So I guess I'll talk to you in three weeks?"

"You will. And thank you."

"Good luck, sweetie."

*

"Oh, no," Billy lamented as he sagged dramatically against the metal bistro chair at Mueller's Bakery. "I can't *possibly* have a draft finished in three weeks."

Stacy looked at him, stunned. She'd tracked him down the moment she'd come off the phone with Emmerson, anxious to share the good news because she thought he'd be eager to get to work.

"What do you mean you can't do it? You asked for this—you came to my house and begged me to help you. Do you have any idea what it took me to get this extension?"

He dropped his gaze to his lap and she glared at him, fuming.

People were starting to stare, so she leaned forward, lowering her voice to a hiss.

"You told me you wrote the first book in a week. Now you have three." A thought occurred to her, so terrible it took her breath away. She leaned back and stared at him. After a moment, she found her voice. "Were you lying to me, Billy? Were you lying when you said you wrote the first book in a week?"

"No, of course not." He looked up. "Everything I told you was true."

"Then what's the problem?" She squeezed her hands together in her lap, frustrated at his shift to apathy.

Billy reached for a paper napkin and began to tear it. "I never expected the first book to go anywhere. I told you why I wrote it. The second book is different. I have loose ends to tie up, characters who need attention. It'll take months just to outline."

"We have an outline. We made it six years ago."

He threw up his hands in frustration. "I've had *ideas* since then. Different directions for the characters and the story."

"*You* came to *me*, Billy." She leaned forward again, leveling him with a stare she'd learned from her mother. "Let me tell you what it took to make this happen. I tracked down Emmerson and leaned heavily on our friendship to convince him to give you another chance. He offered you an extension despite waiting six years for this book and never seeing so much as a draft. For my part, I am sacrificing three weeks of summer vacation with my family because I believe in your talent." She dropped her voice to a low growl. "So, let me tell you what's going to happen now: You will write from the existing outline, stopping only to sleep and eat. On August fourteenth, we will deliver a complete draft of *A Promise of Spring* to Emmerson."

Billy blinked. "Fine. Let's go get my stuff." He heaved a great sigh as he rose from the table. "You didn't have to be so mean about it."

The Dewberry Beach Motor Lodge was located in a relatively isolated section of town, away from the shops and beach access. Years ago it had been marketed as a family campground; the wide flat lawn was perfect for pitching tents, and the banks of tall trees provided shade and privacy. When the founder died, he left the camp to his children with the hope they'd continue to run it. The children had other ideas. They converted the outbuildings into single-room cabins for tourists, but the construction was cheaply done and the result was a disaster.

Billy pushed open the chain-link gate. The metal frame was warped, the fittings rusted. It screeched as he walked through. "Don't ever tell me I don't suffer for my art."

"I thought they shut this place down years ago," Stacy commented.

They walked across the courtyard, past the drained and chipped swimming pool, the twisted lounge chairs and the broken umbrellas, to a cabin on the far end of the lot. It seemed to be the only one open.

"Ignore the smell." Billy inserted the key and twisted. The door creaked as he pushed it open.

The room was a throwback from the seventies, still decorated in shades of yellow and brown. The wallpaper was a faded mess of yellow flowers splattered against a muddy dark background. Two narrow twin beds were covered with polyester bedspreads in the same faded yellow, with a lumpy pillow at the head of each bed. The room's only window was covered with the remains of an old shower curtain, cracked and spotted with mold. Finally, at the far end of the room, a tiny pedestal sink and a dull mirror indicated the bathroom, and a wheeled clothes rack served as a closet.

Stacy pulled the curtain from the window and kicked it to the side. The window was filthy, but letting the sunlight in was an improvement. "There. That's better."

She turned, taking in every detail of the room. There really was no angle that made it seem less dire, but of course she couldn't tell Billy that.

Billy moved past her, toward the clothes rack, and set his suitcase on the bed. "The pictures were very different. You think I'd stay here if I had a choice?" He pulled a shirt off the plastic hanger and threw it in the bag. "Anyway, it's over now. I'll just be a minute."

"Where are you going? Did you find another place to stay?"

Billy hesitated. "I assumed I'd be staying with you, in one of your guest rooms. I'd prefer something on the top floor, near those sweet dormer windows, but I can be flexible."

Stacy sat on the edge of the desk chair, careful to avoid an unidentifiable stain. "Billy, we don't have any spare bedrooms. There are seven people in that house; we're using every bit of space."

"Well, in that case I'm sure you know another place I can stay." Billy went back to tossing clothes into his suitcase. "I'll leave the details to you, but my preference is a room filled with natural light that overlooks water—the ocean or the bay. The sounds of seagulls overhead and waves crashing to the shore would do wonders for my inspiration." His smile shrugged as he turned to his work. "But really, anything is fine."

"Billy, you're not going to find anything like that here. We don't have oceanfront hotels with room service, or concierges, or spa services. Nothing you're used to. Dewberry Beach is a family town, very low-key."

He tossed a pair of sneakers in and zipped the bag closed. "I admit to being disappointed, but I'm nothing if not a team player. If you don't have the right hotel, we'll just have to widen our circle a bit, branch out. I don't mind traveling."

They had three weeks to produce an entire novel. According to the schedule that Stacy had drawn up, there would barely be time to sleep. And if he allowed himself to be distracted by hotel amenities like room service or a minibar, they'd never meet their deadline.

"This is fine," Stacy said.

"What's fine?"

"This room. It's perfect, in fact." Stacy set her work bag on the plywood desk. "We're going to work here."

"Oh, no. No. No. No." Billy held up both hands and squeezed his eyes shut. "This place is horrid, you said it yourself. It *smells*."

Stacy retrieved the schedule from her bag and set it on the desk. "I'll bring you a lavender candle. You won't even notice the smell after a while."

He pointed to the trail of insects in the corner of the room. "There are ants."

"Applegate's sells bug spray. I'll get you some."

He pointed to the windowsill, thick with cobwebs. "Spiders."

"I'll bring you a broom."

"This place doesn't even have Wi-Fi. I can't *possibly* work here."

Billy was beginning to hyperventilate, and Stacy was afraid she might have gone too far. She reached for his hands and squeezed. "Billy, listen to me. You don't need Wi-Fi. You don't need anything but your imagination and a laptop. This is our shot. Our only shot. I'm going to do everything I can to keep us on track, but I need to know that you're committed too.

"I have a schedule." She tapped the spreadsheet she'd drawn up. "You write during the day and I'll edit what you wrote at night. Every morning, we can exchange work. It'll be hard, but it will be worth it. In three weeks, you'll be finished."

He visibly deflated as he let out the breath he'd been holding. "Okay. I can stay here for three weeks." He pointed to the bed. "But not with those pillows."

"I'll bring you sheets and blankets from home, and a mattress topper for this bed. You're going to need your rest."

"And a pillow."

"Okay, a pillow too. I'll be back in about an hour."

The last thing she heard before she closed the door was Billy sighing as he opened his laptop and switched it on.

Stacy hoped she wasn't wrong about this.

Chapter 20

Three days later, Kaye discovered a party invitation propped on the corner of Chase's dresser, which was odd for several reasons. In Dewberry Beach, social functions were always arranged by the wives, the invitations issued verbally as part of a casual conversation. The invitation Chase saved had been *printed on stationery*. Kaye knew for a fact that there wasn't a custom printer within twenty miles of Dewberry Beach, leading her to believe that this party had been planned for quite some time. She would go, though she wasn't familiar with the host and she wasn't particularly interested in expanding her social circle at the moment.

"Tell me again why my loafers aren't good enough for a clambake?" Kaye grumbled as she reached to the back of the closet for the box that held her linen espadrilles.

The invitation said the party was to be a New England clambake. Messy affairs, if done correctly, so guests understood to arrive in their most washable clothes. Tubs of steamed crab, lobster, and clams would be upended onto newspapers spread across a long trestle table. There would be ramekins of melted butter and saucers of cocktail sauce for dipping. Traditional food also included platters of corn on the cob dripping with parsley butter and steamed red potatoes so delicate they crumbled when speared with a fork. Guests were given a platter to hold shrimp, lobster, clams, and corn, a mallet to crack the shells, and a bib that did absolutely nothing to protect their clothes.

Kaye slipped on her shoes, though she thought it was a mistake to dress up. She stood, then glanced at her husband. "You're wearing a *tie*?"

In place of his usual printed Bermuda shorts and a soft cotton shirt, Chase wore an ironed dress shirt, black slacks, and tassel loafers. It looked as if he were going to work and Kaye wasn't sure she liked it.

Chase looped the edge of his tie and pulled the end through. "I'm just following the guidelines on the invitation."

"You read the invitation? You never read the invitation," Kaye scoffed as she glanced in the mirror at the dress she'd chosen to wear. The baggy linen shift now seemed all wrong, especially given Chase's outfit. "Fine." She changed into a navy blue silk, although the dress was almost guaranteed to be ruined.

Chase glanced at her change of clothes and smiled. "You look nice. I like you in blue."

"Thank you." Kaye felt herself blush. She touched his shoulder as she crossed the room to her jewelry box. There wasn't much need for jewelry at the shore house. As a rule, Kaye left her best pieces in the safe at the Princeton house. But the silver cuff she'd bought at the art gallery a few weeks before with Brenda might go well. She slipped it on and added the matching silver earrings.

"Who are these people again?" She added a swipe of lipstick. "How do you know them?"

Chase dribbled a bit of cologne into his palm and dabbed it on his face. "The hosts are Marc and Jill Goodman, and I don't know them, not personally. Marc is one of Jim McKean's newest clients and the invitation is through Jim."

"Is this a work thing then?" Kaye asked warily.

Chase added cufflinks, a monogrammed pair she'd given him the Christmas before his illness. "No. Just something to do with people you might like to meet."

"Hm," Kaye replied. She'd known her husband for most of his life and could always tell when he wasn't telling the complete truth. This seemed like one of those times, but she couldn't be sure so she said nothing.

The property was close enough to walk to, so they did. They left the shore house just as the sun had begun to set and watched as the sky was splashed with shades of orange and purple. It was a lovely walk but Kaye was still uneasy. Every clambake Kaye had ever attended was a full-day affair, so it seemed odd that one should begin so late in the afternoon. She reminded herself that this was Chase's event and she would need to keep an open mind. She even allowed him to take her to a section of town that she'd purposefully avoided for eight years.

When Hurricane Sandy hit the coast of New Jersey eight years before, it decimated the shore, changing the coastline, and destroying entire neighborhoods and whole towns. Despite the seawalls and the plywood, the sandbags and the prayers, the hurricane had been unstoppable and it was terrifying. For six days and nights the wind and rain had been relentless, pounding the shore and flooding the streets. Eventually the storm dissipated, but it was weeks before the National Guard let any of the shore residents through the roadblocks to check their property and the things they'd left behind. The Bennett home had suffered flood and wind damage but the damage was reparable.

Others weren't so lucky.

The section of town they walked to now was one of several that was hit the hardest. These homes were original to Dewberry Beach, built back in the 1920s, without the benefit of seawalls or sand dunes or any protection at all from the storm. When the hurricane came for this side of town, there had been nothing to stop it. It sucked two family homes into the sea. It filled surrounding homes with sand and debris that required heavy machinery to remove. Mary-Pat Blatch, one of Kaye's dearest friends, watched events unfold on television. From the safety of her sister's house, she saw her family's summer home collapse and couldn't bring herself to return to Dewberry Beach to see it in person. Mary-Pat and her husband Paul were one of the first couples to accept an offer from a New York developer and had never returned.

"That's the one." Chase gestured to a Dutch colonial with a gambrel roof, a second-floor deck that overlooked the ocean, an attached three-car garage, and landscaping so new that Kaye could smell the cedar bark mulch atop freshly turned soil. "What do you think?"

"Isn't that something." Kaye managed a tight smile, though she hated everything about it.

It looked like a caricature of what New Jersey shore houses were supposed to be, built by someone who was looking to make a quick buck. It was wildly out of proportion to its neighbors, making it look like a hotel in a neighborhood of cottages. The siding wasn't real cedar, though it was painted to look as though it was. And the structure itself seemed to be built just far enough behind the new dunes to be legal.

She and Chase passed a trio of uniformed valets collecting car keys and shunting sleek black cars to a reserved lot a few blocks away. They joined the throng of guests making their way up the front steps to the entrance, and Kaye didn't recognize anyone in the group. The women were younger than her by far and seemed to be dressed in evening wear. Black silk dresses and threads of gold jewelry shimmered against perfectly toned and tanned bodies. The men wore crisp polo shirts with upturned collars, silk pants, and shoes that probably cost more than Kaye's first car.

She smoothed the fabric of her dress, thankful she'd changed and annoyed with herself for feeling out of place. She'd been a resident of Dewberry Beach far longer than these people had. She had nothing to be ashamed of.

"Hello." A young blonde woman met them in the foyer. She looked no more than twenty-five years old, dressed in a simple black shift, her gold bracelets clinking together as she offered her hand. "Thank you for coming." The woman's smile revealed a row of perfect white teeth. "I'm Brittney, the shore house manager. I'm helping Marc and Jill tonight."

"It's nice to meet you, Brittney," Chase replied as he shook her hand. "I'm Chase and this is my wife, Kaye."

The house was massive. As an open-concept, the entire first floor was one room and had been decorated in various shades of white. The hardwood floor had been bleached a soft gray to look like driftwood, and scattered across the room were large area rugs woven from seagrass. There were several conversation areas in the room, arranged with upscale furniture and accessories that wouldn't last a single day in a real shore house. The whole arrangement gave Kaye the impression that the owners had paid an expensive decorator to curate a presentation of what they thought the shore should be. But they'd missed.

"Would you look at that," Chase whispered, lifting his chin toward the back of the house.

"Wow."

Even Kaye had to admit it was stunning. The back of the house was a wall of windows that overlooked the ocean. It gave the impression of being directly on the beach and the effect was amazing.

She turned her attention back to her husband in time to see Brittney gesturing toward a floating set of metal steps at the far end of the room. "The bar is on the second floor and the outside deck has a magnificent view. Jill and Marc have put together a fresh take on the traditional clambake and they hope you like it."

Before either Chase or Kaye could reply, Brittney turned her attention to the next couple in line. So they made their way across the room then upstairs, to find the host.

"I've never seen anything like this," Kaye murmured to Chase as they crossed the room. "Who is this guy?"

"Real-estate investor out of Manhattan," Chase answered as he looked around. "He must be doing well."

Kaye scoffed. "I'll say."

At the bottom of the stairs, a waiter approached them with a silver tray of hors d'oeuvres. He lowered the tray and offered them a napkin. "Smoked clams and potato in puff pastry. Would you like one?"

"Not quite yet, thank you," Kaye answered for both of them and the waiter withdrew. Puff pastry was not a good choice for Chase's heart.

They climbed the stairs to the deck. A uniformed bartender served drinks, and side tables were set with appetizers, bowls of corn salad, and platters of potato quiche. Outside, the view of the ocean was vast and unobstructed. Kaye wondered how the builder had got the permits past the town review.

"Chase. Glad you could make it." Like everyone else, Jim McKean shook Chase's hand and smiled at Kaye. "Kaye, nice to see you. How's the family?"

"They're fine, Jim. Thank you."

"I hope you don't mind if I steal your husband for a minute or two?" Jim draped his arm across Chase's shoulder. He called over to her as he guided Chase away, "Jill's downstairs. You'll love her."

This was definitely a work function and Kaye felt her annoyance grow at what appeared to be deception. There had to be an explanation and she hoped it was that Chase hadn't realized it himself. She would like to believe that he wouldn't go back on his word, his promise to retire. But things did not look good, especially since he'd dressed for work.

She wandered around for a while, before deciding to try and find the hostess. Her fingertips skimmed the banister as she descended the floating staircase. It was jarring to see such a wide space between the steps, without anything to anchor them.

"This is one weird party, right?"

"Ginny!" Kaye hugged the woman before her. "How nice to see a familiar face. I didn't think you'd have time to come down. Isn't Ava off to college this year?" She tutted. "Even saying that sentence makes me feel so old. I remember when Stacy used to babysit your girls."

"I came down especially for this party, believe it or not. These owners are supposed to be very well connected." Ginny glanced at her husband, who was circling a group that included Chase. While Kaye thought the world of Ginny and the girls, she'd never warmed to her husband. He was too slick, too aggressive, too pretentious; an outsider in a town that preferred to leave business behind in the summer.

"Well connected?" Kaye repeated. "How so?"

"I don't know the details, but Rick says that knowing Marc Goodman is always good for business. Rick wants to expand his practice and Marc will probably invest." She glanced back toward the group. "Rick says Chase is part involved, too, so it's almost a sure thing."

The comment felt like a punch. "That's not possible. Chase has retired. His partners bought him out last spring."

"Oh… then I must be mistaken." Ginny shrugged. "I probably misunderstood."

A respectable three hours later, Kaye strode across the room to her husband. She took his arm and pulled him aside. "I'd like to go home soon please."

"That wasn't so bad, was it?" Chase was positively chirpy on the way home. They left the party before the hosts ignited fireworks on the beach, but Chase didn't seem to mind. His step was light, his conversation animated. "Not a conventional party, that's for sure, but a nice change. Did you get a chance to meet Jill?"

"No."

"The food was good, I thought. Did you try the potato quiche?"

"Yes. It was good."

"And that deck, what a view." He clasped his hands together in a way that grated on Kaye's nerves. He glanced at her. "I know you're upset about this area being rebuilt, but aren't you glad they've taken away the last traces of the hurricane? I know I am."

"I saw Ginny Maxwell."

"You did? How is she?" Chase slipped off his jacket and offered it to Kaye. She shrugged it off.

"She told me this was a work party. That Rick is expanding his practice and wants financing."

"Is that so?"

She stopped suddenly, turning on him. "Are you planning to work with Marc Goodman? Is that why Jim invited us?"

"What?" Chase's brow creased in confusion. "No. Where would you get an idea like that?"

"Why else would we be invited to a fancy party thrown by people we don't know? Money people were there, Chase. People you used to work with—Jim McKean, and all the others."

Chase stared at her as if he couldn't tell if she was serious. "It's true, Marc had a couple of questions about how to structure a new investment but that's all. What he wants to do is interesting. As for Rick, I have no interest in working with him."

"But you talked to Marc. You discussed business with Marc," Kaye pressed, her voice rising.

"Yes. What he wants to do has interesting implications. I told him I'd have coffee with him later in the week to discuss it."

"Coffee with him?" Kaye repeated. "That doesn't sound like 'not working with him.' In fact, that sounds very much like working with him. You told me you'd retire from all this when your partners bought you out. You *promised*."

"And I have."

"You haven't. Meeting with Marc for coffee is not retiring. That's working!" Her body vibrated with anger, furious that he'd lied to her.

"Kaye." Chase's expression changed; his tone was icy. "You wanted my partners to buy me out—and they did. You wanted me to stop going into the office—even though I love what I do—and I did. But I have to find something to do, something more than morning walks and watching the ball game on the television in my den."

"You promised." Kaye stepped back, stung at his reproach, furious with him for twisting the conversation to make their situation her fault. "Have you forgotten the last three years? Because I can't. The panicked phone call, the anguish of seeing you in the ICU, the uncertainty of your recovery. For the first six months, *I wasn't even sure you'd survive.*"

"That was three years ago, Kaye, and I've recovered," Chase answered. "You have to know that even you can't control the future. No one knows when their time is up. I could drop—"

"Do not finish that sentence!" Kaye warned, her fists balled at her side. "I will not listen to you being so cavalier about a life that took the best cardiologists in New Jersey weeks to save and an entire team of physical therapists two years to rebuild."

"Kaye…" Chase began.

But Kaye wasn't listening. A fog of hysteria and panic had descended on her, shielding her heart and leaving her fighting for breath. "You promised me, Chase Bennett. You promised me and I believed you."

"Kaye—"

"If you intend to pick up the threads of your life as if the past three years meant nothing to you, then you can do it without me!" She spat the words at him, jagged and raw and filled with fear. "I will *not* watch it happen again."

And for the first time in three years, Kaye Bennett left her husband's side without knowing when she'd return.

Kaye left Chase alone on the sidewalk and headed toward the only person she knew would understand, who knew how difficult Chase's recovery had been, and who had always taken her side. Even though it was dark and much too late to visit, Kaye found herself at Brenda's doorstep. The house was quiet, but Kaye knocked on the front door anyway.

After a moment, the porch light flicked on and Brenda pushed open the screen door. She tied her bathrobe and rubbed the sleep from her eyes. "Kaye, is everything all right?" Her eyes widened. "Oh my gosh, is Chase okay?"

"He's fine," Kaye scoffed.

"Come in, come in." Brenda stepped aside so Kaye could enter.

In the calm of Brenda's house, Kaye felt her anger fade. She looked at the blanket on the couch and glanced at her friend. "Were you asleep, Bren? I'm sorry to wake you up."

"No, don't be silly." Brenda led the way into her kitchen. "I'm just watching an old movie."

"Really? Which one?"

"No idea," Brenda replied as she reached for the remote and flicked off the TV. "It was just on in the background." She moved toward the cabinet, then looked at Kaye. "Is this a wine problem or an herbal tea problem?"

"Wine."

"Wow." Brenda uncorked a bottle and filled two glasses, then brought them to the table. She sat opposite Kaye and waited.

"If you're still planning to go on that artists' trip next month, I want to go with you," Kaye blurted.

"The trip to Asheville?"

"Yes. Exactly. That's the one." Kaye averted her gaze and sipped her wine. If Chase could live as he pleased, then she could too.

"When did you start sculpting?"

"I'll learn."

"That bad, huh?" Brenda laughed. "The workshop in Asheville is about technique and most of the day will be spent in the studio. You'd hate it."

"I'll stay in the room and meet you for dinner then. I don't care. I'm sure there are gift shops I can browse in town while you're working."

"Without Chase?"

"Absolutely without him." Kaye frowned. "It's better without him anyway."

Brenda set her wine glass on the table with a gentle tap. "What's going on?"

"He wants to go back to work."

"Of course he does. Did you expect him to sit around all day, doing nothing?"

Kaye pressed her palms to her forehead and closed her eyes, as if she could somehow blot out the image of her husband hooked up to machines. "I expected him to keep his promise."

"What happened?" Brenda leaned back in her chair.

So Kaye told her the whole story: the party, the investment project.

"It's going to happen again; I know it will. The doctors warned it would if he didn't slow down." Kaye drew a ragged breath. "I can't go through it again, Bren. I can't watch him work at that pace anymore knowing what it will bring."

"How do you know he's going to? And what makes you think that whatever he's doing now will lead to a repeat of what happened three years ago?"

"I just know it." Kaye shuddered.

"That's the thing, Kaye: you *don't* know." Brenda left the table, returning with a soft blue blanket that she draped over Kaye's shoulders. She squeezed Kaye's shoulder through the blanket, then collected the wine glasses and took them to the sink. "Just out of curiosity, what would you have him do instead?"

"I don't know—nothing. Retire. Get to know his grandchildren."

"Okay." Brenda shrugged. "Say he does that—sits around the house all day long. He gets to know his grandchildren, knows all about them—what they like, who their friends are. And then what?"

"What do you mean, 'and then what'?"

"I can see this is going to be a longer discussion." Brenda lifted the dish towel that had been draped over a cake container and unsnapped the lid.

"Are you still doing that?" Kaye snorted. "Hiding cake from yourself?"

"Yep." Brenda reached into the cabinet and removed two hand-thrown ceramic plates.

"Does it work?"

"Not yet." The silverware drawer rattled as she opened it.

"What kind did you make?"

"Coconut."

"My favorite. Is that a Christmas plate?" Kaye peered closer at the design on the plate Brenda set in front of her. A reindeer with a bright red nose stood in the center, circled with alternating snowflakes and evergreen trees.

"It is, and don't change the subject," Brenda remarked, settling back into her chair. "Just so I'm clear, you're angry at Chase because he's not doing exactly what you want him to do?"

"No, that's not it at all," Kaye protested, stung at Brenda's over-simplified explanation. "I'm annoyed because he's not taking care of himself. He promised me he would and he's not. He lied to me."

"Really?" Brenda dragged her fork across the frosting. "Has he stopped the sale of his share of the company and decided to return full-time to work?"

"No, the sale was finalized in March."

Brenda nodded thoughtfully. "And has he stopped going to the physical therapist? Or refused to see the cardiologist?"

"They both released him for the summer. Although he's got appointments with both for follow-ups." Kaye pointed her fork at Brenda. "I see what you're doing and it's not going to work."

"Then explain it to me." Brenda set her fork on the plate and fixed Kaye with a pointed look. "What, exactly, is your husband doing that's got you so wound up that you want to join me on a ceramic retreat in Asheville?"

Kaye swallowed the lump in her throat. She put her own fork down and drew a shaky breath. "It's going to happen again, Brenda," she whispered as she felt the breath leave her body. "I can feel it."

"Oh, honey." Brenda reached across the table for Kaye's hand. "Lemme tell you something: you married a good man, Kaye. A good one. Chase reminds me of my Eddie, God rest his soul." She squeezed. "And three years ago, you saved your husband's life. You found the right specialists. You forced him to go to physical therapy, even though he didn't want to. You scheduled his meds and made sure he took every dose on time. You saved his life, no doubt about it. But that doesn't give you the right to run it now."

"But—"

"Let me finish." Brenda's eyes were sharp, though her tone had softened. "A man like your husband needs something to do. More than just reading the newspaper or walking to the duck pond with his grandchildren. He was a titan of industry, as the expression goes. It's who he is, who he's always been. It's why you married him."

"So what am I supposed to do? Wait until the next heart attack? Because I can't do that."

"God forbid," Brenda answered. "I wouldn't wish that on anyone." She straightened. "You know I love you like a sister, Kaye. I really do.

But when you decide you're right, you dig in your heels and no one can convince you otherwise."

Kaye was silent, so Brenda continued.

"Chase has done everything you've asked. You've taken very good care of him and he's gotten better. Now you both need to go out and find a new normal, a new way to live. That's the only fair thing to do."

If Kaye were being completely honest, she didn't care about being fair; she cared only about keeping Chase well. She'd spent the past three years in a state of readiness, watchful for signs of something amiss so she could prevent catastrophe this time. The tools she used to dampen the hum of anxiety weren't working anymore and she didn't know what to do.

Brenda rose and took the blanket from Kaye's shoulders. "You need to go home and talk to your husband. Be honest about what you're feeling and he'll understand."

Brenda was right.

Kaye allowed herself to be led down the hallway and shuffled out the door.

"Call me later." Brenda waited for her to reach the sidewalk, then turned off the light.

Chapter 21

Fueled by their excitement, the first week of work was productive and passed quickly. They stuck to the schedule Stacy had set: Billy writing new pages during the day and Stacy editing the pages at night. As promised, Ryan took care of the kids every day, and if he didn't always hear Sophie waking at night, that was okay. Stacy was up anyway and could put her back to sleep.

The second week was more challenging. Billy dissolved into a puddle of despair several times and once threatening to give up entirely. But they pushed past that and ended the second week with almost three hundred pages completed and ready to go.

Now, the second morning of the third week, Stacy could see light at the end of the tunnel, however dim. As was her habit, she started her day by walking across town toward Billy's room, carrying edits from the night before and a cooler of food for Billy's day. Though it wasn't the sort of food he was used to, or even liked, he seemed grateful to have it. As their work progressed and he seemed to be running out of steam, she'd added bars of dark chocolate and cans of double-shot espresso drinks, which seemed to do the trick.

She crossed the weedy yard and made her way to his room, knocking sharply on his door. She wasn't surprised when he didn't answer; they were both exhausted. She pulled out her key and swiftly unlocked the door then dropped the cooler on the floor with a thud. "Good morning, Billy."

"Go away." He buried his head under the pillow.

"I've got good news today." She snapped open the drapes, letting in shafts of weak sunlight across the dull brown carpet.

"I don't care."

"You'll care about this." She slipped a cup of strong black coffee from the carrier. "Emmerson likes what you've written so far."

"You showed him?" Billy poked his head up, like a meerkat.

"The first few chapters, yes." She set the coffee on the nightstand and clicked on the bedside light.

He buried his head back under the pillow. "If Emmerson likes what you showed him, he'll like the book." His voice was muffled. "Tell him to extend our deadline. I can't take this pace anymore."

Stacy suppressed a surge of exasperation. Of course he was tired—they both were. But she would not let him give up.

She pried the lid from her coffee and settled into his desk chair. "You know it doesn't work that way."

Sitting up, Billy pulled back the sleeves of his ratty denim shirt and thrust his arm toward her. "Do you *see* how pale I've gotten?" He massaged his throat with his fingertips. "And I think I'm coming down with something. My vitamin D levels are dangerously low, probably because you keep me in this dungeon without any sunlight at all."

"I'll bring vitamins tomorrow."

"I'm *tired*." Billy turned over and stared at the ceiling.

"We're both tired, Billy." Her voice broadcast a calm she didn't feel, but it would be useless to take her frustration out on him. She needed him to focus on the work. "I've had the same headache for a week and my left eye started twitching two days ago." Setting her coffee down, she rose from her chair and stood next to his bed. "You have four chapters to write and three days to do it. You can sleep when we're finished—the whole day if you want to. But right now, we have to get to work."

With a dramatic sigh, he rose from his bed and crossed the room. He accepted the flash drive with her corrections and plugged it into the computer. "Fine."

Stacy took the shortcut back to the house, her mind on the day ahead. She'd left Billy working and was optimistic about their ability to finish. It would be tight, but if they stayed on schedule, Emmerson would have his book by Friday's deadline.

Once home, she followed the front path to the gate, knowing it would take a firm push to open it. That gate had always been temperamental; the wood swelled in the summer's humidity, and the springs rusted in the winter snow. There was a trick to opening it, depending on the weather of the day. This time, however, the gate opened smoothly, without effort. It seemed that someone—Brad, no doubt—had fixed it. It looked as though he'd replaced the hardware, sanded and repainted the wood too. Stacy ran her fingers across the join and was impressed with her brother's work.

In the yard, she heard the tinny sound of a portable radio mixed with the occasional clink of tools. Curious about what her brother was up to, she crossed the side yard and headed for the workshop. Brad was seated at the workbench, a pool of yellow light shining on a collection of rough sketches.

He looked up as she approached. "Hey."

"Hey yourself." She leaned against the doorframe. "Good job on the front gate."

"Thanks." Brad's attention returned to the papers in front of him. "What are those?"

"Mrs. Ivey's friend hired me to build a gazebo. These are some ideas."

"That's really pretty." Stacy reached for the lamp clipped to the shelf and adjusted it. The bulb was weak and needed replacing. "But you need more light. How can you see anything?"

Brad swatted his sister's hand away. "This is Gramps's lamp and the light is fine."

"Fine." Stacy took a step back, then spotted the kids playing in the yard. "Have you seen Ryan?"

Brad gestured to her old beach car. "He thinks he can get it working again."

"You're back early." Ryan emerged from beneath the car and came over to meet her, his T-shirt smudged with dirt from the garage floor. "Did things go well over at Billy's?"

"We're almost finished. Billy's doing his best, but he's slowing down. I have pages of stuff to get through, then I'm going back to check on him. But first I need a quick nap. Everything okay with the kids?"

"Yeah." Ryan wiped his hands on a rag and tucked it into his back pocket. "They're playing in the yard. They're fine."

"They've been 'playing in the yard' a lot lately," Stacy observed. "Maybe you should take them somewhere?"

"Maybe. We'll see."

Parking the kids in the yard and letting them play by themselves wasn't her definition of caring for them, but even though she was annoyed, she was too tired to argue.

*

Stacy crossed the backyard and went around the house to the mudroom entrance. Inside, she stopped to kick off her shoes and shelve Billy's empty cooler from the day before.

"Is that you, Stacy?"

"Yeah, Mom. I just got back."

"Are you finished with the book then?" Her mother wiped her hands and draped the towel over the oven handle.

"Not quite yet." Stacy brought her work bag in and set it on the stool.

"Are you sure you want to continue working in your condition?"

"Yes. I like working." Stacy pulled a bottle of mineral water from the refrigerator, popped the top, and sipped.

"I'm serious, Stacy." Her mother frowned. "Ryan mentioned that he's not working anymore. That he lost his job?"

"He didn't lose it. He quit," Stacy clarified.

Her mother frowned. "What I'm trying to say is that your family needs you. I'm not sure this is the right time for you to—"

"Mom." Stacy matched her mother's tone. "I don't think this conversation is going to end well."

"Stacy, all this hard work can't be good for the baby. Connor and Sophie need you. I can see Ryan is trying, but a mother's attention is different. Children always need their mother."

"Is that all?" Stacy closed down the conversation by crossing the kitchen and tossing her bottle into the recycle bin.

"Stacy, think about what I'm saying—"

Stacy held her hand up, a wave of exhaustion washing over her. "No, Mom. I will not think about it. I want to do this. Ryan has agreed to support me by caring for *his own children*. End of discussion."

Grabbing her bag, she left the kitchen and made her way upstairs without another word.

Once in her room, she pulled out her phone to set an alarm, then flopped onto her bed. In the stillness of the room, doubt bloomed. What if her mother was right? Logically, what she'd said didn't make sense—Ryan had offered to watch the kids, and more importantly, he wasn't exactly doing her a favor because they were his kids too. But her mother had a point. Ryan's approach *was* much more relaxed, and Stacy worried they weren't spending much time together. That her husband appeared more interested in her old beach car than he did his own children.

The debate continued in her head as she drifted off to sleep.

"Stacy, wake up." Her mother's tone was urgent, bringing Stacy fully awake.

"What is it, Mom?" Stacy sat up, blinking the room into focus. "Are the kids okay?"

"They are, but your father and I have to leave so you'll need to watch them."

"Where's Ryan?"

"He went with Brad to the hardware store."

As she pushed aside the cotton blanket, her heart squeezed. "And he left the kids alone?"

"He left them with me," Kaye corrected. "But, as I said, your father and I are going out now and you need to get up."

"Okay. I'll be right there." Stacy rubbed her eyes, glancing up as her mother withdrew from the room. "Is Dad all right?"

"He's fine." Kaye's tone seemed unnecessarily sharp. "But you need to hurry."

After her parents left, Stacy set herself up at the kitchen table. Her plan was to let the kids play in the yard for a few more minutes until Ryan returned and could take over. Then she'd move upstairs to the quiet bedroom where she could concentrate and finish her work.

She didn't account for the fact that Connor and Sophie had been playing in the yard all week and were tired of it. They came inside almost immediately and asked for things repeatedly. A popsicle. A drink of water. A hug. They asked Stacy to take them crabbing and whined when she refused. Their demands to be taken places were relentless—the swings at the park, the ducks on the salt pond, a walk to the candy store. Stacy refused each one, explaining she had to work, and feeling a wave of guilt each time. Finally, she bribed them with ice cream—any kind they wanted—if they went outside and let her work. They agreed, then clambered back inside a few minutes later.

"Mommy, we're hungry!" Sophie stood at the back door, her shoes caked with dirt.

"You know the rule. Shoes off in the house." Stacy pointed toward the mudroom. "Put them in there."

"But Daddy tied the laces too tight." Sophie dropped to the floor in a dramatic heap. "He doesn't do them like you do."

"You should learn how to tie your own sneakers, Sophie." Stacy put down her pen and crossed the room to help. "Then you can make them however you like." She slipped the grass-stained sneakers off and handed them back. "Put them away please."

As Sophie reluctantly trudged to the mudroom, Stacy glanced at Connor who stood in the doorway, holding back.

"You okay, bud?"

Connor frowned; his bottom lip quivered. "Bibi's right. You don't like us anymore."

"What?" Stacy gasped. "Bibi said that?"

Instead of answering, Connor looked away, so Stacy crossed the room and knelt in front of him. "You know that's not true, right?" She reached for his hands. "I'm working for a little while, just like Daddy does."

"Daddy doesn't like us either when he works. He tells us to be quiet and now you're telling us that too."

The comment took Stacy's breath away. "Is that what you really think?"

Connor nodded slowly.

She squeezed his hand. "Just a few more days, buddy. Then I'll be finished and we can play."

Even as she spoke, she knew "a few days" meant nothing to a six-year-old; she may as well have said "a few years." She glanced at her work bag and the pages spread across the counter. It was true that she'd barely seen her children since she and Billy began work. They were used to seeing her every day and it must be hard for them.

"Okay." Stacy rose. An afternoon off might be a good idea, a chance to clear her head. And she'd bring her work with her, just in case. But the pool had closed for the season and the kids had already been to the duck pond more times than they could count.

She needed to give them something bigger.

"Go get your suits on, we're going to the beach." She blurted it out quickly, before she had a chance to take it back.

She scribbled a note for Ryan and headed for the beach.

*

The parking lot was full by the time they arrived, rows and rows of cars shimmering in the summer heat. Driving to the beach had seemed like a good idea because they had so much stuff to bring, but the only empty space they found was blocks from the beach and they'd end up walking anyway.

"Make sure you put on your flip-flops before you leave the car." Stacy turned off the engine and glanced toward her kids in the back seat. "The asphalt's hot this time of day and you'll burn your feet."

Sophie scrambled out of the car the moment she was released from her car seat, excited for the afternoon. Stacy grabbed her hand and pointed to a patch of grass beside the curb. "You stand right there, Sophie. Do not move from that spot."

She turned to Connor. "Buddy, watch your sister, okay? I don't want her running into the street."

"Okay." Connor grasped his sister's hand as Stacy unlocked the trunk and began unloading everything they needed for two hours at the shore.

"Connor, can you carry this bag?" Stacy handed him the canvas boat tote filled with sand toys. It was bulky but light, and he should be able to manage it. She waited while he lifted it from the ground.

"Yes, Mommy."

"Good boy." Stacy pulled Sophie's pink bag from the car and handed it to her daughter. "Sophie, you take this. Both of you stay right there while I load up." Stacy pulled the wagon from the car and clicked the wheels into place. Out came a stack of beach towels, more sand toys, a snack bag, a cooler of drinks, sunblock, floppy hats, and sunglasses. Finally, she jerked a tangle of rusty beach chairs free from the back of her car and balanced them on top.

"You guys ready?" Her face was covered in a mask of perspiration and the back of her shirt was damp with sweat. She smiled at her children, despite the uneasiness she felt at being this close to the ocean.

The area became more congested as they approached the beach stairs. The small parking area beside the entrance, designed for loading and unloading, was packed with cars, most of them double parked. The spillover lined both sides of the street and the queue for beach badge checking snaked down the stairs and into the parking lot.

"Mommy, we're here!" Sophie broke free from her brother's grasp and ran toward the line, her flip-flops slapping against the bottoms of her feet.

Connor dropped his bag and ran after his sister.

Stacy felt the start of a blister as the edge of her sneaker cut into the back of her heel, and the baby kicked in protest as she bent to pick up the canvas bags her children had abandoned. As she straightened, someone bumped her cart and jostled a beach chair free from the load. A rusty tip of metal scraped her shin as she retrieved it and pushed it back on top.

By the time she caught up with her children, Stacy was light-headed with exhaustion. The line inched forward as the attendant checked badges that allowed entrance to the beach. The wooden stairs radiated the heat from the sun and her temples began to throb. She'd packed hats for the kids but had forgotten her own. They crested the stairs to the platform and Stacy glanced at the beach, groaning in frustration.

This had been a mistake.

The beach was a patchwork of neon towels and wide umbrellas stuck into the sand. The shoreline was clogged with people, swimming, wading, and surfing. It had been so long since Stacy had been to the beach she'd forgotten how crowded it could become, especially on a sunny summer afternoon.

"Next."

Stacy tipped her badge toward the attendant and moved forward, fighting the anxiety filling her chest. She'd promised the kids an afternoon at the beach. Two hours, and then she could go home. She could stand anything for two hours.

They descended the ramp to the bottom of the stairs and paused briefly to rearrange their load. A thread of sand trickled into her sneakers and Stacy made the mistake of kicking them off. She'd forgotten how hot summer sand actually was.

"Keep your flip-flops on and stay close to me," she told them as she grabbed the handle of the beach cart and pulled it forward.

Luckily, Stacy spotted a family packing up to leave. She sent Connor running over to reserve the spot. The proximity to the water's edge made her nervous, but it didn't seem like they had much of a choice. She staked the umbrella while Connor and Sophie spread their towels. It took them a while to unpack, but in the end Stacy was satisfied. There was a shady spot for the kids to play with their buckets and shovels and sandcastle molds, and room for Stacy to work on Billy's pages. The space was tighter than she would have liked, but it was workable.

She unzipped the snack bag. "You guys take whatever you want." She gave them each a juice box. "We'll have lunch a little later."

The kids seemed happy enough, scooping sand and eating snacks, so Stacy began her work. The sound of the surf and the murmur of conversation receded as she focused on the words.

"Mommy—look!" Sophie's squeal of excitement pulled Stacy from Billy's story. She glanced to where Sophie pointed, to a pair of trawlers headed off to sea.

"They're going fishing," Stacy said.

"Can we go fishing too?"

"On a big boat like that? I don't think so, sweetheart. I think that's just for fishermen."

Connor upended a bucket of dry sand and the wind caught it, scattering sharp grains across their towels.

Stacy brushed her pages clear. "Connor, you have to be more careful."

"Sorry, Mommy."

"It's okay, buddy."

The kids played together for a while and Stacy finished a few more pages.

This isn't so bad after all.

"Mommy, can I take my tugboat over there to play with those kids?" Connor pointed toward a shallow tide pool well away from the breaking waves. A few other children were there already, kids about Connor's age, and with adults seated nearby it seemed safe to let him go.

"Do *not* go in the water. You stay on the sand. You got it?"

"Okay, Mommy." Connor scooped up his tugboat and went to join the others.

Sophie had fallen asleep under the umbrella and Stacy returned to her work. After a few paragraphs, she found her rhythm and immersed herself in the story. Billy's second book might just be better than the first…

"Stacy, there you are!"

Startled, Stacy jumped. It was jarring to be pulled back into this world after being so engrossed in Billy's. Shielding her eyes from the sun with her hand, Stacy looked up at the voice.

"I brought you all something to eat." Kaye glanced at Sophie, napping in the shade, and lowered her voice. "I wasn't sure what food you had."

"We're fine, Mom," Stacy said coldly, remembering their previous conversation. "I know how to feed my children."

"About what I said earlier…" Kaye began. "Maybe I owe you an apology."

"I'd say so." Stacy waited.

Kaye set the bag of food on the edge of the blanket. "Where's Connor? I have his lunch too."

Stacy glanced at the tide pool and her heart slammed into her chest. The tide pool where she'd sent Connor to play with his little plastic boat had disappeared. In its place, ocean water swirled and foamed as the tide surged in. Waves raced across the beach toward the jetty, then receded, leaving nothing in their wake.

The tide pool was gone.

The children and the adults watching them were gone.

Her son was gone.

Stacy bolted to her feet, abandoning her work, and sprinted across the sand to where the tide pool used to be. Panic clawed at her throat, sucking out her breath. She didn't stop running until she was knee-deep in water, calling her son's name with a primal howl.

She ran toward a group of adults seated a little higher up the beach. "Have you seen my son?" She clasped her shaking hands together to keep them steady. "He's six years old. This tall. White T-shirt. Wavy brown hair. Red bathing suit—have you seen him?"

The world slowed as Stacy watch them look at each other and back at her. One of the women rose from her chair. Stacy felt hands on her shoulders, but she shook them off and ran back to where the tide pool had been.

The water was deeper now as the tide rushed in. Stacy watched as the waves snatched a forgotten beach towel from the sand and slammed it into the jagged rocks before sucking it back under water. She imagined her son in place of the towel, his body broken by the ocean waves. She pictured him being carried out to sea, losing his breath and calling for her.

A sob rose in her throat as she ran into the water again, the waves pushing against her legs, slowing her progress. A wave crested, breaking against her body and she lost her balance. She thrust her hands in front of her body to protect the baby from her fall, and when the wave receded, she righted herself and continued into the ocean, thrashing her way past the breaking waves, on her way to rescue her son.

She was aware of a frenzy of activity behind her but she didn't pay attention. Her only concern was rescuing him from the waves. In the distance, a lifeguard whistle sounded, shrill and sharp on the beach. Another wave slammed into her chest, this one knocking her off her feet. She felt a pair of strong hands pull her to shore. She'd lost the strength to shake them off, but she howled in protest. Stacy tasted her heartbeat, her blood pressed against her skin as she watched the waves carry the towel out to sea.

Her son was out there. She knew he was.

She dropped her head onto her knees and sobbed.

"Stacy, it's okay!" A hand reached for her, smoothed her hair away from her face. "Stacy, listen to me."

Stacy drew a ragged breath and looked up. She felt strangely detached, as if she were watching a movie about a woman on the beach who'd lost her child.

"They found him." The voice sounded as if it came from far away. "Stacy, they found Connor. He's okay."

"Where?" Her body was heavy as she rose to her feet. "Where is he?"

"He's fine." Her mother wrapped her arm around Stacy and helped her up. "He went to play with a boy named Miles. He said he didn't tell you because you were working."

Stacy stopped, unable to move as shame washed over her.

She'd lost her child because she thought work was more important than caring for him. Her mother had been right. It was crazy to think she could do both.

Connor came back to them, red-faced and apologizing for running away.

Stacy dropped to her knees and held him tight, feeling shame and relief pressing so heavily on her body that she could barely speak.

Eventually, she watched her mother pack up the beach things and allowed herself to be led back to the car.

Chapter 22

When they arrived home, Kaye guided Stacy upstairs to her room as if she were a child. She found a soft nightgown in the drawer and turned down the bed. While Stacy changed in the bathroom, Kaye drew the curtains and switched on the air conditioner. She tucked her daughter into bed and smoothed the creases from the blanket.

"You rest now. We should talk later," her mother said as she closed the door behind her.

But there didn't seem to be anything to say.

Sometime during the night, Stacy woke feeling the weight of the ocean press against her chest as if she were drowning. She lay in the darkness, gasping for air, the sheets wrapped around her legs like a rope, her pillow hot and damp. She reached across the bed for Ryan, but his side of the bed was empty.

The next time she woke, it was light. The air conditioner had been turned off, the window opened, the curtains pushed back, and daylight flooded the room. Outside, there were sounds of children playing, riding their bikes in the street and calling to each other. Stacy sat up in bed. It was time to get up and face judgment for what she'd allowed to happen.

There was a soft knock on the door.

"Come in."

The door creaked as it opened and Ryan entered. "You're up." He carried a steaming mug of what smelled like peppermint tea.

"What time is it?" Her head felt fuzzy.

"Around four in the afternoon, I guess—on Thursday. You were out for a long time."

So she'd miss tomorrow's deadline, which seemed appropriate punishment for what she'd done. She only regretted that her judgment would include Billy. He didn't deserve that.

Stacy sat up to accept the mug of tea. The warm liquid soothed her raw throat. "This is good, thank you."

They sat in silence for a while, listening to the children play outside and feeling the late afternoon breeze from the open window. Ryan wandered to the window and sat in the chair.

"I guess you heard what happened?" Stacy said finally, her gaze focused on the contents of her mug. She wouldn't blame him if he left her.

Ryan shifted his position to look at her. "I did, and I'm really sorry, Stace."

She frowning in confusion. "Why are *you* sorry?"

"Because what happened is my fault. I promised to watch the kids while you worked, and I pawned them off on your mother first chance I got. I shouldn't have."

"Ryan, I think you're missing the bigger picture here. I lost your child."

He scoffed. "You know how many times my parents lost me when I was a kid? Or lost my brothers? More times than I can count. And Connor's fine."

Stacy hadn't the vaguest idea how to reply, so she didn't.

"Can I tell you something else?" Ryan continued. "The reason I left them with your mother?"

"Sure."

He rose and paced the length of the room "You're better with the kids than I am. I didn't know what to do with them."

"I don't understand."

"You make it look easy, Stace, and it's not." He sighed. "You know how many times Connor bugs me to go crabbing or to the beach? That kid is a bundle of energy. And then Sophie—she's always asking for a juice box."

"Only one," Stacy said automatically.

He paused and looked at her. "What?"

"Only one juice box," Stacy said. "She'll ask a million times, but she only gets one a day because the sugar makes her hyper."

"That little stinker," Ryan muttered as he raked his fingers through his hair. "But you see? I don't know stuff like that. You do."

"Ryan." Stacy gaped at her husband. "I *lost your child* at the beach. No one's giving me any parenting awards."

"Our kid ran off. It could have happened anywhere."

Ryan was dismissive, but Stacy couldn't be. It was true that she'd lost track of her kids before, at Target or the grocery store, but this was different. She'd never felt this kind of terror before and it shook her, making her doubt herself, her ability to keep them safe.

"It's not your fault." Ryan crossed the room and stood before her. "Stacy. What happened is not your fault."

Stacy managed a weak smile. She didn't agree with him and she never would, but she appreciated his words.

"I'd like another chance with them," Ryan said suddenly.

"Another chance?" Stacy echoed. "Ryan, they're your children. You can have as many chances as you want."

"You don't get it." The mattress dipped as Ryan sat on the edge of the bed. "I'm embarrassed to know that I can only last a few days with the kids before foisting them on your mother. That's not good. So, I've been thinking." He leaned forward, placing his elbows on his legs and lacing his fingers together. "What if I don't go back to work right away? We'll cash in my options now and I'll take some real time off. If we're careful, we could do it for maybe a year or two."

"That sounds like a lot to talk about right now..." Stacy said as she set her mug on the nightstand. "I'm not sure I can handle any big discussions."

"Yeah, sure. Of course," Ryan amended. "We'll talk later."

She settled back into the bed, expecting Ryan to leave, but he didn't.

"There's just one more thing to add..." Ryan glanced at her. "You seem to really like working with Billy, and I remember how much you loved your job at Revere. If I stay home, you can see if the freelance job they offered goes anywhere? Or you can start something new, whatever you want."

Stacy thought about how disappointed and angry Billy would be when he learned they'd miss the deadline. She closed her eyes to block it out but still, she saw his face. And that was her fault too.

"Thanks, but I don't think Billy—or anyone—will work with me after this. Technically the deadline isn't until tomorrow, but we'll miss it. I had a hundred pages left to edit and Billy had more to write. We can't do all that in a couple hours."

Ryan laughed, shaking the bed.

"What's so funny?" Stacy said, stung that he seemed to make light of this after everything that had happened.

He laid his hand on her knee. "Stace, you aren't going to miss your deadline."

"I will," she insisted. "The manuscript is due at nine o'clock tomorrow morning. I still have a hundred pages to edit and Billy has more to write. There's no way to catch up now."

He laughed again and stood. "You should talk to your mother."

Stacy rubbed her face with her palms, not understanding the abrupt change of topic. "No. I can't take a conversation with my mother right now."

Ryan lifted a summer dress from the hook and brought it to her. "Trust me, you're going to want this one."

Chapter 23

Kaye had asked the boys—Ryan, Chase, and Brad—to take the kids away, and they had agreed not to return until they heard from her.

She tidied the kitchen as she waited for her daughter to come downstairs; wiped down the kitchen counter, though it didn't need to be done. The lunch dishes were on the drying rack, the floor mopped, everything put away. There was nothing that needed her attention. Nothing, except her daughter and a conversation that was long overdue.

The distance between them was Kaye's fault; had always been her fault. She had been closer to Brad, probably because he'd been easier, willing to go along with anything Kaye decided. But Stacy had known her own mind from a very young age and that was difficult to control. The more Kaye tried, the further they had drifted apart, until they had become polite strangers. And that was Kaye's fault too.

Kaye heard the back stairs creak as Stacy descended and she froze, unsure.

Stacy entered the kitchen, making her way to the table and the pot of tea Kaye had set out for her. "Everyone's giving me tea today," she said, her voice flat.

Kaye opened her mouth to speak, but the words wouldn't come. She cleared her throat and tried again. "Are you hungry? Do you want a sandwich?"

"Where is everybody?" Stacy glanced toward the yard.

Kaye forced herself to the table, to a seat opposite her daughter. "They went to feed the ducks. I asked them to give us time to talk."

Stacy's shoulders stiffened, but she didn't reply.

"How are you feeling?" It seemed to be a good place to start.

"I'm fine." Stacy's reply was clipped. "Let's get this over with, Mom. I'm tired."

"How long have you been afraid of the ocean?" Kaye blurted out.

"What?" Stacy glanced at her mother, and this time it was Kaye who looked away.

She folded her hands in her lap and forced the words to come. "The clues were there all summer. How upset you were when the club's pool closed for repairs. That you'll take the kids anywhere except the beach. Even today, Connor told me you don't ever let either of them go into the water."

Stacy's temper flared. "I don't have time to listen to you catalogue all my faults. I feel bad enough about what happened. I don't need your judgment to add to it."

"That's not it, Stacy." Kaye's voice cracked. "I'm not judging you and I'm hoping you won't judge me after you hear what I have to say.

"When you and Brad were little, I brought you to the beach one day. You loved the waves when you were little. You were three, I think, and fearless. Your brother was still an infant, so I left him on the shore with your grandmother and took you into the water myself. The swells were higher than usual, and I wanted to teach you how to jump the waves. It was early in the season and there weren't many people in the ocean. I should have taken that as a sign, but I was a young mother. Young and ignorant.

"We walked into the surf, about chest high. I had you on my hip. We jumped the first wave. The power of the water lifting us from the bottom was exhilarating. It felt as if we were flying and you loved it. You squealed, patted the water with your little hand."

Kaye felt her chest tighten with panic but pushed it away. She had to continue, for both their sakes.

"We jumped a few more waves before I noticed the undertow. Every time we jumped, the receding wave pulled us a little further away from the shore, a little further out to sea. And when it set me back down, I wasn't as sure-footed as I'd been before. Very quickly, I could only scrape the sandy bottom with my toes. By then, the waves were coming faster. I held you tighter against my body and started to swim to shore but I couldn't. The undertow was too strong. I knew I had to get the lifeguards' attention."

Kaye swallowed, clenching her fist as she finished her story.

"I thought I could hold you. I held you to my side with my arm and raised the other to get help. Then a rogue wave, bigger than any of the others that came before, picked us up and broke, sucking both of us under the water. The force of the wave ripped your body from mine. I couldn't right myself, no matter how hard I tried. And I couldn't find you. I remember clawing at the water, fighting the undertow, opening my eyes and seeing nothing but sand and foam, churning in the current. In reality, it happened quickly, but to me, it seemed to last a lifetime.

"After an eternity, I could finally feel the sand beneath my feet and I could stand. The ocean had spat you out too, further down the beach. Your hair was tangled, your suit was full of sand, your skin mottled with sand-burns. And you were hysterical, screaming and crying."

"That was real?" Stacy drew a sharp breath. Her face was white. "I've had nightmares about being sucked into the ocean and drowning my whole life. I never once thought it really happened. Why didn't you ever tell me?"

"Honestly, I hoped that you were young enough that you might eventually forget." Kaye swallowed and continued her story. "And for a long time, I thought you had. You went back in the water, were on the swim team. But that was the pool, not the ocean. I don't think you've been in the ocean since that day. I should have known that but I didn't. I guess I didn't look closely enough. I suppose I didn't want to." Kaye looked away. "I'm so sorry to have put you in danger so many years ago."

"Mom…"

Kaye glanced up, her vision blurred. Whatever punishment Stacy decided, Kaye would accept.

To her surprise, Stacy reached across the table for her hand. "That's a terrible thing to live with."

A sharp knock on the back door interrupted their conversation, startling them both.

"Hello?" The screen door creaked as it opened. "Anybody here?"

"Billy?" Stacy gaped at him.

Kaye slipped on her company manners, rising to welcome him. "Are you hungry? Would you like something to eat?"

"Billy, you've showered," Stacy said.

Billy glanced down at his clothing and smiled. "So I have."

"And you look *happy*."

A mischievous smile crept across his face. "I guess I am." He slid a large envelope across the table, toward Kaye. "This is the last of it."

"Thank you, Billy." She moved toward the refrigerator, pulling out sandwich fixings. "Your sandwich will be ready in a minute."

"What's going on?" Stacy interrupted, frowning. "Billy, you should be furious at me for disappearing on you. Why aren't you?" She poked the envelope. "And what's—" Her voice faded and her expression cleared. "Wait. Is this the book? Are you finished?" she ended with a whisper.

"Yes, it is." Billy slapped the table with an open hand. "All finished and ready to go."

"How did you—" Stacy sputtered.

Billy giggled, clearly delighted with himself. "Your mother, Stacy dear, is a formidable woman. She came to my room day before yesterday and told me what had happened." He straightened, reaching for a peach in the fruit bowl. "Then she demanded I finish the story right there and then, didn't you, Kaye? She edited while I wrote."

Kaye set a sandwich in front of him. "I did." She turned to Stacy. "I won't pretend to know as much as you about editing, but I gave it my best shot." She touched Stacy's shoulder on her way out of the kitchen. "I'll leave you two to work out the details."

Chapter 24

On the first Saturday of September, Kaye woke early and crept downstairs to a quiet house. She padded into the kitchen and opened the window to let the early morning breeze into the shore house. Throughout the morning, the salty fresh air would ruffle the curtains and fill the house with the scent of the ocean, and she would remember. On snowy winter days in Princeton, she would remember the smell of the ocean in Dewberry Beach.

She poured water into the coffee machine and made her way to the pantry. Pushing aside the tin of decaffeinated green tea she'd bought for Chase earlier in the summer, she reached instead for the strong dark roast he preferred. She slipped a paper filter into the basket and measured in the grounds. The aroma of rich coffee filled the room.

As she turned toward the bread box, a note on the kitchen table caught her attention. On top of a stack of printed pages was a bright orange sticky note written in Stacy's hand.

We're finished
You get the first read.
PS: Keep it secret.

She brushed the manuscript with her fingertips, proud that Stacy would choose to share such an accomplishment with her. Kaye intended to find a quiet moment and bring the book to the deck and read it all the way through. Their relationship had improved. Stacy had heard Kaye's confession and had forgiven her. For that, Kaye was grateful.

Kaye glanced out the kitchen window at what had been Santos's work shed, now gifted to Brad with Chase's blessing. Brad and his grandfather had always had a special connection, and Brad seemed pleased to work where his grandfather had spent so much of his time.

What had started as a favor for Mrs. Ivey was beginning to grow into a small business. Brad had asked about staying on at the shore house after the summer season to explore the idea. Kaye had overheard Chase offering to help organize the financials, maybe even offer some seed money. Mrs. Ivey was all for it. As Brad's first and best client she made no secret of her wish that Brad would put "those city people" out of business.

Kaye lifted the carafe and poured two cups of coffee, adding a bit of cream and a touch of sugar to both. On her way out the door, she paused to examine the butterfly costume she and Sophie had created for the Firefly Festival later that evening. Kaye reached to tap a streak of glitter with her finger and was pleased to see the glue had held.

She pushed open the screen door and took the coffee to the deck.

"Caffeinated?" Chase glanced up from his morning newspaper, one eyebrow raised.

"Not a chance." Kaye set the mug on the table beside his chair. There were some concessions she wasn't willing to make.

"Just checking." Chase folded his paper and set it down. "Are we the only ones up?"

"So far." Kaye sipped her coffee and looked past the bank of cattails to the pond. The ducks were stirring, quacking loud enough to let everyone know they were awake and ready for bread. The morning air held the first hint of fall, and it wouldn't be long before they'd need sweaters to sit on the deck. "Stacy's author friend was over again yesterday."

"Is that right?"

"It is. And what's more, I think they might work together on a third book. *And* I overheard Stacy tell Ryan that Billy might be interested in buying that motel property, can you believe it?"

"Is that so?"

"Yes, it is." Kaye smiled into her coffee cup. "If Billy decides to settle in Dewberry Beach and starts work on the third book, it just might be easier if Stacy, Ryan, and the kids stay too, don't you think? Maybe Ryan can even lend a hand guiding Brad's new business."

"What are you planning?" Chase's eyes twinkled as he looked at her.

"Nothing at all." Kaye shrugged. "I *may* have mentioned what a good school Dewberry Beach Elementary is, but that's all."

Chase's laugh warmed her heart. "I just bet that's all."

"I spoke to Nancy and George the other day. Their Christmas plans for Austria fell through, something about finding dry rot on the riverboat. They're renting a cabin in Maine instead and want to know if we'd like to join them."

"Maine in December?"

"Not December. They moved it to October instead, to see the fall foliage. I thought you might want to go."

Chase reached for her hand. "Thank you."

"Don't thank me yet. Nancy's bringing over the details this afternoon." Kaye sipped her coffee, felt the warmth spread throughout her body. "I think it might be fun, but we'll see. If this doesn't work out maybe we can go somewhere else, just the two of us."

"I'd like that."

Outside, she heard a work crew blocking off streets for the Firefly Festival later. Inside, there was a hum of conversation coming from the kitchen and the clatter of pans on the stove.

It looked as if Labor Day at the shore had begun.

"I'd better go inside, start getting ready for the parade. Connor asked me to walk with him." Chase beamed as he rose from his chair and gathered his things. "You coming?"

"Absolutely. I'll be there in a minute," Kaye replied.

She heard the slap of the screen door as Chase went into the house, and the buzz of conversation as he chatted with his grandchildren. She listened to all the sounds inside and smiled. This was exactly what she wanted, her family around her at the shore house. She wanted just one more minute to soak it all in.

Finally, she rose and went to join them.

It had been a wonderful summer.

A Letter from Heidi

Thank you so much for choosing to read *The Shore House*. If you enjoyed it and want to keep up to date with all my latest releases, please sign up at the following link. Your email address will never be shared and you can unsubscribe at any time.

www.bookouture.com/heidi-hostetter

The best stories come from writing what you know. For me, writing about the New Jersey shore felt like coming home. I grew up in New Jersey and spent summers at my grandparents' shore house in a town very much like Dewberry Beach. I remember sparklers and fireflies at night, the ice-cream truck making the rounds in the evening, and daily trips to the salt pond to feed the ducks. My grandfather taught us to crab off the pier, using fish heads tied to the end of a long string because he insisted old ways were the best ways. Applegate's Hardware is gone now, but when I was a kid, it sold everything you could possibly need—or want—for a summer at the shore. It's not a stretch to imagine Ryan buying an antiquated fire extinguisher there.

As I wrote this story, I wondered what it would be like for a family coming together after a sudden illness and a long recovery. And because no family is perfect, I knew there would be bumps in the road, old hurts to address, misunderstandings to clear up. With a little time and a lot of work, they'd remember what made them a family in the first place. I didn't know when I started writing that the Bennett family would stay at the shore house after the summer was over, but I'm happy they did.

My next book will be set in Dewberry Beach too, this time with a different family and different circumstances to address. I'm looking forward to visiting the shore again and I hope you'll join me.

I hope you loved reading *The Shore House*. If you did, would you mind writing a quick review? It doesn't have to be long and I'd be so grateful. Reviews make it so much easier for new readers to discover my books for the first time. Thank you again.

If you want to contact me directly, that's great too—I love hearing from readers. You can find my author page on Facebook or you can join my reading group on Facebook. You can also find me on my website. The links are below.

My Author Page on Facebook:
www.facebook.com/AuthorHeidiHostetter

My Reading Group on Facebook:
www.facebook.com/groups/636728933179573

And, my website:
www.heidihostetter.com

Again, thank you for reading and I really hope you enjoyed the story.

Warmly,
Heidi

Acknowledgments

My deepest and most sincere thanks go to my editor, Kathryn Taussig. She knows what makes a good story great and her patience is infinite. Thank you for *everything*. You're the best. I was thrilled to work with you on this book and I'm so excited to work with you on the next.

Next, I'd like to thank the entire Bookouture team. Your enthusiasm for my work and your attention to detail show that my stories are in very good hands. Thank you all.

I am not exaggerating when I say that I'd be a mess without my writing group. Seven years, you guys. We have been through it all and what an honor it is to be in the company of such a talented group of authors: Laurie Rockenbeck, Sandy Esene, Heather Stewart McCurdy, Ann Reckner, and Liz Visner.

Thank you to David Anderson who reminds me every time I call that a complete and utter breakdown is part of my creative process. You have a way with words and I'm glad you're my friend.

Finally, to my readers. Thank you for reading and thank you for reaching out to tell me how much my stories have meant to you. It's an honor to write for such an engaged audience.

Made in the USA
Middletown, DE
23 July 2020